A RALPH COMPTON NOVEL

SO-AWA-510

RALPH COMPTON:
BROTHER'S KEEPER

DAVID ROBBINS

WHEELER PUBLISHING
A part of Gale, Cengage Learning

GALE
CENGAGE Learning®

Farmington Hills, Mich • San Francisco • New York • Waterville, Maine
Meriden, Conn • Mason, Ohio • Chicago

LIBRARY OF CONGRESS CATALOGING-IN-PUBLICATION DATA

Names: Robbins, David, 1950– author. | Compton, Ralph.
Title: Ralph Compton : brother's keeper : a Ralph Compton novel / by David Robbins.
Other titles: Brother's keeper
Description: Large print edition. | Waterville, Maine : Wheeler Publishing, 2016. | © 2015 | Series: Wheeler Publishing large print western
Identifiers: LCCN 2015050970| ISBN 9781410488817 (softcover) | ISBN 1410488810 (softcover)
Subjects: LCSH: Large type books. | GSAFD: Western stories.
Classification: LCC PS3568.O22288 R327 2016 | DDC 813/.54—dc23
LC record available at http://lccn.loc.gov/2015050970

Published in 2016 by arrangement with New American Library, an imprint of Penguin Publishing Group, a division of Penguin Random House LLC

Printed in the United States of America
1 2 3 4 5 6 7 20 19 18 17 16

THE IMMORTAL COWBOY

This is respectfully dedicated to the "American Cowboy." His was the saga sparked by the turmoil that followed the Civil War, and the passing of more than a century has by no means diminished the flame.

True, the old days and the old ways are but treasured memories, and the old trails have grown dim with the ravages of time, but the spirit of the cowboy lives on.

In my travels — to Texas, Oklahoma, Kansas, Nebraska, Colorado, Wyoming, New Mexico, and Arizona — I always find something that reminds me of the Old West. While I am walking these plains and mountains for the first time, there is this feeling that a part of me is eternal, that I have known these old trails before. I believe it is the undying spirit of the frontier calling me, through the mind's eye, to step back into time. What is the appeal of the Old West of the American frontier?

It has been epitomized by some as the dark and bloody period in American history. Its heroes — Crockett, Bowie, Hickok, Earp — have been reviled and criticized. Yet the Old West lives on, larger than life.

It has become a symbol of freedom, when there was always another mountain to climb and another river to cross; when a dispute between two men was settled not with expensive lawyers, but with fists, knives, or guns. Barbaric? Maybe. But some things never change. When the cowboy rode into the pages of American history, he left behind a legacy that lives within the hearts of us all.

— *Ralph Compton*

CHAPTER 1

Thalis Christie knew he was in trouble moments after he opened his eyes. Dawn was about to break, and he lay there debating whether to get up or wait a few minutes.

That was when something brushed against his leg.

Thal nearly jumped out of his skin. There shouldn't be anything under the tarpaulin and blanket that covered him — except him. It didn't help matters that before he'd turned in, he'd stripped off every stitch of clothing.

Thal was on his side, with just his head poking out of his bed. Goose bumps erupted as the thing that had crawled in with him slithered onto his shin. *Snake,* his mind screamed, and it was all he could do not to scramble out. He didn't move for two reasons. The first was that he would rather die than let the other Crescent H punchers see him naked. The second reason mattered more. The snake might be a rattler. If he moved his leg, the thing might bite.

No one else was up yet except the cook, Old Pete, who was over at the chuck wagon fixing breakfast. A few of the hands were snoring. His pard, Ned Leslie, was closest to him and snoring the loudest.

"Ned!" Thal whispered.

Ned went on sounding like a bear in hibernation.

Thal tensed as the snake inched up his leg. It was the creepiest feeling. Worse than that time a black widow spider had crawled up his arm in the woodshed. At least he could see the spider.

His mouth was so dry Thal had to try twice to say a little louder, "Ned, consarn you. Wake up."

Another puncher muttered and rolled over, smacking his lips.

Thal swiveled his eyes from side to side, seeking anyone else who might be awake.

The snake reached his knee.

Thal blamed himself for his predicament. He shouldn't have used the tarp, as hot as it was. But thunderheads had been noisily rumbling in the distance when he turned in, and he hadn't cared to be soaked. It never did rain, though. The storm had passed them by.

Because of the heat, Thal had left a gap for air to circulate. That was how the snake had gotten in with him.

Of all the ways for a man to meet his Maker, Thal reflected, being bit in his bed was downright dumb. He'd be the laughing-stock of the hereafter.

He saw the tarp bulge slightly as the serpent inched up his thigh, and he broke out in a cold sweat.

To the east the sky had brightened and the stars were fading. Others would wake up soon. The first puncher who did, Thal would ask for help. He didn't know what anyone could do, but there had to be something.

Luck was with him, for just then Ned Leslie slowly rose onto his elbows and sleepily gazed around. Ned's hat was off, and his usually slick black hair stuck out at all angles. He yawned and gave his head a slight shake, then saw Thal staring at him. "Mornin', ugly."

"I need help," Thal whispered.

"What's that, pard?" Ned said, scratching himself. "Didn't your ma ever teach you not to mumble? You'll have to speak up."

"I need help," Thal whispered a little louder.

"You sure do," Ned said, his green eyes

twinkling. "That filly over to the Mossy Horn Saloon wouldn't warm to you nohow the last time we were there. And Lordy, how you tried."

Thal smothered a few choice cusswords. Ned had been needling him about his attempt at romance for weeks now. "Snake," he whispered.

"Shake?" Ned said, and sat up. "You got cottonmouth or somethin'? I don't see how you could, seein' as how we haven't had a lick of liquor for days." He ran a hand over his hair to smooth it down. "Maybe more whiskey would have helped you with that filly. Get a gal drunk enough and she'll do just about anything."

"Snake," Thal said.

Ned didn't seem to hear him. "The problem with that is, by the time the gal is drunk, you are too. Some of those doves hold red-eye like it's water. The last time a gal and me got drunk together, I woke up in an outhouse with no idea how I got there or what happened to her. So gettin' drunk ain't no guarantee you'll get lucky."

"Ned, snake, damn you."

"What's that, Thalis?" Ned jammed his hat on. "You're actin' awful peculiar. Quit whisperin'. My ears haven't quite woke up yet, although the rest of me has."

10

Thal took a gamble. He said out loud, "There's a snake in my beddin', you lunkhead."

"You don't say?" Ned said calmly.

Thal could have hit him. The reptile had reached his hip and was posed along his unmentionables. He shuddered to think of the thing's fangs sinking into his private parts.

"That's what you get for bundlin' in all that canvas in the summer," Ned was saying. "Snakes like hot spots, and the inside of your beddin' must be an oven."

"Ned," Thal said, "I'm unshucked."

Ned started to laugh, and caught himself. "You're buck naked?" he said, and then did laugh. "Well, ain't this a pickle?"

"It could be a rattler."

"Has it rattled yet?"

"Not that I've heard."

"That's good," Ned said. "They usually only bite when they're riled, and they usually rattle before they bite. So long as it doesn't, you should be all right."

"Ned, for the love of heaven."

"Oh, all right." Ned cast his blanket off. He had gone to sleep with his shirt and pants on. He'd taken off his boots, though, and now he commenced to pull one on.

Much too slowly, for Thal's liking. "Any

11

chance you could hurry it up? Bein' snake-bit ain't nothin' to sneeze at."

"Maybe it's not the heat," Ned said, tugging harder. "Maybe it's how you smell."

"What?"

"You and your baths," Ned said. "Always goin' on about how you like to smell clean when we go to town so the gals will fancy you more. But bein' clean didn't help with that dove, did it? And after you sat in that river water for pretty near ten minutes, scrubbin' yourself raw. I don't see why you bother. You probably gave the fish fits."

Thal couldn't believe his pard was ribbing him, yet again, about his fondness for baths. Not at a time like this. "If I get bit and die, I'm comin' back to haunt you."

"That's the spirit," Ned said, reaching for his other boot.

"I mean it. I'll come back and make you take baths just to get even."

Ned paused. "Can a ghost do that? Make somebody do somethin' they don't want to do? If so, you can keep your darn baths. Twice a year was good enough for my pa and twice a year is good enough for me. That's why wash pans were invented. Our face and our hair are all that count. Who cares about the rest of us? No one can see how dirty we are if we have our clothes on."

Thal felt a feathery touch on his thigh. The snake's tongue, he reckoned. "Ned, honest to God."

"Don't be bringin' the Almighty into this. It's not His fault He gave you a brain and you don't use it."

The snake was on the move again. Thal felt it creep past his hip, climbing higher.

Ned stood and stomped each foot a couple of times. "There. I'm all together. Or pretty near." Bending, he scooped up his gun belt and proceeded to strap on his six-shooter. When he was done, he patted his Colt. "I'm not Jesse Lee, but I reckon I can hit a snake in a bedroll."

"Like blazes you will," Thal said. "You're liable to hit me." Neither of them was much shakes with a revolver. They only ever used their six-guns, ironically enough, for snakes and such.

"I know what made it crawl in with you," Ned said, and snapped his fingers. "It's not the heat or your smell. It's that yellow hair of yours. I bet the snake mistook it for the sun and you for a flat rock."

"You're not even a little bit funny." Thal was whispering again. The snake had reached his chest. He nearly shuddered.

"Some folks might not think so," Ned said. "But I like to start my day with a grin.

It puts me in a good mood for whatever comes after."

"The snake," Thal whispered.

"Oh, Thalis," Ned said with an exaggerated sigh. "The way you harp on the little things. It's not as if you've got a bear in there. That filly doesn't know how lucky she is that she didn't let you lead her to the altar. You'd have harped her to death with all your gripin'."

"I swear," Thal said. The snake was almost to his shoulder. Peering down in, he imagined he saw the tips of its forked tongue.

This whole time, others had been waking up and rising. A pair of them ambled over. Like Thal and Ned, they were pards. Unlike Thal and Ned, who were both in their twenties, one of the pair was past forty and the other was the youngest hand in the outfit.

Jesse Lee Hardesty was seventeen. He hailed from North Carolina, and was Southern through and through. He liked to wear a gray shirt as a kind of tribute to his pa, who had lost an arm in the War Between the States. His shirt matched his gray eyes. His bandanna was red. Another splash of color decorated his hip. Where the rest of the punchers got by with an ordinary Colt, Jesse Lee's sported ivory handles and nickel plating. He was uncommonly quick on the draw, and accurate. Around the campfire at night, he loved to hear stories about shootists. Some of the more seasoned punchers worried that if the boy wasn't careful, he'd turn into one himself.

Crawford Soames was one of those worriers. He'd been Jesse Lee's pard for going on a year. A lot of the men figured that Crawford had taken Jesse Lee under his wing to keep him out of trouble.

"What's goin' on?" Crawford now asked Ned Leslie. "Why is your pard still in bed? Is he sick?"

"Thal has come down with a case of snake," Ned said with mock gravity.

"He's done what, now?" Jesse Lee drawled.

"A snake has crawled in with him," Crawford had realized. "That happens from time to time. I remember Charley Logan, over to the Bar H. A snake crawled in with him one time and bit him when he rolled on top of it. Lucky for him it was a copperhead and not a rattler. Copperhead bites don't always kill, but he was in misery for months."

Thal was about to burst with exasperation. "Are you three goin' to stand there jawin' or are you goin' to help me?"

"Someone flip that tarp off," Jesse Lee said, placing his right hand on his ivory-handled Colt. "I bet I can shoot the side-winder before it bites him."

"Sidewinders are desert rattlers," Ned said. "Southwest Texas is a lot of things, but it's not no desert."

"Most likely the snake's a diamondback," Crawford said. "Timber rattlers like trees, and we're not near any woods."

"We have diamondbacks in North Carolina," Jesse Lee said. "Folks say they're the most dangerous there is."

"They are," Crawford said.

The snake reached Thal's shoulder. Now he definitely could see its tongue darting out and in. "I hope you all die," he said.

"We'd better do somethin'," Ned said. "I don't want to have to break in a new pard." He came over to the tarp. "I'll grab this side. Craw, you take the other. When I count to three, we'll flip it off and Jesse Lee can try and shoot the serpent before it can strike."

"Try?" Jesse Lee said.

"Hold on," Thal said, breaking out in even more sweat. "There's got to be a better way."

"What would you have us do?" Ned said. "Ask it 'pretty please' to not bite you and come out and leave you be?"

Jesse Lee chuckled. "Wouldn't that be somethin'? A snake with manners."

16

"The things you come up with," Crawford said.

"Let's hear your plan," Ned said to Thal. "Do you have a trick for lurin' the reptile out?"

Thal was about to say that all he cared about was not being bitten when the snake's snout appeared at the edge of the tarp. Eyes with vertical slits peered back at him with what he took to be malignant purpose. He recollected his grandma telling him once that snakes were evil, that they were Satan's progeny on earth, as she'd put it, constant reminders of the fact that Satan had disguised himself as a snake to cause the Fall. "It's right here," he whispered.

"Here where?" Ned said.

The rattlesnake slithered into the open.

Thal nearly cried out. It was indeed a diamondback. Over three feet long and as thick as his wrist, the snake glided by within inches of his face.

As if it had become aware of the others, the rattler suddenly streaked toward a patch of high grass.

Just like that, Jesse Lee's Colt was in his hand. He fired once, from the hip, and the snake's head exploded. The body stopped cold, writhed spasmodically, and was still.

Shouts came from different quarters,

17

cowhands demanding to know what was going on.

"Just a rattler!" Ned hollered, and smiling, he squatted and tapped Thal on the head. "Are you fixin' to lie abed all day? Or did you wet yourself and you need a towel?"

"What I need," Thal said, "is a new pard."

CHAPTER 2

The Crescent H was one of the largest ranches in that part of Texas. Two-thirds of it was hilly, with a lot of brush. The cattle loved that brush. They'd hide in it during the day.

Thal and Ned and ten other punchers, among them Crawford and Jesse Lee, were searching for those hard-to-find critters to add them to the growing herd that would be shipped to New Orleans.

Thal had donned chaps on account of all the thorns. His were batwings. So were Ned's. Crawford was fond of bull-hide chaps because they were thicker and offered more protection. As for Jesse Lee, he liked Angora chaps. Made from goat hair, his were as white as snow.

The four of them were working a section together. Crawford was the best tracker, and found some fresh sign.

"Made this mornin'. Over a dozen or

more. And lookee here." Bending low from his saddle, Crawford pointed at a particular set of prints. "The size of those, it's got to be a big ol' steer."

"Wonderful," Thal said. Older, wilder animals were notorious for giving cowpokes a hard time. The animals would run and have to be roped, and sometimes would fight when cornered, and their horns weren't to be taken lightly.

"He went up thataway," Crawford said, bobbing his chin at thick timber ahead. "Why don't you boys split right and Jesse Lee and me will take the left side, and we'll work our way in?"

"Sounds good to me," Ned said.

Thal had his rope ready. Shorter than the rope he'd use in open country, it had a smaller loop. Both were essential. In heavy brush a long rope with a wide loop became entangled too easily. "Maybe he'll let us herd him."

"I love an optimist," Ned said.

Jesse Lee laughed, and he and Crawford went their own way.

Clucking to his roan, Ned assumed the lead. "I've been meanin' to ask you somethin', pard."

"I'm listenin'," Thal said, although he'd rather they didn't jaw. An old steer could be as quiet as an Apache when it wanted to, and might slip by if they didn't stay alert.

"How long do you aim to keep at this?"

"At what?" Thal asked absently. "Brush poppin'?" They had been working the brush country for pretty near half a year, and he had gotten darn good at it, if he did say so himself.

"No, you knucklehead. This cowboyin'."

The question so startled Thal that he tore his gaze from the undergrowth. "Where did this come from? I thought you liked it."

"I do," Ned said, nodding. "I like the outdoors. And I like to ride. So the work agrees with me."

"Why talk of quittin', then?"

Ned shifted to look back at him. "I didn't mean quit all cowboyin'. I meant quit the Crescent H and find cow work somewhere else."

Thal had never given it any thought. The wages were good, they were treated decent, and Old Pete had a knack for tasty victuals. "What in tarnation is wrong with the Crescent H?"

"Not a thing," Ned said. "But it's not the only cow outfit in the world. There are heaps of them, from Oklahoma to Montana."

"Wait," Thal said. "You're hankerin' to

21

leave *Texas*?" He'd only come to the Lone Star state about four years ago, and had fallen in love with it. He'd never considered going anywhere else in a million years.

"Texas ain't all of creation, you know," Ned said. "There's a whole wide world we haven't seen yet."

"Why, Ned Leslie," Thal scolded him, only half in jest. "You've had me snookered all this time. I took you for a Texan through and through." His friend had been born and bred there.

"I'm as Texan as you or anybody," Ned said defensively, "and I'll thrash anyone who says different. But would it hurt to travel a little? Would it hurt to see what else is out there?"

"I know what this is," Thal said. "You've come down with a case of wanderlust." He had a cousin who'd come down with it. An itch to see what lay over the next horizon, and the one after that, and then the one after that. The last he'd heard, his cousin was up in Oregon country and could go no farther west on account of the Pacific Ocean. That was where wanderlust got you.

"I suppose I have," Ned admitted. "Although it didn't come on me suddenlike. I've been thinkin' about seein' more of the world for a while now, and was waitin' for the right time to bring it up."

"What makes this the right time?"

"That snake. It spooked you. I could tell. You reckoned you were a goner, and I don't blame you. That rattler was proof that none of us know when our time is up. We could be bucked out tomorrow, for all we know."

"They call that 'life,' " Thal said.

"All the more reason for us to see some more of this world before we cash in our chips. We could hire out on a drive to Kansas, or anywhere you wanted."

"This is your brainstorm, not mine."

"And you're against it," Ned said.

"The notion is new, is all," Thal said. "You've sprung it on me out of the blue. I need to ponder on it some."

"Ponder all you need to."

Thal tried to concentrate on the brush but couldn't. "Do you have somewhere particular in mind or do you aim to ride from here to Canada to find a place you like?"

"I'm not lookin' for somewhere to plant roots," Ned said, sounding irritated. "I just want to look."

Thal never savvied that attitude. His cousin, for instance, had always gone on and on about what was over the next horizon. The answer was simple. Another horizon. A fella could chase horizons from now until the day of doom, and what would it get him? A sore backside from all that riding, and not much else. To Thal, one prairie wasn't much different from another, one mountain peak wasn't any more exciting than the next. Sure, there were some wonderful sights in the world, but riding around looking for them would get boring after a while. How many sunsets did a man have to see, how many sparkling lakes and grand canyons, before he realized that when he had seen one, he'd seen them all?

A sudden snort brought Thal out of himself.

Ned drew rein and pointed at a patch of thick brush ahead and to the left. Deep in the patch, something moved.

Unlimbering his rope, Thal nodded. It must be the big steer they were after. He looked for sign of Crawford and Jesse Lee coming from the other direction. With their help it would be a lot easier.

Another snort heralded the crash of brush as the steer hurtled from cover, making to the northwest.

"Almighty!" Ned blurted.

Thal didn't blame him. The steer was huge. The biggest he'd ever seen, two thousand pounds or better, with a horn spread of eight feet, at least. It was a monster, and it plowed through the oak brush as if the vegetation were paper.

Ned let out a whoop and took off after it, bawling, "Craw! Jesse! It's comin' your way!"

Thal used his spurs. The mare he was riding was one of six horses he'd picked from the remuda. Small and wiry, she was a natural at brush popping. He'd picked her for just that purpose. Larger and slower horses were of no use in the brush.

The longhorn hurtled along like a steam engine, its legs pumping like pistons, leaving a swath of flattened vegetation in its wake. The animal was moving so fast they were falling behind.

Ned resorted to lashing his reins. "Get on there, horse! Get on!"

Acting on inspiration, Thal veered onto the path of destruction and followed it as if it were a road. He quickly gained to where he was only a few yards from the longhorn's tail.

"Stick with him, pard!" Ned hollered.

Thal had every intention of doing so. A peeve of his was letting a steer escape. He'd only ever had it happen a few times, but it galled him. He took it personal, the way some men took insults. And in a way, it *was* an insult. A cowhand worth his place at the feed trough should never let a cow get away.

The longhorn abruptly broke sharply to the west.

Reining after him, Thal saw the reason why. Crawford was barreling in from the northwest. Almost instantly the older puncher reined to cut the longhorn off, but the monster flew by before Crawford could throw a loop.

Thal bent over his saddle horn to avoid a tree limb. The noise they made was tremendous. Between the pounding of hooves and the crashing of brush, he could barely hear himself think.

Two wide white stripes appeared and grew into Angora chaps as Jesse Lee, yipping like a Comanche, bore down from the west.

Again the longhorn changed direction, to the southwest this time. Jesse Lee tried a toss, but it fell short.

Thal could have told him that would happen. The youngster had misjudged. It took experience to know when to let fly. And if there was anything in the world Thal was good at, it was roping. He practiced all the time, and why not? Roping was one of the main skills of his trade. A man who couldn't rope was worthless as a brush thumper and at riding herd.

The longhorn was going all out. The wily

critter knew from experience that if it could stay ahead of them long enough, their horses would tire and they'd have to give up.

Not this time, Thal thought. The steer had met its match in the mare, who had more stamina than most three horses put together. That might be bragging, but it was close to the truth.

They swept down one slope and up another, the longhorn a living engine of destruction, the mare a credit to her kind. The chase might have gone on for a while, if not for the unforeseen.

The steer was racing down yet another hill. Thal, still glued to its tail, eagerly watched for a chance to throw. Without warning the mare squealed and pitched into a roll. Kicking free of the stirrups at the last moment, Thal pushed clear. He struck hard on his shoulder. His hat went flying and he lost his hold on his rope.

The next he knew, Thal was flat on his back. His shoulder and the back of his neck throbbed with pain. Grimacing, he raised his head and turned it from side to side. Nothing appeared to be broken.

Her nostrils flaring, the mare was back up. Her eyes were wide and she was quaking.

A bellow explained why.

Thal's blood went cold at the sight of the longhorn not twenty feet away. Its legs planted wide, it snorted, pawed at the ground, and tossed its head from side to side. He recognized the signs. It was about to charge.

Springing to his feet, Thal dashed to the mare. He reached her just as the steer exploded into motion. In a bound he was in the saddle and reined around to get out of there. He realized he wasn't going to make it and braced for the impact of a ton of sinew and bone.

Out of nowhere, Ned Leslie galloped up. His loop was in the air even as he broke clear of the brush, and it settled as neatly as could be — but only over one horn. That was enough to slow the steer but not stop it. The next instant, though, Jesse Lee was there, whooping as he tossed his own rope. It flew over the other horn and down over the critter's head, but not quite far enough. The steer snorted and pulled back.

"Hold him!" Ned bawled.

There wasn't much either man could do other than dally his rope and hope for the best.

Thal had drawn rein. Thinking to help, he swung down and ran to his rope, which lay

28

on the ground not six feet from the struggling longhorn.

"What do you think you're doin'?" Ned yelled.

Scooping his rope up, Thal coiled it for a throw. He wasn't watching the steer, and looked up when Jesse Lee shouted a warning.

A shorn tip sheared at Thal's face. Ducking, he dropped to his hands and knees and scrambled out of there before he was gored or kicked. The steer tried to reach him but was hindered by the ropes.

With a great rending of brush, Crawford finally arrived. He didn't waste time with a head toss. He threw just as the longhorn reared back with its front hooves off the ground. His loop passed under and up, and with a swift dally and a jerk on his reins, he brought the monster crashing down on its side.

Darting around, Thal threw his own loop over the rear legs, and the job was done. Only then did it hit him how close he had come to not seeing the sun set.

"That was plumb fun," Jesse Lee declared. "Let's add him to the herd and go find another."

"Kids," Crawford said.

"Are you all right, pard?" Ned asked Thal.

"You look a little shaken."

"First the snake and now this," Thal said. "I'm havin' a wonderful day."

"Look at the bright side," Ned said. "You're still breathin'."

CHAPTER 3

Cowboys liked to eat. After a long, hard day, they loved to stuff themselves and relax around the fire. If the food was bad, it affected their outlook, and their work. The last thing a rancher wanted was a bunch of unhappy punchers. Which was why it was often said that the most important person in any outfit was the cook.

Most, like Old Pete, were older men. Most, again like Old Pete, wouldn't qualify to hire on as a culinary wizard with a fancy restaurant. They didn't make dishes that dazzled the brain. But they did take pains to make the best food they could. Their meals were always hot, and ready on time, and varied enough that their fare wasn't always the same old thing.

An outfit's cook was the lord of the collective outfit's stomach, and as such, he enjoyed a sort of power no one but the rancher rivaled. When a cook said he needed help with this or that task, he got that help, no questions asked. Tote water? No problem. Help to clean the pots and pans? You bet. His wishes were the cowpokes' commands.

The Crescent H punchers adored Old Pete, even if he was as cantankerous as could be. Most cooks were. It was sort of a tradition. But Pete worked hard to fill their bellies with food they liked, and that counted more for them than anything.

On this particular evening, Old Pete had prepared stew and sourdough biscuits.

Thal and his friends were the last to reach camp. The sun had already set. They weren't worried about there not being any food left. Old Pete always made plenty. He'd never let a puncher go hungry.

As Thal came up to the pot with his plate in hand, Old Pete cocked a crinkled eye at him.

"About time. I thought maybe I'd have to keep this food warm till midnight."

"I'm so hungry I could eat the wagon," Thal said.

"You do, and you'll be pickin' splinters out of your teeth from now until forever." Old Pete ladled a heaping portion and added two biscuits. "If you need more, just say so."

"I could hug you."

"You do, and I'll wallop you with this ladle." Old Pete shook it at him, then motioned for Thal to move on so Ned could take his turn.

His stomach growling, Thal sat cross-legged facing the fire and dug in. He was famished.

Ned, Crawford, and Jesse Lee joined him. Not much was said until they had cleaned their plates and were sipping coffee from their tin cups.

"That was more than all right," Crawford remarked. "If Old Pete ever leaves this outfit for another, I reckon I'll go hire on with them just so I can go on eatin' his food."

Thal chuckled. Some punchers did that. They'd follow a good cook wherever he went. "You old men and your bellies."

"I can still whip my weight in wildcats," Crawford said.

"He's not that old." Jesse Lee came to his pard's defense. "It'll be a year or two yet before we can call him Methuselah."

Thal laughed.

"Speakin' of leavin'," Thal said, "Ned told me today he's hankerin' to leave the Crescent H."

"Whatever for?" Crawford said in surprise. "This here is a good outfit."

"You got another in mind?" Jesse Lee asked.

"He does not," Thal answered before Ned could. "He wants to wander around seein' the world."

"For real?" Jesse Lee said.

Thal nodded. "I was plumb flabbergasted myself. We do have it good here. I'd as soon stay on until I'm as old as Craw."

"Keep it up," Crawford said.

"Mind if I speak for myself?" Ned said. "I agree the Crescent H is top-notch. But there's a big old world out there I haven't seen much of, and lately I've been hankerin' to have a gander at some of it before I'm too old to sit a saddle."

"Stop talkin' about old," Crawford said.

"Where he goes, I go," Thal said, "even if I'd just as soon not."

"Thanks," Ned said drily.

"I don't know," Jesse Lee said.

"No one is askin' you or Craw to tag along," Ned said. "I haven't even made up my mind yet. It's just a hankerin'."

"Some hankerin's should be nipped in the bud," Crawford said. "Like goin' barefoot to take a leak in the middle of the night. You never know but when a rattler might mistake your toe for a mouse."

"My pard knows all about rattlers," Ned

said. "He's an expert."

Jesse Lee laughed.

"I knew a puncher once who got a hankerin' go be an ore hound," Crawford went on. "So he took himself to Arizona, bought a mule and a shovel and a pan, and went to it." He paused. "Apaches staked him out and skinned him alive."

"I'm not about to be no prospector," Ned said.

Thal gazed up at the sky, which had darkened and was filling with stars. "Thank you, Lord."

"There's a lot of talk about gold up the Black Hills way," Jesse Lee remarked. "Ever since Custer found some."

"There's also a lot of Sioux in the Black Hills," Crawford said, "and you might recollect that they wiped out Custer and most of his command."

"They're as unfriendly as the Comanches," Jesse Lee said.

"I'm not hankerin' to go to the Black Hills either," Ned informed them. "I was thinkin' more like driftin' up Denver way, and maybe Montana, after."

"News to me," Thal said. "A pard is always the last to know."

"What's in Denver besides whores?" Crawford said. "I hear tell they've got more than just about anywhere."

"More than New Orleans?" Jesse Lee said.

Crawford nodded. "More than a thousand work the line, I've heard. They call it the Row, and it's wide-open."

Jesse Lee whistled. "That's a heap of whores."

"I wouldn't go to Denver for the whores," Ned said, sounding irritated. "I'd go to take in the sights."

"Which?" Jesse Lee said.

"How the blazes do I know? I ain't been there yet."

"It seems to me," Crawford said, "that you've got ants in your britches, and unless you scratch powerful hard, they're liable to lead you to who knows where."

"Now it's ants," Ned said in disgust.

"Well, it's somethin'," Thal said. "But you're my pard and I'll stick by you."

That was what pards did. He'd tried to explain that once to a drummer from back East. The drummer wasn't acquainted with cowpoke lingo and thought that a pard was the same as being a friend. Thal had set him straight. A pard was more than that. A pard was a range mate, a bunkhouse companion, confidant, adviser. A pard was more a brother than anything. Pards were inseparable, and would do anything for each other.

Which was why most chose their pards with care. A bad pard could bring a man to ruin.

"Don't pack your war bag just yet," Ned said. "I ain't even decided if I'm goin' to go."

"I hope you don't," Jesse Lee said. "You two are the best friends Craw and me have."

"If you were to drift, I might even go with you," Crawford said.

Jesse Lee gave him a sharp glance. "For real?"

"You say that a lot," Crawford said.

"For real?" Jesse Lee said again.

Crawford chuckled, and shrugged. "I haven't seen much of the world my own self, and as you three chipmunks keep pointin' out, I'll be sproutin' gray hairs any day now."

"Chipmunks?" Ned said.

"Ever see how a chipmunk's cheeks bulge when it's gatherin' up nuts and such?" Crawford said.

"I have," Ned replied.

"Well, your heads are a lot like their cheeks."

"Are you sayin' we're the cheeks or the nuts?"

"Guess," Crawford said, and laughed.

"If anyone ever tells you that you have a sense of humor," Ned said, "shoot him."

Now it was Thal who laughed. It struck him how much he liked these three, and working at the Crescent H. He hoped Ned didn't give in to his wanderlust. It would be a shame to give up the good life they had.

Off in the growing darkness, hooves drummed.

A puncher who was spreading out his blanket looked up and said, "Someone is comin'."

"Who's left that ain't here?" another man asked.

They all looked around, and then Old Pete said, "No one is left except the two ridin' herd. And the rider ain't comin' from that direction."

Thal rose to his feet, and he wasn't the only one. Whoever it was was riding hard, and that was unusual unless there was an urgency involved.

"He's in an awful hurry." Ned had said the very thing that Thal was thinking.

No sooner were the words out of his mouth than the rider drew rein in a flurry of dust and dismounted.

"Why, it's Hank," Jesse Lee said.

Hank Winslow was the Crescent H foreman. Like their cook, he had a reputation for being one of the best in the business. He had more experience with cattle than just about anyone, and he was fair in all his dealings. So long as a puncher did his job to the best of his ability, Hank was willing to forgive the occasional mistake. But cross him, and he came down on the offender like a stampede.

Hank didn't look all that tough, which was deceptive. He had a square jaw and a scar on his chin from the time he was kicked by a bronc. Now he nodded and said simply, "Boys."

Old Pete produced a cup of coffee. "Here's some Arbuckle's to wash down the dust."

"I'm obliged," Hank said.

"If you came to check up on us," a cowboy named Fisher said, "you'll be happy to hear there hasn't been a hitch."

Another puncher nodded. "The roundup is goin' exactly as you wanted. We're even ahead on the count."

"It's not the cows I'm here about," Hank said, and shocked Thal by pointing at him. "It's Christie here."

"Me?" Thal blurted.

"There's been a development," Hanks said. "The big sugar sent me to fetch you back."

"Me?" Thal blurted a second time. He couldn't imagine a single circumstance that would call for the ranch owner to send for him.

"He's not bein' fired, is he?" Ned said. "Because if he is, when he goes, I go."

"Why would we fire a good hand like Thalis?" Hank said, and grinned. "Now, you, on the other hand . . ."

Old Pete cackled and some of the others joined in.

"It's nice to be loved," Ned said.

"What can Mr. Hooper possibly want with me?" Thal asked. "I haven't done anything."

"He got a letter," Hank said.

"Mr. Hooper did?"

"It wasn't President Grant."

Old Pete did more cackling.

"Mr. Hooper got a letter that has somethin' to do with me?" Thal was unable to hide his bewilderment.

"It's from your sister," Hank said.

"Ursula?"

"If she's the only sister you've got, that's who it must be."

Thal could have been floored with a feather. He'd left home nearly six years ago and hadn't heard from them the entire time. Not that he blamed them. He'd only ever sent word to them once, about hiring on at the Crescent H, and how much he liked it.

"Is it my ma or my pa? Are they sick or dead?"

"Mr. Hooper didn't say and I didn't ask," Hank replied. "The letter was addressed to him. I wasn't there when he read it. All I know is that he sent for me and told me to fetch you right back, and here I am. We'll leave at first light." He turned and went over to some other punchers.

Ned placed his hand on Thal's shoulder. "Don't look so stricken. Maybe it's good news."

"Sure," Thal said. He didn't believe it for a minute. Letters from home were rare, and nearly always brought bad tidings. Something was wrong. He felt it in his bones.

"You should turn in early and try to get some sleep, pard," Ned advised.

"Fat chance," Thal said.

CHAPTER 4

Ezekiel and Carmody Hooper were third-generation Texans.

Zeke's grandfather had come West from Ohio with a small inheritance. He'd bought up all the land he could and took to ranching like a duck took to water, which was remarkable given that back in Ohio he'd made his living as a store clerk. He started with a small herd and grew from there. Zeke's father expanded the herd, and their range, even more, and turned the Crescent H into a prosperous example of what a ranch could be when it was run right.

Their prosperity was reflected in the ranch house. Three stories high, it had a porch that ran around the entire house, with whitewashed pillars and a railing carved in a flowery design. Inside, the home was downright extravagant. Polished mahogany floors, a music room, a den and library — the house had it all.

Thal had only stepped foot inside twice before, and each time had intimidated him. He wasn't used to so much wealth. It made him nervous to walk on floors so clean he could eat off them. He wanted to take his spurs off before going in, but Hank didn't give him time. No sooner did they dismount than the foreman ushered him and Ned inside.

Thal had asked if his pard could come along, and Hank didn't object.

Now, standing in the cool hallway with their hats in hand, they waited for Hank to return. He'd gone to announce them, as he put it.

"Lordy, this place is somethin'," Ned said quietly, as if they were in church. He gestured at a small table with a vase that held fresh flowers. "I'm afraid to touch anything for fear it might break."

"I know what you mean," Thal said. He was more concerned, though, about his sister's letter.

"I wonder if you and me will ever live high on the hog like this."

"I doubt it."

"What kind of way is that to talk?" Ned said. "Where's your confidence? You and me could start our own ranch someday, and it could do right well. You never know."

"I know I'm not as smart as Mr. Hooper," Thal said. His pa always used to say that a man should know his limitations, and Thal liked to think that he knew his. He wasn't a fast thinker, like some. He knew a lot about horses and cows, and that was about it. As for running a business, especially a large operation like a ranch, that took more than he felt he had in him.

"I bet we could do it," Ned persisted. "We'd learn as we go, like most folks. Maybe we'd make mistakes, but we'd have a good ranch, and make do."

"I admire your pluck," Thal said.

"I wish you had more of it yourself."

Thal was taken aback. Ned hardly ever criticized him. Not a serious criticism anyway. "Well, we are how we are."

"Not so," Ned said. "We can change. No one stays the same their whole life long."

"I meant in how we think and what we can do."

"So did I. It's not like we go from the cradle to our grave always the same. We grow, don't we? We start out as babies and end up as old men."

"That's our bodies," Thal said. He was watching down the hall for Hank to reappear.

"So what? Our minds can grow just like

our bodies do. I don't think the same way now as I did when I was wavin' a rattle around and poopin' my diapers. That's because my mind has grown."

"Maybe you only think it has," Thal said. "Maybe it's the same mind, but all you did was fill it with words."

"That's ridiculous. It's not only words. We do things. We experience things. We grow from that too."

Thal shrugged. "All I know is that I'm the same person now as I was when I was ten. I'm bigger, sure. And I know more stuff. But I'm still the same person."

"You have a strange —" Ned began, and stopped.

Hank had stepped out of a doorway and was beckoning.

"Here we go," Ned said.

Thal had butterflies in his belly. For all this fuss to be made, he had a hunch either his ma or his pa had died, or maybe his younger brother, Myles. His sister had to be all right. She wrote the letter.

"Mr. Hooper will see you," Hank said, and stepped aside so they could enter the parlor.

Mr. and Mrs. Hooper were seated on a plush settee. She wore a lovely dress with a high collar, and her shoes were polished to a sheen. He wore a suit, which wasn't

45

unusual, as he only donned work clothes when he had work to do.

"Howdy, men," their employer said, rising to greet them.

As nervous as a cat in a room full of dogs, Thal shook and nodded and said, "Mr. Hooper."

"Call me Zeke. I prefer that."

"Yes, sir."

Thal smiled at the wife. "Pleased to see you again, ma'am."

"Same here, ma'am," Ned said.

Mrs. Hooper had remained seated. She smiled in return but didn't say anything.

"Have a seat," Mr. Hooper directed, indicating nearby chairs.

"We're not all that clean," Thal said. He hadn't been able to take a bath in over a week, and he sorely missed it.

"Nonsense. Be seated."

Roosting as delicately as if he were sitting on a flower, Thal complied. He began to wring his hat, and caught himself.

"We won't keep you in suspense," Mr. Hooper said. "As Hank has no doubt explained, I've received a letter from your sister."

"Ursula," Thal said.

"Yes. It was addressed specifically to me and not to you. I hope you won't mind, but

I've let my wife read it too. Only us. No one else knows the contents. Not even Hank."

"Do you want me to go, then?" the foreman asked.

"No, you stay," Mr. Hooper said. "You should know his decision as soon as he makes it, since you might have to reassign some of the hands."

"My decision?" Thal said.

"You'll understand shortly." Mr. Hooper sat back down on the settee and touched his wife's arm. "I'd like Carmody to read the letter. Since it's from your sister, that's only fitting."

Thal didn't see how, but didn't say so.

Mrs. Hooper reached down beside her and picked up an opened envelope. Extracting the letter, she unfolded it, smoothed it in her lap, and gave a slight cough. " 'My dearest brother,' " she began.

Thal felt his ears grow warm. Ursula and he had always gotten along well. She was five years younger, only seventeen to his twenty-two. Their brother Myles was twenty.

Mrs. Hooper had looked over as if expecting him to say something, and when Thal merely sat there, she went on. " 'I'm writing this to your employer. I would have written to you, only you can't read.' " She stopped and looked up again.

Thal squirmed in his chair. "That's true," he felt compelled to say. "Not real well anyhow. My ma taught us the alphabet and such, but I always had to wrestle with the words to make sense of them. The letters never look right."

"How's that again?" Mr. Hooper said.

"The letters," Thal repeated. "When I try to read, they're jumbled or upside down. I don't know why that is."

"How unusual," his employer said.

"I've heard of one or two people with a similar condition," Mrs. Hooper remarked. "They're born that way, I've been informed. It's very sad."

"Yes, ma'am," Thal agreed, although reading had never been high on his list of favorite things to do.

Mrs. Hooper bent to the letter once more. " 'Please ask your employer to forgive my boldness, but I am at my wit's end and have nowhere else to turn. Ma and Pa can't help, so that leaves you.' "

Thal sat straighter. He had been right; something terrible must have happened.

" 'Myles has left home,' " Mrs. Hooper continued. " 'He's older than you were when you left, and went off to make his mark in the world. What is it with you men that you have to leave your marks?' " Mrs.

Hooper paused, and chuckled. "She has that right. You men truly do."

"Carmody, please," Mr. Hooper said.

"Sorry." Mrs. Hooper gave another light cough. " 'I asked Myles not to go. I told him Pa can use his help around the farm. But Myles wouldn't listen. He has that mark to make. I did persuade him to write to me every chance he got, and he did so regularly for a while. He'd heard about that gold rush in the Black Hills and wrote that he was thinking of going there to make his fortune. I wrote back, warning him how dangerous it was. The Sioux have been scalping folks. And the country is infested with cutthroats. Ma says she's heard that there are killings and robberies and lynchings all over the place, and that no God-fearing Christian should go anywhere near that country. I wrote and told Myles, but he wrote back that he was going anyway. It about brought me to tears.' " Mrs. Hooper stopped.

"Is your throat dry, my dear?" Mr. Hooper asked. "Would you like a glass of water?"

"I'm fine," Mrs. Hooper said. She was staring at Thal. "Your sister cares for your brother and you very much." It was a statement, not a question.

"Yes, ma'am."

"You're fortunate in that regard. My own

49

sister and I have never gotten along. Even less so after I married Zeke. She's jealous, I believe."

Mr. Hooper frowned. "Do you deem it wise to air our family linen in public? It's none of their concern."

"I was only making conversation," Mrs. Hooper said. "But very well." She continued. " 'In his last letter, Myles went on and on about someplace called American City. I never heard of it and don't know where it is except that it's supposed to be right in the heart of the Black Hills. I wrote back asking him to let me know when he got there and how he was faring, but three months went by and I didn't receive a single letter. So I wrote to American City, general delivery, care of the marshal. I don't even know if they have one, but most towns do. I asked about Myles, and if there was any chance someone could inform me of his whereabouts and his health. To my surprise, I received a letter from a Mr. Tweed. He didn't say who he was or what he does. It was short and to the point, and said only that Myles had been shot and was recovering.' "

Thal almost came out of his chair. "Shot?"

"There's more," Mrs. Hooper said, and resumed yet again. " 'I am heartbroken at the news. I'd like to go find Myles and make sure he is all right, but Ma and Pa won't hear of it. I pleaded with Pa to go, but Ma got mad and won't let him. She said she's sorry about Myles, but he brought it on himself, and she's not willing to lose Pa on his account. I think that's cruel, but that's just me.' "

"Sounds sensible to me," Mr. Hooper marked. "I don't blame the mother one bit."

Nor did Thal. His parents were both in their fifties, much too old to be traipsing around the Black Hills in search of his brother. Not with all the dangers they might encounter.

Mrs. Hooper went on. " 'Thalis, I know I can count on you. I appeal to you for help. Please, please, please ask your employer for time off and go to the Black Hills and find Myles. I won't rest until I hear he's safe, and I doubt you will either. If I am asking too much, I apologize. But I'm sister to both of you, and love you both dearly, and would do for you as I'm trying to do for him.' " Mrs. Hooper glanced at Thal. "I said it before and I'll say it again. You are indeed a most fortunate man, Mr. Christie."

"Thank you, ma'am," Thal said. He supposed he was, at that, to have a sister so devoted.

Once more Mrs. Hooper bent to the letter. " 'If you can do so, please visit home on your way to the Black Hills. You have to come north anyway.' "

"Where are you from, Mr. Christie?" Mr. Hooper interrupted. "I don't believe I've ever heard."

"My pa has a farm near Salina, Kansas," Thal revealed. "I was raised there."

"Kansas is a fine state," Mr. Hooper declared.

"There's only a little left to read," Mrs. Hooper said, and finished with, " 'Can you have your employer or a friend write to me whether you will or you won't come? If not, I'll find someone else to go look for Myles. Again, if this is an imposition, I'm sorry. But we're family, and this is what family should do.' " She paused a final time. " 'In deepest affection, your loving sister, Ursula.' "

"Well, now," Thal said, not knowing what else he should say. He looked at the floor and shook his head in amazement at the unexpected turns of events. When he looked up, everyone was staring at him. "What?"

Mr. Hooper rose from the settee. "I imagine I know what your decision will be, but let me hear it. And don't worry about your job. I'll hold it open for you for, say, three months. If you haven't returned by then, I'll take it that I should hire new hands to replace you."

"Yes, what will you do, Mr. Christie?" Mrs. Hooper. "Will you go to your sister's aid, or not?"

"I believe I will," Thal said.

CHAPTER 5

The Texas Panhandle was mostly grassland, and at that time of year, mostly dry. It was also largely uninhabited. Ranches were few, although Thal had heard tell that Charles Goodnight was starting one up. If anyone could succeed at ranching in the Panhandle, it was Goodnight. The man was well-known for his partnership with John Chisum over to New Mexico, and for the Goodnight-Loving trail they'd established to take cattle to market.

Thal admired Goodnight greatly. From all he'd heard, Goodnight was just about the best cattleman anywhere, and had a great head for business. Thal would give anything to be like him. He was thinking that when Ned, who was riding ahead, abruptly drew rein and pointed at the ground.

"Do you see what I see?"

Thal brought his chestnut to a stop and peered down. His skin crawled at the sight of a lot of horse tracks; not one was shod.

"Comanches," Ned said.

Thal nodded. "Thank goodness they're headin' east, and not north like us."

"What are they doin' here at all?" Ned said. "They're all supposed to be on reservations."

The Comanches were once the terrors of Texas. Their warriors ranged far and wide, taking white lives wherever they could. Constant warfare, and disease, nearly wiped them out. The slaughter of the buffalo, on which they'd depended, completed their downfall. Only a couple of years ago, the last of the holdouts, Quanah Parker, had surrendered.

"These must be wild ones," Thal said. There had been reports of warriors slipping away from the reservations to raid and kill. For nomads like the Comanches, who'd always wandered wild and free, being cooped up on a reservation was a sort of living death. Thal hated to admit that, after all the people they'd slain, he felt more than a smidgen of sympathy for their plight.

"Just our luck," Ned said, gazing anxiously about. "Young bucks on the warpath, I reckon."

"It will be a cold camp for us tonight, to be safe," Thal said.

"I hear that, pard."

They rode on more warily than before. When specks appeared in the distance, they both stopped and placed their hands on their six-shooters.

Thal braced for the worst even though he didn't think it likely the specks were the Comanches.

Together, they cautiously advanced until the specks acquired shape and substance.

"Well, I'll be," Ned declared, and chuckled in relief. "Look at those horns and humps."

"Buffalo, by golly," Thal said. He well knew that the enormous herds of yesteryear were gone. Killed for their hides more than their meat, they'd been slaughtered, their carcasses left to rot. Only a few small herds remained, and to see any these days was rare.

Thal counted fourteen, ambling along as if they had somewhere to go. Enormous animals, they stood five feet high at the shoulders and were up to eleven feet in length. He couldn't imagine trying to bring one down with a puny bow and arrow, yet Comanches and warriors from other tribes had done it all the time.

"They've seen us," Ned said.

The buffalo were swinging wide to the west to avoid them. Apparently the buffs had learned from the demise of so many of their shaggy brethren, and were fighting shy of humans.

"Dang, they're somehin'," Ned said. "Look at how big they are, and how they move."

"Take one for a pet, why don't you?"

"Would that we could," Ned said. "Or at least tend them for their meat like we do cattle."

Thal grunted. It had been tried a few times but not with any success. Buffalo were too huge and too powerful to be contained by a fence. Not even barbed wire could stop them. Combine that with their temperamental natures, and they were trouble on the hoof.

This small bunch trotted on into the heat haze and were presently out of sight.

"I'm glad I got to see that," Ned said. "It'll be somethin' to tell my kids about."

"Seein' buffalo?"

"Sure. There might not be any at all before too long. It's like those birds back East. Those pigeons. Once there were millions of 'em and now they're all gone. The buffalo might end up the same."

Thal hoped not. He didn't think any living thing deserved to be wiped out entirely, unless it was rattlesnakes.

That night they camped in a hollow, without a fire. Any light, however small, might give them away, and with Comanches on the prowl, Thal believed in being safe rather than sorry.

They were eating cold beans with the stars for a canopy when Ned asked out of the blue, "What's this sister of yours like?"

Thal paused with his spoon halfway to his mouth. "Why do you want to know?"

"You never even told me you had one. Are you ashamed of her or somethin'?"

"You heard the letter. Ursula is a sweet gal. Our whole family thinks the world of her."

"A fella would think you'd talk about her more."

"My own sister? To a passel of randy cowpokes?" Thal snorted. "Not on your life." He had a sudden suspicion. "Why this sudden interest in her anyhow?"

"Just curious," Ned said, chewing noisily. "I don't have a sis, but I always wanted one. Ma said after six boys, she wasn't havin' any more kids."

"Curiosity, huh?" Thal said skeptically. "Just remember. You're to be on your best behavior when you meet my family."

Ned stopped chewing. "Why, pard, I'm stricken. Would I do any less for you?"

"I mean it. I know how you get around females."

"I have no idea what you're talkin' about."

"Do you recollect the Red-Eye Saloon? And how you danced on the bar to impress that dove? I was plumb embarrassed."

"I was plumb drunk," Ned said, "so no, I don't remember a whole lot about it except that it must have worked because I woke up in her bed the next mornin'."

"Brag, why don't you?"

"Can I help it if my dances make females swoon?"

"Since when is stompin' your heels dancin'? I've seen broncs dance better than you when they're tryin' to buck the peeler."

"Where do you think I learned it from?" Ned said, and laughed.

Despite himself, Thal laughed too. "Just don't be stompin' your heels at my sister. I don't think she ever dances."

"How would you know? I bet you never asked her to."

"Dance with my own sister? No one does that." Thal shuddered. "That'd be almost as bad as dancin' with your own ma."

"I danced with my ma a couple of times," Ned said. "At church socials. Waltzes, they were. She was teachin' me how so when I took to courtin' I could impress the gals."

"How did you go from a waltz to heel-stompin' in a saloon?"

"When you've had enough whiskey," Ned said, "a waltz just won't do."

Thal hardly ever danced because he was as ungainly as a bird with its wings clipped. When he tried, he was all elbows and knees. And once he'd tromped on a poor girl's toes.

"You know," Ned said thoughtfully, "if I wasn't so fond of cow work, I wouldn't mind dancin' for a livin'."

"Who ever heard of a such a thing? No one does that, you simpleton."

"Sure they do. Back East. They have schools where they teach folks to dance."

"You're makin' that up."

"As God is my witness," Ned said. "My ma told me about them. You pay money and some gal teaches you the steps so you can do the dances proper."

"Well, that would be an improvement over your stompin'," Thal said, "but I wouldn't waste good money on somethin' as silly as dance lessons."

"Why not? You could stand to improve your chances at romance. You're not exactly a marvel at it."

"There you go again," Thal said. "Bringin' that up."

"I'm only tryin' to help," Ned said. "Sooner or later you're bound to hanker after a bedmate who smells of perfume instead of cows. You'll need to impress her if you hope to have her say 'I do.' "

"I can do without perfume."

"Is your nose broken? Any man with sense would rather smell a flower than a cow's backside."

Thal spooned more beans, and froze. He'd heard something, out on the plain. Their horses had heard it too. Both animals had raised their heads and were staring to the east. "Did you hear that?" he whispered.

"What?"

"I don't rightly know. But it was somethin'." Thal put down his beans and spoon, quietly rose, and moved toward the east rim of the hollow.

"The Comanches, you reckon?" Ned whispered, following.

"I said I don't rightly know. It could have been a horse. It could have been a wild animal."

A sea of pale grass in the starlight, the plain stretched for as far as the eye see could in all directions.

After a minute or so, Ned whispered, "I don't hear or see anything."

Neither did Thal. "If it was Comanches,

we won't."

Ned drew his Colt. "I'm too young to be pincushioned with arrows."

"For all we know it was a bear."

"Bears like hills and mountains and woods, not prairies."

"There are plains bears too. Most have been killed off, like the buffalo, but some are still around."

"You're sayin' that to scare me," Ned said. "You know I'm as fond of bears as you are of snakes. I was mauled once, if you recollect."

"Yes, you told —" Thal stopped.

Out on the plain figures moved. Riders, passing like phantoms in the night.

"Comanches!" Ned whispered.

Thal couldn't tell much other than the riders were in single file, as Comanches liked to do. He guessed they were a couple of hundred yards out, if that, and was doubly glad he'd insisted on not making a fire.

A low nicker about made his heart stop.

Thal spun. His chestnut must have smelled the other horses. Rising and tucking at the knees, he ran down and rushed over to place his hand over the chestnut's muzzle. "Enough out of you," he said in the animal's ear.

Ned stayed on the rim awhile. When he finally descended, he announced, "They're gone, and good riddance."

Thal let go of the chestnut. "We'd better keep watch. I'll go first and you can go second unless you'd rather it was the other way around."

"Fine by me," Ned replied, "but it's early yet to turn in."

They resumed their meal.

Thal barely tasted his beans. The close shave had reminded him of how perilous the wilds were. It wasn't like back East, where things were so tamed down a man could go around without a firearm or even a knife and not be in fear for his life. The West would be like that one day, some believed, and truth to tell, Thal wouldn't mind. He wasn't Jesse Lee. The prospect of a shooting affray didn't excite him one bit. He'd be content to live out the rest of days without ever having to shoot anyone, hostiles included.

"What are you thinkin' about?" Ned asked. "Your sister?"

"Not her again."

"Then what? Your brother?"

"I'm thinkin' how much I like to breathe," Thal said. "I don't want to die this young. There's a lot of life I haven't lived yet."

"That's the spirit," Ned said, grinning. "It's exactly what I've been talkin' about."

"No, you want to waltz all over creation. That's not the same thing."

"Are you pokin' fun at my dancin' again?"

"No. Why?"

"You said 'waltz.' "

Thal sighed. "There are days when I wonder why I took you for a pard."

"That's easy," Ned said. "Because I'm popular with the ladies and you're not."

"You and your fillies," Thal said. "There is more to life than females."

"Oh, Thalis," Ned said with mock gravity. "You worry me. You truly do. Without females there wouldn't be any life. Or any romance. The way they walk, the way they laugh, how their eyes twinkle when they're playful, those red lips of theirs. Don't you know that females help make life worth livin'?"

"What I know," Thal said, "is that if you so much as wink at my sister, I'll shoot you."

CHAPTER 6

Salina, Kansas. In its early days, life was precarious. Its residents had to fend off hostile war parties, and later, during the Civil War, an attack by guerillas. After the war, Salina boomed.

The Kansas Pacific Railroad had a lot to do with the growth of Salina's economy. It turned Salina into a shipping hub for cattle. Almost overnight, as it were, Salina became a rowdy cow town. But the saloons and the fallen doves didn't sit well with the majority of Salina's everyday folk, who weren't upset at all when the cattlemen took their trade elsewhere.

Salina became a farming hub instead. Wheat was grown in abundance. So was alfalfa, thanks to a local resident who saw its potential.

Nowadays, Salina was as peaceable as a town could be. Flour mills provided employment for a large workforce. Her churches were well attended. They had a school. Their law officers discouraged riffraff from staying. The worst problem Salina had was invasions of grasshoppers.

There were worse places to grow up than a God-fearing community like Salina.

"So this is where you're from?" Ned Leslie remarked as they rode down Main Street.

"I was five or so when my pa moved here," Thal replied. "Back then, Salina wasn't much more than a trading post. It even had a stockade at one time."

"What do they for entertainment? Listen to the grass grow?"

"Poke fun all you want," Thal said. "Salina is as civilized as anywhere. Take a gander at the new wooden sidewalks."

"Sidewalks don't impress me much. Saloons do. I ain't seen a single one yet. What do they do? Hide them?"

"We're not Dodge City. We don't go for rowdy behavior."

"It looks to me like you don't go for any behavior beside walkin' around smilin' at each other."

"We don't have time to drink anyway," Thal said. "We're goin' straight to my pa's place."

"My throat wouldn't mind a sip or two. We've been ridin' for days and days."

"The sooner I talk to my sister, the better. She might have heard word from Myles since she wrote me."

"I forgot about her," Ned said. "You're right. Let's forget the coffin varnish and go pay a visit."

"I won't tell you again to behave."

Ned grinned. "I'll be as gentlemanly as can be."

"You better."

Their horses were tired or Thal would have gone at a gallop. He was impatient to see his family again. Not once down in Texas had he been homesick, but he was now.

A rush of recollections filled his head, stirring fond memories. Milking the cows, collecting eggs from the chicken coop, the plowing and the planting and the harvesting, Thal had helped with all of it and would have made a good farmer. He'd disappointed his pa and ma terribly when he announced that he had heard so much about the cowboy life he'd like to try it awhile and see if it agreed with him.

His pa was hurt the most. In large part, Thal reckoned, because his pa had planned to leave the farm to him someday. He'd naturally figured that with him gone, his pa would leave it to his brother. But now Myles had gone off too.

The sight of it brought a lump to Thal's throat. The house and the barn, the tilled fields, they were exactly as he remembered. The house wasn't as huge as the Hooper ranch house, but it was a wooden house and not a soddy like those a lot of Kansas farmers lived in. The house was painted white, the barn red. The outhouse, thanks to his ma, was the same blue as the sky. That never made any sense to him, but his mother insisted their outhouse should look "pretty."

Ned had noticed his reaction. "That's it yonder, I take it?"

Thal nodded.

"Your folks are doin' better than mine. We lived in a cabin, and our farm is small compared to yours."

"A roof is a roof," Thal said.

"Lessen it leaks."

They came to the turn into the lane, and Thal drew rein.

"What's the matter?"

"I'm just lookin'," Thal said. Truth was, he was awash in emotion. It had been years since he left, without a word from them the entire time. Then again, since he could hardly read, thanks to his condition, why would they bother? It had taken a crisis like

68

Myles being shot for his sister to send that letter.

"Look all you want," Ned said. "It choked me up too, the last time I was home. I couldn't get over how old my folks looked. They'd aged ten years in just two or three. It was spooky."

Someone was moving about in the front yard. A pink bonnet gave Thal a clue who. "Don't forget what I told you about winkin'," he said, and gigged the chestnut.

"Is that her?"

"It's not Betsy Ross."

Ursula was wearing one of her plain "everyday dresses," as she liked to call them, and had sunk to her knees by their ma's flower garden. Her back was to them, and she was so engrossed in whatever she was doing that she didn't hear them until they were almost there. Glancing over her shoulder, she squealed in delight, leaped to her feet, and flew toward them with the biggest smile in the world on her face. "Thalis! Thalis! You're home!"

"Land sakes, she's pretty," Ned breathed.

Thal had never thought about it, but he supposed she was. Ursula had golden hair, blue eyes, high cheekbones, and a clean complexion. She'd grown since he saw her last, from a girl into a young woman. He drew rein and dismounted, and was nearly bowled over when Ursula flung herself at him and wrapped her arms tight.

"Oh, Thalis. It's so good to see you again."

Thal couldn't speak for the constriction in his throat. He returned her hug and thought his eyes might mist over, but fortunately they didn't.

Ursula drew back and studied him. "You got my letter, then? Oh, I'm so happy. I'm worried sick about Myles."

"Me too," Thal got out. "It's why I came."

"I hope that's not the only reason." Ursula clasped both his hands in hers. "Didn't you miss us even a little? I've missed you."

"Sure," Thal said, and coughed.

Just then Ned said, "Are you goin' to introduce me or am I a bump on a log?"

"Oh." Thal couldn't take his eyes off Ursula. "Sis, this is my pard, Edmund Horace Leslie."

Ned reacted as if he'd been slapped. "You didn't just tell her my whole name."

"He likes 'Ned' for short," Thal said.

"Mr. Leslie," Ursula said, bestowing a warm smile on him.

"I'm hardly much older than you, Miss Christie," Ned said. "Just 'Ned' will do."

"So long as you call me Ursula."

Ned seemed to be entranced. "Whatever

you like, ma'am. I am yours to command."

"Why, listen to you," Ursula said. "Aren't you gallant?"

Thal almost laughed when Ned's cheeks turned red. "Oh, he's that all right. Just ask any saloon girl in Texas."

"Oh, Thalis," Ned said.

Ursula laughed. "Let's put your animals in the barn and go inside. Ma is takin' her afternoon nap. She'll be overjoyed to see you. She frets something awful, about you and Myles both."

"Pa?" Thal said.

"He's out in the fields. Unless he saw you ride in, he'll be back along about suppertime. You know how he is."

"I do," Thal said. Their pa was one of the hardest workers he'd ever known. From dawn until dusk, day in and day out, year after year, their pa worked his fingers to the bone.

"What's your pa's name anyhow?" Ned asked. "Your ma's too, for that matter. I don't believe you've ever said."

It was Ursula who answered. "Pa's name is Frederick. He answers to 'Fred' but likes 'Frederick' better."

"Frederick it is, then," Ned said.

"Ma was christened Elizabeth Collandar Beckwith," Ursula revealed. "Everyone calls her Beth."

"It'll be Mrs. Christie for me," Ned said. "To show my respect."

"You sure are courteous," Ursula said.

"For you, ma'am, I'll be anything."

Thal glared.

"What?" Ned said.

The barn was as it had been the day Thal left: the same stalls, the same hayloft, the same feed bins for the cows, and the same hog pen with the same stink. The shade inside was welcome after the heat of the sun. As he stripped his saddle, he recalled the time he stabbed himself with a pitchfork. He'd been breaking apart a bale of straw and misjudged, and a tine went through his middle toe. He was twelve. It had hurt like the dickens, but he'd refused to cry.

Ursula rocked on the balls of her feet and stared at him as if she couldn't credit her eyes. "You're really here."

"You sent for me, didn't you?"

"I didn't know you'd come. It's been so long since we heard from you. . . ." Ursula shrugged, and looked sad.

Stung by her comment, Thal said, "You know I can't write any better than I can read."

"You could have someone write for you. Like Mr. Leslie here."

"It's Ned, remember?" Ned said. "And I'm afraid I wouldn't be much use. My writin' is chicken scrawl. Mostly all I can do is make my mark."

"You never had any schooling?"

"I'm from the hill country of North Carolina. Readin' and writin' don't count for much. We're more partial to coon huntin' and fishin'. And pretty gals."

Thal glared again.

"I like your friend," Ursula said.

Thal grunted. "It's nice somebody does."

The front porch had three rocking chairs now, instead of two. Thal touched the brass knocker on the door that hardly anybody ever used but that his ma had insisted they'd needed just as she'd insisted the outhouse should be blue.

"Your room is just as you left it," Ursula remarked as he opened the door for her. "Myles didn't change anything after you left. Ned here can have Myles's bed. I'm sure Ma and Pa won't mind."

The parlor's main fixture was a sofa, not the usual settee. Another of their mother's extravagances, on which she took her daily nap.

Thal stood in the doorway, staring at her, and was flooded with more reminiscences. Of his mother taking a large splinter out of his thumb and drying his tears, when he was little. Of her delicious meals, and especially her apple pies. Of quiet evenings on the porch, with his folks rocking and him and his siblings playing in the yard. They had been wonderful, glorious days. The bedrock of his life, you might say.

"Maybe we shouldn't wake her," Ned whispered.

"She'll be upset if we don't," Ursula said, and going over, she gently shook her mother's shoulder. "Ma? Ma? Your oldest is here. The prodigal has returned."

Thal had never seen his mother move so fast. She was awake and off the sofa and coming toward him with her arms outstretched before he could get out, "It's good to see you again, Ma."

Ursula joined in the hug, and they stood there a minute or more, until Ned shifted his feet and a spur jingled, reminding them he was there.

"I'm so pleased," Thal's ma said, stepping back. "Your pa and I are worried sick about your brother."

"I'll find him," Thal vowed.

"You've heard about the Black Hills, haven't you?" his mother said anxiously. "Our parson says no decent soul should go there. They're full of killers and thieves and confidence men, and worse. It's worse than Sodom and Gomorrah, he says. Why your brother took it into his head to go there, I'll never know."

"Myles was hopin' to strike it rich," Ursula said.

"A foolish notion," their mother declared. "He's my own son and I love him dearly, but he's not mature enough, by half. Now's he gone and got himself shot and might be dead for all we know."

"Ma, don't talk like that," Ursula said.

"Well, he might be." Their mother placed her hand on Thal's shoulder and fixed him with misting eyes. "Promise me you won't do the same. Promise me you won't get yourself killed."

"I'll try my best," Thal said.

CHAPTER 7

That night, long after their ma and pa had turned in, Thal and Ursula rocked on the front porch in the cool of the Kansas night. Ned had gone to bed too, in Myles's old room, although it had been plain to Thal that his pard would rather stay up and talk to his sister. But Thal wanted to be alone with her, and asked Ned that favor.

"Bein' your pard is hard sometimes." Ned had grinned, and gone off to sleep.

Now, with a cool breeze on his face, and the farm lying peaceful under the stars, Thal brought up what was on his mind. "So, tell me, sis," he began. "What got into Myles? What was that whole makin'-his-mark business you wrote me about?"

Ursula's golden hair was like a halo in the dark. "It wasn't the same as with you," she replied. "You wanted to be a cowboy. Why, I'll never know. But you went off to Texas to tend cows."

"Texas suits me," Thal said, "down to my marrow."

"It's changed you," Ursula said. "And I don't mean just your clothes or that six-shooter. You've picked up a drawl, and you talk different. I think it's cute."

"Of all the things you can call a man, that's the worst."

Ursula laughed. "Your friend is cute too, but don't tell him I said that."

"I believe I will," Thal said. "It will take him down a peg. He likes to think he's candy for the ladies."

"Does he, now?"

"Back to Myles," Thal said.

Ursula commenced to slowly rock. "You remember how he was. Farm life never did agree with him. He complained about the cows, he complained about the hogs, he complained about the chickens. The cows were dumb, the hogs were always rolling in the dirt, and the smell of the chicken coop made him want to wring their necks. We used to laugh about it. We thought it was funny, him griping so much. But looking back, he was sour through and through, and we didn't see it."

"That could be," Thal said.

"Anyway, after you left, he talked more and more about how he wanted to leave too.

He didn't tell Ma and Pa. Just me. If he brought it up once, he brought it up a thousand times. It got so I was tired of hearing it."

"Why did he go to the Black Hills, of all places?" Thal asked. "It's dangerous up there. Everybody knows that."

"The dangers haven't stopped the hordes who have gone. That's how the newspaper described it. As a 'hungry horde.' Hungry for gold, that is."

"Myles had gold fever?"

"He has money fever — that's for sure. Had it long before he left. He and I would sit out here like we're doing, and he'd go on and on about how wonderful it would be to not have to scrape for a living. He wanted money, and a lot of it. For fancy clothes and a fine horse and all that. You should have heard him."

"He changed after I left," Thal remarked.

"Or maybe he was that way all the time and didn't show it much," Ursula said. "People hide how they are sometimes."

"Did Ma and Pa know about his money hunger?"

"Myles brought it up with them a few times. Pa would always say that there was more to life than money. That having a family and a roof over your head and good, decent work counted for more. It didn't impress Myles much. Nor did Ma when she'd remind him that the Bible says the love of money is the root of all evil. Do you know what he said to her?"

Thal shook his head, realized she hadn't noticed in the dark, and said, "I wasn't here."

"Myles told her that it was easy for the Bible to say it's wrong to love money because the Bible doesn't have to eat and wear clothes and get along in this world."

Thal could imagine how his mother reacted to a statement like that. "Did she take him to task?"

"Did she ever! She wagged her finger at him and told him that Scripture is the word of God and God is never wrong, and if God says that the love of money is the root of all evil, then it by God is."

"What did Myles say?"

"He just sat there. He never spoke back to her. Not even when she warned him that the Bible is the one true and good book there is, and if he didn't take it to heart, he'd come to ruin." Ursula lowered her voice. "Later that night, when him and me were talking about it, he called Ma a fool."

"He didn't." Thal was genuinely shocked. Their ma had her faults. Everyone did. But her faith wasn't one of them, and she loved her children dearly.

"As surely as I'm sitting here," Ursula said. "I scolded him for being so mean. All he did was shake his head and say it would be best for all of us if he went off into the world to make his mark."

"That again."

"He said it a lot. You ask me, he was money-hungry, plain and simple. That's all his mark was. He hankers after more money than he knows what to do with."

"That explains the Black Hills."

"It was all he talked about after he heard about the gold rush," Ursula said. "How a lot of men were going to be rich, and he should be one of them." She drummed her fingers on her chair arm. "You know, looking back, I can see we missed a few signs."

"How do you mean?"

"Don't you remember how he'd bring up gold rushes now and then? That time we were helping Pa with the hay, and Myles went on and on about the California gold rush, and how he wished he'd been born back then and could have gone so he could have made his fortune."

Thal sighed. That fortune stuff was bunk. Anyone with any sense knew that most who took part in a gold rush never saw any gold, let alone got rich. It was a pipe dream, as folks would say.

"Myles was always interested in gold rushes. I remember him talking about that one up in Idaho, and another in Canada, and wishing he was old enough to go to those too."

"It's too bad we never had a gold rush in Kansas," Thal joked, but his sister didn't laugh.

"Then Myles heard about the Black Hills. Day in and day out, it was all he talked about. How gold was there for the taking. How if he didn't get there soon, he's lose out on his share."

"The simpleton."

"Myles isn't stupid," Ursula said. "It's the gold fever. It's made him deaf to listening to reason."

"I wonder how he got shot," Thal said, and instantly regretted it.

Ursula stopped rocking and let out a low groan. "Don't remind me. I'm worried sick. The man who wrote us didn't say what the circumstances were. I wish he had. Not knowing is killing me."

"Don't you worry," Thal said. "If I find Myles I'll bring him home, whether he wants to come or not."

"He's a man now, Thalis. He can do as he

81

pleases."

Thal looked at her, trying to read her expression. "If you don't want me to bring him back, why did you send for me?"

"To find out if he's all right. Or even alive. I'd have gone myself if it was safe to do."

"Thank golly you didn't." Thal shuddered to think of her fate if she were cast among the wolves of the world, as young and innocent as she was. He'd seen enough to know that innocence was no protection against evil. In fact, evil preyed on innocence, like a wolf on sheep.

"I'm counting on you, Thal, to do what I can't."

"You've said that before. I'll do the best I can. But don't get your hopes too high."

"I only have one hope, and that's you, big brother."

Thal would hate to disappoint her, but they must be realistic about things. He was about to suggest she'd be wise to brace for the worst when he heard the faint beat of hooves out on the lane. Sitting forward, he asked, "Do you hear that, sis?"

"What?" Ursula said, and then: "Oh. Who would be paying us a visit at this time of night?"

Thal stood. It was only ten o'clock or so, but in farm country that was well past bedtime for most. Farmers were early risers, like his pa, usually up by five a.m. They needed to go to bed early to get their rest. "A neighbor, maybe."

"I can't think of any who would stop by this late."

Moving to the steps, Thal waited. He wasn't expecting trouble. Not here.

"There are two of them," Ursula said at his elbow.

Thal had already seen the dark outlines of a pair of riders. Going down the steps, he moved to meet them, saying, "Who are you and what are you doing here?"

"You can't tell who we are?" one of them said.

"We're lookin' for you, you lunkhead," said the other.

Thal forgot his ma and pa were asleep, and whooped for joy. "Craw? Jesse Lee? Is that you?"

Slumped in fatigue, the pair drew rein and grinned.

"Did you miss us?" Jesse Lee said.

"We rode like the dickens to catch up to you," Crawford said. "It's a good thing you used to talk a lot about your folks and their farm so we knew where to find you. Or almost. We had to ask in town for directions."

83

"And here we are," Jesse Lee said. Suddenly stiffening, he doffed his hat. "Why, lookee there. An angel has come to earth to pay us a visit."

Ursula had come down the steps. "Oh my," she said.

Thal was trying to collect this wits. "What are you two doing here?"

"Is that anything to say?" Crawford said. "After we've ridden so hard and so long?" The older puncher touched his hat brim to Ursula. "Ma'am. You must be his sister. He was always sayin' how you were the prettiest girl in these parts."

"He did?" Ursula said.

"And he was right," Jesse Lee declared. Lithely swinging down, he gave a slight bow. "Jesse Lee Hardesty, at your service, Miss Christie."

"Oh my," Ursula said again.

"Quit tryin' to impress my sister and tell me why you're here," Thal said, a trifle ruffled.

"Should you even have to ask?" Jesse Lee said, his gaze fixed wonderingly on Ursula. "We're your friends. When we heard about your brother, we went to the big sugar and told him we'd be obliged if'n he'd let us come help you in your hunt."

Crawford nodded. "It was Jesse's doin'

84

more than mine. I was worried Mr. Hopper would say no and Jesse would go anyway and we'd be out of work."

Still looking at Ursula, Jesse Lee said, "Mr. Hooper might have, at that. But Mrs. Hooper was there, and it pleased her that we were concerned about you, and she asked him to let us come."

"And here we are," Crawford said.

"I'll be switched," was all Thal could think of to say.

Ursula was returning Jesse Lee's stare with a peculiar expression on her face. "Such wonderful friends you have, and you've never said a word about them."

"Why would I?" Thal said. "It's Myles I'm here about."

"And Myles we'll help you find," Jesse Lee said. "The four of us together can do anything we put our minds to."

"Aren't you something?" Ursula said.

"Until a minute ago I didn't know what I was," Jesse Lee said to her.

"Behave," Crawford said.

Thal was growing annoyed. "Yes. Behave. This is my sister you're makin' cow eyes at. You're worse than Ned."

"Who?" Jesse Lee said.

"Would you like some food?" Ursula

asked. "Or something to drink? Water per-haps?"

Crawford was climbing down. He moved stiffly, which was unusual for him. "We're fine, ma'am. Except that we're worn out. Point us to where we can bed down and we'll be happy."

"You can sleep in the barn," Thal said. "There's plenty of straw, and you'll have a roof over your heads."

"Who cares about a roof?" Jesse Lee said.

Crawford tugged at his pard's shirtsleeve. "Come on, kid. I'm plumb wore-out. We'll get some sleep and you can make a spectacle of yourself in the mornin'."

"Ma'am," Jesse Lee said, with another bow to Ursula. "May you dream of sugar-plums and flowers."

"Will you listen to yourself?" Thal said, and watched as they walked off leading their mounts. "Sorry about that, sis. He's young and doesn't know any better."

"I think he's gorgeous," Ursula said.

CHAPTER 8

They got an early start.

Thal would have liked to stay another day, but his sister insisted he must reach the Black Hills as quickly as possible. She was so worried about Myles she was losing sleep and didn't have much of an appetite. So an hour after sunrise, Thal bade his father farewell, gave his mother and sister a hug, and climbed onto his chestnut.

"May the Lord watch over you," his mother said.

His father smiled and nodded. They'd shared a short talk the night before. As always, his father didn't have a lot to say, and held his emotions in check. They hadn't even hugged when they greeted each other.

Now Ursula came up to his horse and touched his leg. "Don't let anything happen to you. You're doing this on my account, and it would weigh on me forever."

Thal raised his reins. "I'll be careful," he

said, knowing full well it was an empty promise. Whether he made it back or not wasn't entirely up to him.

"It was a pleasure to meet you, Miss Christie," Ned said. "I look forward to makin' your acquaintance again on our way back."

"You'll have to stand in line," Jesse Lee said. "She already promised me a walk about the property under the stars."

"She did?" Ned said, sounding shocked.

Ursula laughed. "It was the only way I could persuade him to let go of my hand."

"Why, you skunk, you," Ned said to the Southerner.

"Did you just call me a polecat?" Jesse Lee demanded.

Thal nipped their argument in the bud with "Let's light a shuck." He gave his family a last look and reined around. A feeling came over him that he might never see them again, but he shrugged it off. If there was one thing he'd learned about feelings, it was that they were unreliable.

As the four of them swung from the lane onto the road to Salina, Ned brought his animal alongside. "Did you hear your sister back there? That coyote forced her to promise him."

"First of all," Thal said, "Jesse's not a

coyote. He's our friend." The pair had been like roosters on the peck since they woke up, each trying to outdo the other to impress Ursula. "Second of all, she's old enough to take walks with whoever she pleases."

"That's awful liberal of you," Ned replied, "seein' as how you're her own brother."

Against his better judgment, Thal asked, "What would you have me do?"

"Guard her like a hawk, as a brother should," Ned said. "It's your job to keep the wolves away."

"In that case," Thal said, "neither Jesse nor you should go anywhere near her."

"I'm your pard. That gives me special rights."

"To my sister?" Thal said, and snorted. "Do me a favor and put her from your mind until I find my brother. I don't want Jesse Lee and you squabblin' the whole time."

"I'll try, for you," Ned said, "but you better talk to him too."

"I will," Thal said, and since there was no time like the present, he fell back until he was riding next to Jesse Lee and Crawford. "Did you hear any of that?"

"Any of what?" Jesse Lee said.

"He's moonin' over your sister," Crawford said. "He doesn't even hear me when I talk to him."

"I do so," Jesse Lee said.

"I need Ned and you to have a truce," Thal said bluntly. "Not one word about my sis until after I've found Myles. Otherwise you two will nitpick to death, and Craw and me can do without that."

"Can we ever!" Crawford said. "I never saw it fail yet. There's nothin' like a pretty gal to put one gent at another's throat."

"I'd never hurt Ned," Jesse Lee said. "I like him."

"Prove it by not mentionin' Ursula until we're done in the Black Hills," Thal said. "That's not too much to ask. He's already agreed. I want your word too."

"If'n it will make you happy," Jesse Lee said. "But you can't stop me from dreamin' about her."

"Now, see?" Crawford said. "This is why I should partner up with an older hand. Us older ones keep our heads better."

"It's not my head Ursula took," Jesse Lee said. "It's my heart."

"You hardly even know her," Thal said.

"You're not Southern," Jesse Lee said. "You don't understand. Southern men are born with romance in their blood."

"Just make sure it stays there," Thal said.

"I could use some whiskey in my blood right about now," Crawford remarked. "All this silliness gets to a man."

"You won't think it's silly when her and me are hitched," Jesse Lee declared.

Thal had had enough. "You know her barely twelve hours and you're ready to walk down the aisle with her?"

"You're her brother. You wouldn't savvy."

On that note, Thal gigged the chestnut. He had a decision to make and it was an important one. Namely, should they make a beeline for the Black Hills or play it safe and take the longer way around? The beeline involved a more or less straight course across the open prairie. Over four hundred miles, and a lot of it roamed by hostiles. The last two hundred miles or so, they'd be in Sioux territory, and the Sioux were on a tear.

Or they could head for Cheyenne, a distance of about three hundred and fifty miles, and join one of the "expeditions," as they were called, that regularly left for the Black Hills. There was an advantage in that the expedition parties were always large and well armed. Their whole purpose was to offer protection to those bound for the gold fields.

That evening, as they sat around the campfire well north of Salina, Thal put the question to his pard and his friends.

91

"The expeditions are safer," Ned spoke up. "We'd be less likely to lose our scalps."

"I don't care which it is," Crawford said. "Whatever you boys decide is fine by me."

"I say we head straight for the hills," Jesse Lee said. "The sooner we get there, the sooner we find your brother, the sooner I can see your sister again."

"You promised not to bring her up," Thal reminded him.

"Sorry."

"The vote is tied," Ned said. "It's up to you, pard. As it should be. He's your family."

Thal was tempted to try the direct route. They might be able to slip through without the Sioux being aware of it. But if they were caught, they were goners. It was as simple as that. "I reckon we should do this smart, and the smart thing is Cheyenne."

Even that wasn't a sure thing. The Sioux weren't the only tribe who hated that whites were overrunning their land. And then there were outlaws and the like, long riders who roamed the remote regions looking for prey to pounce on.

By the sixth day, they'd left human habitations far behind. Or so Thal reckoned. Then they came to a bluff overlooking a creek bordered by a belt of woods, and across the creek stood a soddy with a large sign that read drinks. To one side was a corral made of saplings, with several horses.

"My eyes must be playin' tricks," Ned said. "A saloon, way out there?"

"I don't believe it neither," Jesse Lee said.

Much to Thal's relief, the pair had been getting along since they buried the Ursula hatchet. "Do we stop or not? I'll leave it up to you."

"A swallow of red-eye wouldn't hurt," Crawford said. "We can rest the horses for half an hour, then push on."

A tiny voice at the back of Thal's mind was urging him not to, but he nodded. "All right. Keep your eyes skinned, though."

"That goes without sayin'," Jesse Lee said.

A game trail brought them to the bottom of the bluff. The creek was so shallow the crossing barely got their horses' hooves wet. As they came up the bank, a plank door attached by leather hinges creaked open and out came a scrawny middle-aged woman wearing a well-worn homespun dress, a soiled apron, and a floppy brown hat. She had stringy gray hair, a pointed chin, and, when she grinned, a gap where several of her upper front teeth should be.

"Howdy, gents. I'm right pleased to see you."

"Who might you be when you're to home?" Jesse Lee said.

"I'm Harriet. This here is my place."

"Strange spot for a saloon," Jesse Lee said.

"It's my house," Harriet said. "I serve drinks to those as wander by to make a few dollars now and then." She motioned. "Climb on down and take a load off. I have victuals, if you're hungry. Includin' a pie I baked only yesterday."

"I do so love pie," Crawford said.

Thal was the last to dismount. That little voice at the back of his head wouldn't relent. No sooner did his boots touch the ground than the plank door opened again and out came two men about his age. There, any resemblance ended. They were as scrawny as the woman, all bone and sinew, and grubby with dirt on their clothes and their faces. They were greasy besides; their hair looked as if it had been slicked back with bear fat. Neither smiled. Each held a rifle in the crook of an elbow, a Spencer for the one and a Henry for the other.

Repeaters, both, fine rifles that didn't come cheap. Thal wondered how the pair could afford them.

"Here are my boys!" Harriet exclaimed proudly. "Cleve" — she nodded at the one with the Spencer — "and Vernon." She nodded at the one with the Henry.

"How do?" Vernon said.

"Same here," Cleve said.

"You take after your ma," Crawford said.

"They're fixin' to do some huntin' for the supper pot," Harriet said. "Ain't you, boys?"

Both nodded.

Thal noticed that Jesse Lee's hand was close to his ivory-handled Colt. "What are you after?" the Southerner asked.

Vernon shrugged. "Whatever we see."

Cleve nodded. "Deer, bear, squirrel, rabbit, fox, it don't make no never mind so long as we can eat it."

"I'd like to find me a snake," Vernon said. "I love fried snake meat."

They made for the woods.

"Ain't they somethin'?" Harriet declared. "It warms the cockles of my heart, how devoted they are. I couldn't get by without them."

"Where's their pa, if you don't mind my askin'?" Crawford said.

"Gone, about two years now."

"Gone as in flew the coop?" Ned wanted to know. "Or gone as in met his Maker?"

Harriet grew sorrowful and answered woefully, "He went off to hunt buffalo and never came back. Me and the boys went lookin' for him and found Injun sign. The Cheyenne or whoever, I couldn't say. But it was red-skins who did my man in."

"Sorry for your loss, ma'am," Crawford said.

Thal didn't have much to say. He was eager to get their drink and get gone. But he felt compelled to remark, "If my pa died, my ma would be heartbroken."

"Enough about my man," Harriet said. With a toss of her head, she stepped to the plank door and held it open for them. "In you go. Stoop as you do. It's a bit short."

Wondering why that was, Thal bent at the knees and ducked under the lintel. Inside, the place was spacious, but dank. The floor was bare earth, the walls and roof sod. A large table made of pine was along the left-hand wall, with chairs. Dark doorways at the back led to where they slept.

"Cozy," Crawford said.

"It keeps the wind out and the rain off our heads," Harriet said. "That's all that matters." Smiling cheerfully, she hustled to a small, crudely constructed bar that appeared to have been fashioned out of the sides of a Conestoga or some other wagon.

"You have your own bar?" Ned marveled.

"My husband's idea," Harriet said, going around behind and taking a half-empty bottle of Monongahela from a shelf. "So those who stop can see we're serious about our liquor."

Crawford pulled out a chair and sat. "Seems like a lot of trouble to go to, as few folks who must stop."

"Oh, you'd be surprised," Harriet said, producing glasses and setting them by the bottle. "Last year there were eleven, I think it was. Most were bound for somewhere to the northwest, as I suspect you boys are."

"To Cheyenne, and from there to the Black Hills," Ned said.

"Have a seat, have a seat," Harriet urged. She brought out a wooden tray, set the bottle and the glasses on it, and came over. "Here you go. Only two bits a drink."

Thal had moved to a chair that let him see the front door and the doorways at the back, both. He was growing uneasy and couldn't say why.

"We're obliged, ma'am," Crawford said.

"Oh, pshaw," Harriet said. "We're just glad to see you fellers. So glad you wouldn't believe."

CHAPTER 9

Thal thought that a peculiar thing to say. But then, everything about the place was peculiar. Or was it just him? Some folks didn't cotton to other people. They liked to live off by themselves. Mountain men, for instance. It could be that this family wanted the rest of the world to leave them be. Yet if that was the case, why offer drinks to people? With a shrug he put it from his mind. In a little while he and his companions would be on their way.

Crawford took the first sip of their whiskey and uttered a happy sigh. "I'll be switched," he said. "It's the genuine article."

"Did you think it wouldn't be?" Harriet said.

"Some saloons water their red-eye down," Crawford mentioned.

"We're not a saloon," Harriet said. "We just do this to get by." She gave them another partly toothless smile and returned to the counter.

Ned swallowed, and nodded. "Just what I needed to wash down the dust. If we weren't in such a hurry, I'd buy a bottle and sit out on the prairie tonight and get drunk."

"Whatever for?" Thal asked. His pard wasn't much of a drinking man. Not like Crawford, who loved to suck the bug juice down but had the presence of mind not to do it when he was out on the range.

"For the hell of it," Ned said. "I haven't been pickled in a good many months. It would be fun to lie there and giggle at the stars."

"Men shouldn't giggle," Thal said. "That's for females."

"I'll have you know I'm a great giggler when I'm drunk. Everything strikes my funny bone."

Thal took a sip and agreed with their assessment. The whiskey was good. He took a second swallow, and warmth spread down his throat into his belly.

Jesse Lee hadn't touched his glass yet. "I don't like it."

"You wouldn't," Crawford said. "You're suspicious of everybody."

"In the hill country where I grew up, you have to be," Jesse Lee said. "All the feuds and such."

"It can't have been that bad," Ned said.

"I lost one brother and two cousins to our feud with the Mallorys," Jesse Lee said. "Don't tell me it couldn't."

"Did you take potshots at each other?" Ned said. "Like people say that hillbillies do?"

"We weren't no hillbillies. We were back-woods folks. When people say hillbillies they mean dumb, and we weren't dumb."

"Shootin' at each other doesn't sound smart," Ned said.

Thal was curious. "What started the feud, if you don't mind my askin'?"

"It was back in my grandpa's day," Jesse Lee said. "Him and Tom Mallory had both taken a shine to a girl who lived over to Possum Flats. She chose my grandpa. Tom Mallory didn't like losin' and took to speakin' ill of my grandpa and her both, every chance he got. Word got back to my grandpa and he went up to Tom Mallory in a tavern and slapped him and called him a cur. Next thing my grandpa knew, someone shot him when he was out choppin' wood. He was lucky and they only hit him in the shoulder. He didn't see who did it, but he knew who it was. Everyone did. When grandpa got back on his feet, he took his rifle and paid Tom Mallory a visit and shot him dead. Mallory had a brother, and he shot my grandpa's brother, thinkin' it was Grandpa. The feud had commenced."

"There was no way to put a stop to it?" Crawford said.

"Not short of wipin' out the other side," Jesse Lee said. "I had a Mallory take a shot at me once. I suspicioned which one it was, a boy my age I'd run into a few times. So I went to Possum Flats and when he showed up, I shot him dead, like my grandpa had done to Tom Mallory."

"I'll be damned," Crawford said.

"Only in my case," Jesse Lee continued, "the sheriff happened to be there. It was just my bad luck that he saw it and came marchin' over to arrest me. I told him I wasn't of a mind to be behind bars, and when he told me I didn't have a choice, I showed him I did have one by clubbin' him with my rifle." Jesse Lee frowned. "My pa told me I'd better fan the breeze or I'd have the law after me from then until doomsday. So I did, and here I am." He gazed about the soddy. "It's strange how life works out sometimes."

"You're from the hills," Ned said. "How'd you end up so good with a six-shooter?"

"Oh, that," Jesse Lee said, as if it were of no consequence. "I'd drifted a spell, takin' jobs here and there. Nothin' appealed to me that much until I was hired on to do ranch work. I told the foreman I could ride, which was true, and could rope, which wasn't. But I learn quick, and I found I liked cowboyin' more than anything I'd done."

"That doesn't explain your ivory Colt," Ned said.

Jesse Lee looked down at his, and smiled. "I'd boughten an ordinary Colt, like every cowhand does. Took to practicin' with it every chance I could. There's somethin' about it. The feelin' when you draw, and when you shoot."

"All I feel is a heavy revolver in my hand," Ned said.

Jesse Lee ignored him. "It got so I was right quick at it. Then one night in a saloon a tinhorn tried to fleece me at cards. I called him on it and he pulled a hideout, but before he could shoot, I shot him dead. The next thing I knew, people were treatin' me like I was some kind of man-killer."

"You were," Ned said.

"They made more out of it than there was. I'd have been fine if everybody forgot about it, but folks love to gossip."

"You've shot others," Ned said. "We heard it was four or five."

"Three," Jesse Lee said. "The second was the tinhorn's brother. He hunted me down and tried to back-shoot me. I thought it was the feud all over again, but he was the only one who came lookin'. The third was a loudmouth who got mad when I talked to a dove he was partial to. He was drunk. I tried to be reasonable, but he wouldn't have it and went for his six-gun."

"The fancy Colt?" Ned wouldn't let it drop.

Jesse Lee shrugged. "I figured that if folks were goin' to brand me as a shootist, I might as well look the part. And you know what? Ever since I put this on, whenever I go into a saloon, troublemakers fight shy of me."

"No wonder," Ned said. "It's like you're wearin' a sign that tells the world if they give you grief, you'll give them lead."

"Who wouldn't?" Jesse Lee said.

Thal had noticed that the woman was listening to every word. She'd frowned when Jesse Lee got to the part about the three men he'd shot, and now she was gnawing on her bottom lip as if she was working something out in her head.

"A reputation can do wonders," Crawford was saying. "Look at Wild Bill Hickok. A gent would have to be plumb loco to tangle with him."

"A reputation can be bad for you too," Ned remarked. "Ever hear of Jack Slade? He got a reputation as a leather slapper, and it got him hanged."

"It's not the reputation, it's the man," Crawford said. "Slade could be vicious. Wild Bill only kills when he has to."

"I suppose," Ned conceded.

"Finish up," Thal said. He hankered to be on their way. It would take long enough as it was to reach the Black Hills. Too long, perhaps, to do his brother any good. He chided himself for thinking like that, raised his glass, and happened to look over at the counter.

Harriet was striding toward them with a double-barreled shotgun at her waist. Both hammers were cocked, and she had a grim expression.

"What are you doin', lady?" Ned said.

"Not one of you is to move," Harriet declared, "or I'll blow you to hell."

"You can't be serious, ma'am," Crawford said. He seemed to think it was some sort of joke.

"Never more so." Harriet planted herself. "Keep your hands on the table and make no sudden moves." Tilting her head toward the door, she hollered, "Come on in, boys! I've got them covered!"

"You shouldn't ought to have done this," Jesse Lee said coldly.

Harriet wasn't intimidated. "You see who I'm pointin' this cannon at? That would be you, gunman. You so much as twitch and I'll splatter you over the wall. Which I'd rather not do, since I'd have to clean up the mess."

The plank door creaked and in hurried Cleve with his Spencer and Vernon with his Henry.

"What's goin' on, Ma?" Vernon said. "We were waitin' for them to step out so we could pick them off."

"Why'd you rush things?" Cleve said.

Harriet gestured with the shotgun at Jesse Lee. "This one's a gun shark. I wasn't takin' the chance he'd get off a shot. You boys mean too much to me."

"We could have handled him, Ma," Vernon said.

"We was well hid," Cleve said.

"Be that as it may," Harriet said, "I'll cover them while you disarm them. Then we'll take them out to the usual place and get it over with."

Crawford stirred in his chair. "You're fixin' to rob and kill us?"

"You're slow but you get there," Harriet said. "Only it's the other way around. We

105

kill you and then we rob you. It's safer that way. A corpse can't raise a fuss when you're helpin' yourself to its poke."

Cleve laughed. "That was a good one, Ma."

"You sure are a caution," Vernon praised her.

Thal was girding himself to do something. He must act before he and his friends were disarmed. Once that happened, they'd be helpless to keep from being murdered. To stall, he said, "How many have you done this to, lady? We're not the first, I take it."

"Not by a long shot," Harriet said, and laughed. "I'd say seventeen or eighteen, although I don't bother to count no more."

"That many?" Crawford said.

"Shucks. I wasn't includin' the kids we had to dispose of. Not that I've ever liked that part of it."

"Kids too?" Ned said, aghast.

"Look at them," Vernon said, and laughed.

"Cowpokes ain't much for brains, are they?" Cleve said.

Harriet looked at them. "Why are you two still standin' there? I told you to take their hardware."

Jesse Lee came out of his chair so fast he stood and drew before anyone could so much as blink. He fanned a shot into Harriet's head, shifted, and fanned the hammer two more times, his hand a blur. The second shot smashed Cleve in the face. The third cored Vernon's forehead. Vernon was dead on his feet, but Cleve jerked his rifle and tried to take aim and Jesse cored his brainpan. The slug burst out the back of Cleve's head and showered gore everywhere. In a span of heartbeats it was over, and Jesse Lee stood staring down at the bodies. "They weren't much," he said.

Thal couldn't find his voice. He'd never seen anyone gunned down before. Let alone a woman.

"Good God, pard," Crawford blurted.

"They were fixin' to kill us," Jesse Lee said.

"Not that. You're so quick."

"Why should it surprise you?" Jesse Lee said, and started to reload. "You've seen me practice enough."

"But still," Crawford said.

Ned was gaping in amazement. "I wouldn't stand a snowball's chance in hell against you."

"I'd never shoot you," Jesse Lee said. "We're friends."

Thal stood and stepped to Harriet. Her eyes were wide in shock and her mouth was wide-open too. He could see her tongue, and that several of her teeth were rotted. Grimacing, he turned away. "We should report this to the law."

"What law?" Ned said.

"We're in the middle of nowhere," Crawford said.

"A marshal or a sheriff," Thal said.

"A marshal only has jurisdiction as far as a town's limits," Crawford reminded him, "and there ain't any towns hereabouts. No county either for a sheriff to get involved."

"A federal marshal, then," Thal said.

Crawford shook his head. "It'll take a month of Sundays to find one."

"It just doesn't feel right not reportin' it," Thal said. Three people were *dead*, after all.

"Federal marshals move around a lot," Crawford said. "They have what they call districts, and each marshal spends most of his time wanderin' over his own, arrestin' lawbreakers and whatnot."

"We might find one in Cheyenne," Ned ventured.

"And if we don't?" Crawford replied. "Where do we go from there? Denver?"

"Why are you makin' a fuss over this?" Ned said.

"If we have to go all the way to Denver, we won't get to the Black Hills for months,"

Crawford said. "And I thought that's the important thing."

"It is," Thal said.

"Then what do we do?" Ned asked.

Jesse Lee had finished reloading and twirled his ivory-handled Colt into his holster. "We bury them. We help ourselves to any valuables and let their horses loose. Then we burn the soddy to the ground."

Thal turned to him. "That's harsh."

"Would you rather leave the bodies to rot? And their horses to starve?"

"If we take their valuables, folks will reckon we're robbers," Thal said.

"What folks?" Jesse Lee said, and gestured. "There's only us."

"He's right, pard," Ned said. "Any money these three had, they likely stole. So it's not as if we're stealin' it ourselves."

Thal reluctantly gave in. "All right. We'll do all of it except the burnin'. We'll leave the soddy as it is."

"What for?" Ned said. "You think someone else will want to move in?"

"No, he's right," Crawford said. "There'd be a lot of smoke. Others might see. Injuns, maybe. We don't want that."

"We surely do not," Ned agreed. He stared at the sprawled figures, and frowned.

109

"The last thing we need is more folks tryin' to kill us."

CHAPTER 10

The plains stretched forever, a rolling sea of grass and sagebrush. On windy days they'd see tumbleweeds tumbling along as if alive. Now and then an island of timber defied the spread of grassland. And along streams there would be cottonwoods and box elders.

In his worry over his brother, Thal became increasingly impatient to reach Cheyenne. But short of riding their horses into the ground, there was nothing he could do except fidget in his saddle from time to time. On the latest occasion, Ned glanced over and chuckled.

"Got ants in your britches, pard?"

"Ants on my brain," Thal said. "It's takin' too long to get there."

"When folks say wide-open spaces," Crawford said, "they mean *wide*-open spaces."

"I never saw so much grass in all my born days," Jesse Lee said.

"All seventeen years," Ned said, grinning.

"You're just jealous I'm so young," Jesse Lee replied. "It gives me an edge with Ursula."

"Says you," Ned said. "She might like older gents, for all you know."

"In that case," Jesse Lee said, "she'd be interested in Craw."

"I'm old enough to be her pa," Crawford said.

"Her grandpa, even," Jesse Lee joked.

"You'll see," Ned said. "When we get back, she'll be so glad to see me she'll throw her arms around me and give me a kiss."

"Dream a lot, do you?" Jesse Lee said.

"Ladies are partial to mature fellas," Ned said. "Ask anyone."

"If you're mature, I'll eat my hat."

"You'll eat crow, at least, when she agrees to let me court her. But don't worry. Once her and me are hitched, you can come visit and talk about the old days when I was a bachelor and lonely, like you."

"You sure are a dreamer," Jesse Lee said. "Gals her age don't want old. They want someone the same age as them so they have more in common." He paused. "Isn't that right, Thal? You know her better than we do. Will she pick someone as young as her or someone who is past his prime, like your pard?"

"Why, you so-and-so," Ned said.

Thal drew rein and turned in his saddle. "I seem to recollect tellin' you mush-heads that my sister wasn't to be discussed. Not for any reason whatsoever."

"We haven't talked about her in days," Ned said.

"This is why," Thal said. "It always leads to squabblin'. And I, for one, can do without the nonsense."

Crawford raised a hand.

"You can do without it too?" Thal said.

"No," the older puncher said, and pointed. "Get off your horses, quick." And he swung down from his.

Thal followed suit, then looked to see why.

To the west figures moved. They were so far away they were as thin as sticks. He thought they might be antelope, but the longer he stared, the more obvious it became that they were men on horseback.

"Injuns, by God," Ned exclaimed.

"Headin' north, toward Sioux country," Crawford said. "There must be ten or more. If they spot us, we're in for it."

Clutching his reins, Thal held his breath until he realized he was doing it, and exhaled. He didn't mind admitting that Indians spooked him. There was no one fiercer than a warrior on the warpath.

"It could be Sioux comin' back from a raid," Crawford speculated. "Or some Cheyenne out after buffalo. Or Arapaho, even."

"Injuns don't scare me any," Jesse Lee said.

"They should," Crawford said. "They might have rifles. If not, their bows can shoot an arrow as far as your pistol can sling lead. Farther, even."

"Farther?" Jesse Lee said skeptically.

"You're more than a fair hand out to twenty-five feet," Crawford said. "An Injun with a bow can hit us from a hundred feet or more."

"We have our rifles too," Ned said.

"Four rifles against twenty hostiles," Crawford said. "None of us are marksmen, not countin' Jesse with his six-gun. I wouldn't rate our chances very high."

"Your pard is a wet blanket," Ned said to Jesse Lee.

"He likes to be practical about things."

"Hold on," Thal broke in. He hadn't taken his eyes off the distant riders. "They've stopped."

The warriors had been strung out in single file, but now they appeared to be congregating in a body.

"Do you reckon they've seen us?" Ned

whispered.

"Why are you whisperin'?" Jesse Lee asked. "They can't hear you, that far off."

"Don't anyone move," Crawford cautioned. "Don't let your horses move either."

"This ain't good," Ned said. "This ain't good at all."

No sooner were the words out of his mouth than the Indians wheeled in a body and came in their direction.

"We're in for it now," Ned said.

"We don't know that," Thal said. But he yanked his Winchester from his saddle scabbard and jacked the lever to feed a round into the chamber.

"Oh Lordy," Ned said, tugging on his own rifle. "I ain't ever done any Injun fightin'."

"Who of us has?" Crawford said. He too was shucking his rifle. He also had the Henry and the Spencer they'd taken from Vernon and Cleve wrapped in his bedroll.

Jesse Lee left his rifle on his horse and moved out in front of them with his hand on his Colt. "Let them come. I'll pit my lead against their arrows any day of the week."

"That's foolish talk, pard," Crawford said.

The Indians approached warily, spreading as they came so they were two or three deep. Those in front had rifles, those behind bows or lances. Except for the one who was bare-chested, they all wore buckskin shirts, leggings, and moccasins. A few had feathers in their hair. A remarkable exception was a stocky warrior who wore a stovepipe hat.

"Which tribe are they?" Ned wondered.

"Beats me," Thal said. He couldn't tell one from another. Especially when so many wore their hair pretty much the same, and there wasn't that much difference in their clothes and their moccasins.

"A scout told me once that he could tell by their faces, but I haven't seen enough Indians to do that," Crawford said.

"I make it to be twenty-three," Jesse Lee said.

"More than enough to wipe us out," Ned said.

"And you called my pard a wet blanket?" Jesse Lee replied.

"Steady," Crawford said. "One thing I do know is that you can't show you're afraid."

"Who's afraid?" Jesse Lee said.

The warriors slowed and finally came to a halt about forty yards out. They talked among themselves and the stocky man in the stovepipe hat jabbed his heels against his pinto and advanced alone.

"What's he up to?" Ned said worriedly.

"No shootin'," Crawford advised. "Not

unless they do."

Thal was trying to tell if the Indians were friendly or not by their expressions. "I don't see any war paint. Could be it's a huntin' party and not a war party."

The warrior in the stovepipe hat came within twenty yards and reined to the right. At a slow walk he circled and studied them, never once attempting to use the rifle he held, the stock resting on his thigh.

"That's an old Sharps," Crawford said. "See the brass tacks in the butt? Injuns like to decorate their guns thataway."

"It's only a single-shot," Jesse Lee said.

"All it takes is one," Crawford said. "A Sharps can blow a hole in you as big around as a dinner plate."

The warrior made a complete circuit and drew rein. He placed the Sharps across his legs, then held his right hand level with his throat, his palm toward them. Extending his first and second fingers, he raised his hand as high as his face.

"What the blazes is he doin'?" Jesse Lee said.

"Unless I miss my guess, it's sign language," Crawford said.

"What did he say?" Ned asked.

"How would I know?" Crawford said. "I don't speak sign."

The warrior stared at them as if waiting for a response. When they didn't do anything, he raised his right hand to his shoulder, again palm-out but with all his fingers and his thumb splayed, and wriggled his wrist back and forth.

"What in the world?" Ned said.

Now the warrior pointed at them, then held both fists close to his chest and made a pushing movement.

"What was all that?" Ned said.

"More sign, you simpleton," Crawford said.

"The Injun is the simpleton," Ned said. "If we didn't savvy his first bit, we sure can't savvy the rest."

"He's givin' up," Thal said.

Reining around, the warrior returned to the others. More talk ensued, with a lot of gesturing in their direction.

"If they were hostiles, they'd have attacked by now," Crawford said.

"For all you know, they're leadin' up to it," Ned said. "That feller with the hat might have told us to surrender, and now they're discussin' how best to wipe us out."

"Do you ever look at the bright side of things?" Jesse Lee said.

"All the time," Ned said

"Look!" Crawford exclaimed.

The Indian in the stovepipe hat was coming back.

"This is it," Ned said. "He'll give a whoop and a holler and the rest will swarm us."

"They do, and six of them won't live to lift our hair," Jesse Lee said, and coiled as if to draw.

"Don't," Thal said. "Let's see what he's up to." He was inclined to believe, as Crawford did, that the Indians didn't mean them any harm.

The one in the hat came to a stop. He acted puzzled more than hostile.

Thal wondered if perhaps the Indians were wondering what he and his friends were doing so far from anywhere. He racked his brain for a way to demonstrate they were friendly. A brainstorm struck, but he hesitated.

"Look," Ned said, pointing. "He's makin' that first sign again. Maybe he's sayin' he's hungry."

"Why would he do that?" Thal said.

"I hear Injuns like to eat."

"So do we."

"What's that got to do with it?"

The warrior in the stovepipe was frowning. Apparently he was disappointed in their inability to respond.

"I wish they'd just ride on," Ned said.

Thal made up his mind. "Hold this," he said, and thrust his Winchester at Ned.

"What are you doin'?"

"Watch and see." Stepping to Crawford's sorrel and the bedroll, he gripped the Spencer's stock and carefully slid it out so the hammer wouldn't catch on the blanket.

"Are you thinkin' what I reckon you're thinkin'?" Crawford said.

"Why not?" Thal said. He extracted the tubular magazine and emptied it, then worked the lever to be sure there wasn't a cartridge in the chamber.

Satisfied, he held the Spencer out in both hands and moved toward the warrior.

"Oh, pard, no," Ned said. "He'll shoot you."

Thal tried not to show how nervous he was. He smiled and raised the Spencer higher.

The warrior didn't seem to know what to make of it. He glanced over his shoulder at the others, and when several made as if to come to his aid, he yelled something that stopped them. Then he sat and waited.

"For you," Thal said as he halted an arm's length from the pinto. "To show we're peaceable."

The warrior's eyebrows were trying to meet over his nose.

"Friends," Thal said. Moving closer, he held the Spencer higher and indicated the man should take it.

With a grunt of surprise, the warrior did. He held it in his left hand and examined it, looked down at Thal, and then at the Spencer again.

"It's yours," Thal said, motioning. "A present."

"Pres-ent?" the warrior repeated.

"Yours," Thal repeated.

A slow smile spread across the warrior's face. Placing his Sharps across his thighs, he reached for a bone-handled knife at his hip.

Thal tensed.

Drawing the knife, the warrior reversed his grip and offered it to Thal, hilt first. When Thal took it, the warrior said something, smiled wider, and with a rifle in each hand, wheeled the pinto and trotted back to his friends. They crowded close for a gander at the rifle, and then the whole bunch rode off to the north. Several smiled and gave little waves.

Thal let out a long breath and returned to the others. He acted casual, but he had butterflies in his stomach.

"That was slick," Crawford said.

"It was all I could think of," Thal said.

Ned was watching the Indians ride off. "First those soddy folks, and now this. I wonder what will happen next."

CHAPTER 11

Early the next afternoon, as they were crossing a particularly flat stretch of prairie, dark clouds appeared on the horizon. Clouds so dark they were almost black.

"I don't like the looks of that," Crawford said.

They were riding four abreast, at a walk, so as not to tire their horses any more than they had to.

"Are you afraid of a thunderstorm?" Jesse Lee teased.

"Some storms are more than that," Crawford said. "They can kill you if you're not careful."

Thal had experience with violent thunderstorms. Kansas was prone to more than its share.

Ned didn't share their concern. "Let me guess," he joked. "We're liable to drown when the water gets up around our toes."

Jesse Lee laughed.

123

Crawford sighed. "I was young like you two once. I was as dumb as you two too."

Now it was Thal who laughed.

"Here, now, pard," Jesse Lee said.

"A storm like that," Crawford went on, "there will be a lot of lightning, and what does lightning strike most? Tall things. Like trees. Only look around you. Do you see any? You do not. Which means the tallest things on this plain are . . ."

"Us," Jesse Lee said.

Crawford nodded. "Then there's the wind. It can get so strong, if you face it head-on, you can't hardly breathe. And the rain can be so heavy, you'll be soaked to the skin in no time. Sometimes the rain changes to hail. And hail can be the size of apples." Crawford cocked an eye at Jesse Lee and at Ned. "You two have any notion what hail that big can do to a man? Or his horse? It can cripple you."

"You're exaggeratin'," Ned grumbled.

"You'd like to think I am," Crawford said, and regarded the approaching cloud bank as if it were a wolf about to bite him. "I hope I'm wrong. I hope that's not the monster I think it is. Because if I'm right, we're in for trouble, boys, and that's no lie."

Thal was inclined to agree. The cloud bank was so huge, extending miles from south to north, that they couldn't go around. The best they could do was hunt cover when the rain started, and hope for the best. He mentioned as much.

"I still say you're makin' a fuss over nothin'," Ned said. "It doesn't worry me any."

"You're not worried about the storm like you weren't worried about those Injuns," Crawford said.

"That's me," Ned said. "Worry-free."

Thal didn't bother to set him straight. He'd learned a long time ago that some people didn't see themselves as they really were. It was as if when some people looked at themselves, they did so through a clouded mirror.

Just then the wind picked up. A gust buffeted them so hard it was like a slap to the face.

"Did you feel that?" Jesse Lee said.

"I'd have to be dead not to," Crawford said.

Thal searched for cover. There had to be a dry wash or a gully, or something. They went another half a mile and then a mile, and all he saw was flat, and more flat. At times the prairie was monotonous that way.

The thunderhead was a lot nearer. Now and then flashes of light briefly lit its black underbelly, and occasionally they'd hear a rumble.

"Yes, sir," Crawford said. "This will be a doozy."

The wind grew even stronger. A cold wind, not a hot wind.

Thal recollected hearing that a cold wind in a thunder-storm was a bad sign.

Crawford must have been thinking the same thing, because he said, "I suspect we're in for some hail, boys."

Thal rose in his stirrups. There was still no sign of a break in the ground.

Not so much as a prairie dog den.

"Gettin' nervous, are you?" Ned said.

The loudest rumble yet issued from the depths of the thunderhead. Underneath, the air glistened with the sheen of falling rain. Not a lot yet, but that would change.

"I hate gettin' soaked," Jesse Lee said.

"You and me both," Crawford said. "We'll need a fire to warm us after the storm passes, and with everything so wet, there'll be nothin' to burn."

"We'll cross that bridge when we come to it," Thal said.

"I wish there was a bridge," Crawford said. "We could take shelter under it."

Off in the distance a jagged bolt cleaved the sky.

"We've got maybe five minutes before it breaks over us," Crawford said.

As if to prove him right, a keening blast of cold wind slammed into them. Thal tucked his chin to his chest and held on to his hat to keep it from being blown off. From under his brim he scanned the prairie, and a tingle of elation shot through him. "There!" he exclaimed, pointing.

"What is it?" Ned asked.

"Somethin'," Thal answered, and used his spurs.

The thunderhead roiled and writhed as if it were alive. The rumblings were constant. As the rain grew heavier, the air darkened until it was almost as black as the clouds. It was a deluge in the making.

Thal galloped for the spot he'd seen, a rift of some kind that widened as he neared it. Smiling, he drew rein on the lip of a dry wash. "We've found our cover."

"None too soon," Crawford said.

The wash was about eight feet deep and half that wide. Its sides were fairly steep, and littered with lots of pebbles and a few large rocks.

Thal went down first and the other followed suit. Dismounting, they took a firm grip on their reins.

"We should hobble our animals to keep

them from runnin' off," Jesse Lee suggested.

Crawford looked up and down the wash, and shook his head. "No. We want to be able to move fast if we have to."

The storm was almost upon them, the wind flattening the grass and causing a horde of tumbleweeds to bounce and whip across the prairie.

"Whatever you do," Crawford cautioned, "don't lose your hold on your horse. If it runs off, we might never see it again."

"I'll be darned if I'll lose mine to some silly storm," Ned remarked.

"Listen," Jesse Lee said.

The wind suddenly commenced to shriek like a banshee. Simultaneously rain fell. Not a lot at first, but increasing every second. Another flash, so bright it made Thal squint against the glare, heralded the elemental rampage to come. There was a tremendous crash, and the ground under them seemed to quake.

The chestnut whinnied and shied. Fortunately Thal had wrapped the reins right around his hand. He gripped the bridle for extra measure.

The next moment, hell on earth was unleashed.

Above them, the sky became a tempest of destruction. The rain fell in buckets, lighting crackled and danced, thunder boomed like cannon. The raindrops were big, and cold.

The brim of Thal's hat bent under the onslaught. In less than a minute he was drenched. Even worse, the rain was so heavy he couldn't see his hand holding the reins.

The screeching wind whipped into the wash, and out again. The sound of the raindrops striking the hard ground was as loud as if they were rocks pelting down.

Ned hollered something.

Thal looked up but couldn't see him. He hoped his pard hadn't lost his animal. It would delay them in reaching Cheyenne.

Then lightning sizzled, and the earth jumped, and one of the horses whinnied shrilly.

Thal didn't blame it. The storm was everything Crawford had warned it would be, and then some.

The air became colder yet.

Thal stooped over so his shoulders and back bore the brunt. Another gust nearly took his hat off, and he jammed it back on and crouched a little lower. All around, the rain pattered. It would take hours to dry his clothes and effects once the storm passed. To say nothing of his revolver and his rifle. Rust, unchecked, could ruin a gun. It pitted the insides of the barrel, and rendered a firearm useless.

Thal was thinking of a fella he knew who had a gun blow up on him and lost a couple of fingers, when a new sound reached his ears. A strange sort of plopping, different from the rain. Keeping his head low, he gazed about. What looked to be white marbles were hitting the ground. Only a few had fallen so far, but more came down even as he looked. One struck next to his boot, and rolled.

Hail, Thal realized. Stones from the sky. He prayed that Crawford wasn't right about how big the hail would get.

The very next moment, a sharp pain in Thal's back almost made him cry out. He glanced down. The hailstone that had caused it was as big as a walnut.

Nickering, his chestnut tried to pull free. Thal held on and sought to soothe it, but there wasn't much he could do. The horse couldn't hear him over the cannonade of thunder and the pounding of the hail.

Ned yelled again, but his shout was swept away by the wind before Thal could make sense of it.

Hail was falling steadily now, crackling and clacking as it piled on top of itself. One hit the knuckles of Thal's left hand, and he winced. Another stung his ear. He resisted the temptation to look up.

The hail, the wind, the thunder. Thal felt as if he were being battered alive.

He would have liked to crouch down close to the ground, but he had to hold on to the chestnut.

A hailstone scraped his neck. Another banged his knee.

Thal recalled hearing about a town once where a hailstorm broke most of the windows and buckled a lot of roofs. At the time, he'd marveled that hail could cause so much destruction.

For long minutes the wind screamed and the hail drummed. Of a sudden, it stopped, to be replaced by rain. The sky wasn't quite as dark.

Thal was grateful for the reprieve, but his gratitude lasted all of two minutes. That was when a new sound drowned out the rest. A great wail arose, as of a thousand souls in torment. The wail became a tremendous hiss, giving the impression that all the snakes on the prairie were hissing at once.

Thal felt a violent tug on his hat and shirt, and looked up. The sight he beheld turned him as icy as the hail.

Almost directly overhead, a funnel was forming. It seemed to be sucking clouds into itself as it spun and spun. The bottom dangled midway to the ground, darting this way and that as if eager to touch the earth and bring destruction to everything in its path.

Thal was terror-struck. Kansans knew all about tornados. Against its unbridled power, they'd be helpless. He could see up into the funnel, see odd blue lights and little baby twisters that broke away from the column of the large one. For a few harrowing heartbeats he feared he'd be sucked up, but the funnel passed over them, sweeping to the east.

Soon the lower end touched down, widening as it advanced. Whole swaths of prairie were violently wrenched into its maw and obliterated.

Thal watched until he couldn't see the twister anymore. By then the wind no longer screeched, and the rain had dwindled to a shower. The worst was over. Slowly straightening, he saw that the others were as waterlogged and miserable as he was.

Crawford draped his arms across his saddle. He looked at Thal and started to smile, then went rigid.

Thal heard it too and spun. A faint swish to the north that quickly grew louder. "What in the world?" he blurted.

"Climb!" Crawford bawled. "Climb for your lives!" He yanked on his reins and began scrambling up the side.

"What's goin' on?" Ned said in confusion.

"Flash flood!" Crawford cried.

Thal pumped his legs for all they were worth. The ground was so soaked it gave way under him. Slipping and sliding, he managed to clutch at the rim. He found a purchase and pulled himself up and over. Balanced on his hip, he hauled on the reins. Out of the corner of his eye, he saw rivulets sweep around a bend to the north, infants to the mother, a watery wall five feet high that crashed around the bend, a liquid force so strong it would carry all before it and drown everything in its path.

With a desperate wrench, Thal gained solid footing and hauled the chestnut to his side.

Below them, the rushing water swept the hail, and part of the bank, away.

Thal moved farther back. The others had made it out and were doing likewise. "We're safe," he said breathlessly.

"We were lucky," Crawford said.

"Wasn't that somethin'?" Ned said, and laughed. "This is more fun than we ever had on the ranch."

"Fun?" Crawford looked at Thal. "Has

anyone ever told you that your pard is plumb loco?"

Ned laughed louder.

CHAPTER 12

The Magic City of the Plains. That was what people called Cheyenne. A strange nickname, given that it had nothing to do with magic. It stemmed from the fact that after the Union Pacific Railroad had rolled in, the city grew by leaps, and more leaps. Now, thanks to the Black Hills Gold Rush, the population had exploded.

Cheyenne was a riotous mix of the frontier and big business, where saloons outnumbered churches ten to one. Where rich cattlemen from the Stock Growers Association hobnobbed at the Cheyenne Club, while the cowhands who worked for them raised Cain at the saloons.

Cheyenne's streets bustled with activity. The ring of hammers on nails and the scrape of saws on wood testified to the ongoing construction of new businesses and homes.

People from all walks of life mingled and

mixed. Townsmen in plain store-bought clothes and dapper suits, women in home-spun and colorful dresses. Railroad crews in their work clothes. Cowhands from outlying ranches, their spurs jangling. Trappers and Indians added splashes of buckskin.

It was, as Ned commented when they drew rein at a hitch rail in front of the Tumble Weed, "A regular jollification of humanity, that's what we've got here."

"A what?" Jesse Lee said.

"A jollification is a celebration," Crawford said, and bobbed his chin at the passersby. "I'd hardly call this that."

"Well, it sure is somethin'," Ned said, and turned in his saddle. "What do you think of it, pard?"

Thal was thinking of his brother, and the quickest and safest way to reach the Black Hills. "Let's ask around inside about expeditions."

It was early yet and the saloon wasn't crowded. Thal made straight for a portly fellow in an apron who was wiping a glass with a towel. The man had watery blue eyes, and the tip of his nose was red. Must like his own stock, Thal reckoned.

"What can I do for you gents?" the bartender asked, setting down the towel and the glass.

"Information would be good," Thal said.

"I might have some, but it doesn't come free."

"That's only fair. Whiskey all around, then."

A painting on the wall drew Thal's gaze. A woman as plump as the bartender lay sprawled on a blue couch with only the sheerest of white lace to cover her ample bosom and hips. She was reaching out, as if to someone, and her full red lips were puckered, as if she was about to plant a kiss.

"Will you look at that?" Ned marveled. "I wouldn't mind hangin' this one over my bunk to give me dreams at night."

"Give me the real article," Crawford said.

"We don't have time for that," Thal said, worried they might decide to visit a sporting house, as they were called.

"I wouldn't anyhow," Jesse Lee said.

"Why not?" Crawford said. "You like females as much as I do."

Before the Southerner could reply, the bartender set four glasses down, slid one to each of them, and produced a bottle of whiskey, which he poured with a flourish.

"Do you dance too?" Ned asked.

"Behave," the man said.

Thal paid, took a taste, and sighed with contentment. He would dearly have loved a bottle back on the prairie after that hella-cious storm soaked them through and through. They hadn't been able to get a fire going, everything was so wet, and the whole night long he'd shivered and tossed.

"Now, what's this information you want?" the barman said.

"The Black Hills," Thal said.

"Head northeast. You'll know when you get there because you'll be up to your armpits in Sioux."

"Hardy-har," Ned said.

"What's the best way to get there that doesn't involve the Sioux?" Thal said.

"You have your pick," the bartender said. "There's the Cheyenne and Black Hills Stage Company. The tickets are pricey, though, and they'd only take you and not the horses I saw you ride up on."

"You're an observant cuss," Ned said.

"I observe you like to flap your gums," the bartender said.

"He has you pegged," Crawford said.

"Now, where was I?" the man said, and rubbed his chin. "There are several outfits that haul mining machines and wagonloads of prospectors to the hills. They'd likely let you ride along."

"Are they the expeditions we've heard about?" Thal asked.

"Ah," the bartender said. "What you want is this." Turning, he opened a drawer, rummaged inside, closed it, and opened another. "Here it is." Taking out a folded sheet of paper, he spread it flat and slid it around so that Thal could read it.

Thal tried, but the letters were a jumble, like always. "What's this?"

"They call it a flyer."

"Let me," Ned said, and picked the paper up. His mouth moved a few times, as if he were practicing, and then he slowly read aloud, " 'Wild Bill has announced an expedition to the Black Hills. . . .' " He stopped, and blinked. "Wait. Which Wild Bill is this talkin' about?"

"Hickok," the bartender said.

"You're joshin'."

"The Prince of the Pistoleers," the bartender said. "Him and Colorado Charley are goin' off to strike it rich like everybody else."

"Wild Bill Hickok?" Jesse Lee said, in clear awe. "Why, I'd give my left arm to meet him."

"Not your right?" the barman said.

"That's the one I shoot with."

"Let me finish," Ned said, and resumed his slow reading. " 'The expedition will leave Cheyenne on the twenty-seventh of

139

June and proceed to Fort Laramie. From there it will travel to Custer City, rest for a week to ten days, and continue on to Deadwood. The cost is eighteen dollars from Cheyenne to Custer City, thirty-five dollars from Cheyenne to Deadwood. Sign up now while you still can.' " Ned set down the paper. "That's all there is."

"I've lost track of my days," Crawford said. "When is the twenty-seventh of June?"

"Tomorrow," the bartender said. "The wagons are gathered over to the freight yards, if you're of a mind to join up."

Thal would very much like to, but they had a problem. "We're obliged," he said. Glass in hand, he moved to an empty table, hooked a chair with his boot, slid it out, and sat.

"What are you lookin' so glum about?" Ned asked, sinking into the chair next to his.

"You heard him," Thal said. "How much money do you have on you?"

Ned fished in a pocket and brought out a handful of coins and crumpled bills.

"How about you two?" Thal said to Crawford and Jesse Lee. "We need seventy-two to go as far as Custer City. One hundred and forty if we go to Deadwood, wherever that is."

"Which is closer to American City?" Jesse Lee asked. "Ain't that where your brother was heard from last?"

"How would I know? I've never been to the Black Hills before."

"We'll have to ask around," Ned said. "As for how much money I have, I'm almost rich. Eleven dollars and change."

"You call that wealthy?" Crawford said.

"For me it is," Ned said.

As it turned out, Jesse Lee had twenty-two dollars, Crawford only had seven, and Thal could boast of eight dollars and twenty-five cents.

"That's barely fifty dollars between all of us combined." Crawford totaled the amount before any of them could.

"Shucks," Jesse Lee said. "We can't even afford to go to Custer City."

"Unless we go by ourselves," Ned proposed. "Let's forget joinin' Wild Bill's expedition. Who needs it?"

"We do," Thal said. "This is Sioux country we're talkin' about, not a walk in the park. We traipse off on our own, we could wind up dead."

"We can wait for another expedition," Crawford said. "A cheaper one."

"Maybe Wild Bill's is the cheapest around," Thal said. "No, I'd rather not wait.

There's my brother to think of."

"What, then?" Ned said.

Thal drummed the table and pondered. If that run-in with the Indians out on the prairie had taught him anything, it was that he shouldn't take anything for granted. They needed the protection a large group offered. "Either we work for the money or we try to win it."

"At cards or at dice?" Ned said.

"Cards," Thal said. "Poker will do." It was his favorite. Dice were too iffy a proposition.

"You're gettin' ahead of yourselves, ain't you?" Jesse Lee said. "We have to sign up, remember? Maybe the expedition is full up. Maybe they're only takin' so many, and we're too late."

"We can learn that right quick," Thal said, and took a long swallow. "Drink up, and we'll go to the freight yards and ask if they can put us on their list."

"Without the fee?" Ned said.

"We'll give them half of what we have as a down payment and tell them we'll have the rest in the mornin'," Thal proposed.

"And if we can't raise it?" Crawford said.

"We're up the creek without a paddle."

"No," Ned said. "We're up the creek without a canoe."

Thal drained his glass and smacked it down. "Let's go find the Hickok expedition."

It proved easy. A long banner announced to the world that a line of wagons were the Hickok-Utter Black Hills expedition. Hardly anyone was around. Thal reckoned most were making last-minute preparations. Stocking up, and the like. He walked around a loaded freight wagon and nearly collided with a man coming the other way.

"You ought to watch where you're stepping, mister." The man was tall and broad-shouldered, with hair that hung past his shoulders. He wore fringed buckskins.

"Are you Wild Bill Hickok?" Ned asked.

The man looked at him is if Ned's mental faculties were in question. "Am I dressed as a gambler?"

"Well, no," Ned said.

"Do you see a red sash around my middle with the butts of two Colts sticking out?"

"I do not," Ned admitted sheepishly.

"Do I even have a mustache?"

Ned shook his head.

"Then it's more than likely I'm not Wild Bill."

Ned brightened and snapped his fingers. "I know. You must be that pard of his, Colorado Charley Utter."

"They shouldn't let you loose unattended," the man said.

"Beg pardon?" Ned said.

"Does my hair look like I comb it and brush it every day? Do you see beaded moccasins on my feet? Or gold and silver pistols at my waist? Do I smell like lavender or lilacs?"

"Why would a man smell like that?" Ned said. "It's a female smell."

"From taking a bath each and every day, come hell or high water," the man said.

"You're sayin' that Colorado Charley Utter is fond of bathin'?"

"You catch on quick," the man said sarcastically, and went to go around them.

"Hold on," Thal said. "If you're not Wild Bill and you're not Charley Utter, then who are you? A scout for the army?"

"I'm Steve Utter, Charley's brother."

Thal was taken aback. "Yet you talk about him the way you do?" Brothers shouldn't ever speak ill of brothers — or to them — was his belief. He'd never once had a harsh word for Myles all the years they were growing up. Sure, they'd had a few childish spats, but nothing serious.

Steve Utter was saying, "Mister, my brother takes more baths than anyone I know or ever heard of. He likes water so

144

much he should have been born a fish." He put his hands on his hips. "Now, what are you gents doin' here anyhow?"

Thal explained that they would like to sign on with the expedition.

"You're too late," Steve Utter said. "We're not taking anyone else on. We've got too many as it is."

"How can you have too many?" Ned said.

"A wagon train ten miles long would be hard to protect, so we have to limit its size," Steve Utter said. "The best I can do is take your names, and if someone drops out, you can take their place."

Thal was crushed but tried not to show it.

"What will it be? Do you want to give your names or not?"

"Christie," Thal said. "My handle is Thal Christie, and I need to —"

Steve Utter held up a hand to stop him. "What is this, mister? Some kind of joke?"

"Sorry?" Thal said in confusion.

"You name is Thal Christie? Then these others must be — what was it? — Ned Leslie, Jesse Lee Hardesty, and Crawford Soames."

"How in hell do you know my last name?" Jesse Lee demanded.

"How do you know any of our names?" Thal said.

"You can stop the act," Steve Utter said. "I'm not amused."

"By what?" Ned said.

"By pretending you want to sign up for the expedition when you already have."

CHAPTER 13

Thal could have been floored with a feather. He looked at his friends and they looked at him.

"You're joshin' us, mister," Ned said.

"Stop playacting," Steve Utter said. "I was standing at my brother's side when he took the money from the little lady and she gave him all your names. I have a good memory for names, so if those are yours, you're the ones."

"Little lady?" Thal said.

Steve Utter tilted his head and scratched his chin. "What's going on here? I'm beginning to think you're really not pretending."

"I don't know how to pretend," Ned said.

"Where is this little lady who signed us up?" Thal said. "We should thank her for her generosity."

"From what I understand, she's taken a room over to the Metropole," Steve Utter informed them.

147

"What name is she going by?"

Utter frowned. "I knew you were joshing me." He wheeled on a heel.

"Wait," Thal said. "I just want to know who she is."

"As if you don't," Steve Utter said in annoyance, and stalked off without a backward look.

"He was halfway riled," Ned said.

"That was dang peculiar," Crawford said.

"Do we go to the Metropole and find this woman?" Jesse Lee threw in.

"Need you ask?" Thal stalked off and the others followed. That tiny voice at the back of his mind was acting up again. He had an awful premonition, and kept telling himself *Surely not.* He stopped to ask an elderly gent for directions to the Metropole, and the man volunteered the information that it was one of the better hotels in Cheyenne.

"It's where the well-to-do and famous folk hobnob."

That eased Thal's worry, a little.

With its fancy facade and decorations, the Metropole was Cheyenne's nod to elegance. The lobby was positively plush, with carpet and sofas and a small chandelier.

Thal had no sooner stepped past the double doors than he stopped in his tracks and blurted, "It can't be."

Seated in a high-backed purple chair, reading a magazine and attired in a new dress and bonnet, was none other than his very own sister.

Marching over, Thal said angrily, "Ursula Marigold Christie, what in tarnation do you think you're doin'?"

Ursula lowered her magazine, which had something to do with ladies' fashions, and beamed sweetly. "Thalis! Finally!" Rising, she gave him a huge hug. "How many times have I told you to never, ever use my middle name? I hate it more than I hate just about anything. It's the only foolish thing Ma's ever done, naming me after her favorite flower."

"Answer my question," Thal said. He was aware of the others coming up behind him. A glance showed they shared his astonishment but not his anger.

"I won't have you talk to me in that tone," Ursula replied. "You're my brother, not my keeper."

"Consarn it all, sis," Thal said. He was so flustered he didn't know which question to ask first, so he blurted all three. "How? Why? What?"

"My goodness," Ursula said in her irritatingly sweet manner. "Aren't you a wonder with words?"

Ned laughed.

"Where's Ma and Pa?" Thal said. "Surely you're not here by your lonesome."

"Surely I am," Ursula said.

"How did you get here?"

"I spread my wings and flew."

Both Ned and Jesse Lee laughed.

Thal felt his ears burn. He was close to losing his temper, which he rarely did. "I'm serious. How did you beat us?"

"I came by stagecoach," Ursula said, then corrected herself with "Stage*coaches,* actually. I left the morning after you did. I was worried I wouldn't make it in time, but here I am."

"My worry is why you're here at all," Thal said. "This is no place for a girl your age."

Ursula went on sweetly smiling as she poked him hard in the chest. "In case you haven't noticed, I'm a woman now."

"I've noticed, ma'am," Jesse Lee said.

"Me too," Ned threw in.

Thal glowered.

"What did we do?" Ned said.

Crawford, who had hung back, coughed to get their attention. "People are starin' at us. Maybe you should take your argument outside."

"I have a better idea," Ursula said. "Let's take it to a restaurant. I'm hungry. How about you boys?"

"I'm whatever you are," Jesse Lee said.

"Me too," Ned said again.

"That's a right good notion, Miss Christie," Crawford said. "We haven't eaten since daybreak, and all we had for breakfast was coffee and leftover beans."

"Then a meal it is." Ursula held out her arm to Thal. "Care to escort me, or are you too mad?"

"My arm is just as good as his," Ned said, "and I'd never be mad at a beauty like you."

"If it's an arm you need, Miss Christie," Jesse Lee said with a grand bow, "mine is always at your service."

"Here we go again," Crawford said.

Thal was trying his best to ignore the simpletons and concentrate on his sister so he could stay angry. Ursula had a knack for charming her way out of things, and he wasn't going to let her this time. He took her arm. "Where'd you get the money for the stage fare and that dress?"

"Ah, ah, ah," Ursula said. "Not until we're at the restaurant. I don't want you foaming at the mouth where everyone can see."

"Foaming at the mouth," Ned repeated, and cackled.

As mad as Thal was, he couldn't help noticing the glances men gave her. With her

151

hair done up, and that dress, she was an eyeful. He hated to admit it, but his little sister really had grown up. "You have an eatery in mind?"

"As a matter of fact, I do," Ursula said.

It was called the Plains Café. A stuffed buffalo head hung on one wall and the head of a grizzly on another. The matron who waited on them was as stout as a tree, and no-nonsense. She gave them their menus, took their orders, and informed them it would be about ten minutes until the food arrived.

"So get to talkin'," Thal said.

"I meant it about your tone," Ursula replied. "Be nice. I don't like it when you're mean."

"I don't blame you," Ned said. "You should see how grumpy he can be in the mornin'. Why, one time —"

Thal's glare silenced him. "No, you don't. This is between me and her. Not one word out of you until we hash this out, you understand?"

"I can't even talk?"

"No."

"Some pard you are. A fella should have a say over what his own mouth does."

"Not . . . one . . . peep."

"See what I mean about grumpy?" Ned

152

said to Ursula. "But all right, if that's what he wants."

"Jesse Lee," Thal said. "It goes for you too."

"What did I do?"

"This is important. Keep your flatteries to yourself until we work it out."

Jesse Lee wasn't happy, but he said, "Out of respect for Miss Christie, I'll go along."

Thal turned to the last of them. "Crawford?"

"This is your silliness. Have at it."

"He can be that way at times," Ursula said.

The anger that had been building inside Thal burst like steam from an overheated teapot. "What's silly about my younger sister travelin' hundreds of miles all alone? What's silly about her comin' to one of the wildest towns west of the Mississippi? What's silly about a brother frettin' over her because of all the cutthroats and lechers in this world?"

"First of all," Ursula said with annoying calmness, "as I told you before, I came by stage, and stagecoaches seldom attack anybody."

Ned snorted and laughed, and covered his mouth with his hand.

"Take this serious," Thal said to his sister.

"I am. The people on stages are mostly courteous and not out to steal a woman's handbag or do her in. I was in no danger whatsoever. As for Cheyenne, yes, it's rowdy, but for wildness, I hear it can't compete with the gold rush towns up in the Black Hills. They have no law up there. Anything goes. Which is why I waited for you and your friends to get here." Ursula's features hardened. "I'm not stupid, big brother, and I resent being treated as if I am."

"Now, look, sis —" Thal began.

"No. *You* look. Myles is my brother too. I'd planned to come all along. But I knew if I brought it up back on the farm, you'd raise a fuss and maybe convince Ma and Pa I shouldn't. So I kept quiet." Ursula put a hand to her new dress. "As far as my clothes and the fares go, I've saved every penny ever given me from the time I was six. Remember Grandma and her inheritance? I had a few hundred dollars socked way."

Now that she mentioned it, Thal recollected the flower vase she kept in her closet, with all her money. Her "little bank," she'd called it.

"I've spent more than half, but that's all right," Ursula was saying. "You're here now, and I have enough to get us all to the hills.

Everything has worked out."

"Hold on. How did you know we'd want to sign on with the Hickok expedition?"

"It's the only one leaving for three weeks. It had to be this one. I was concerned you might be delayed, so I spoke to Mr. Charley Utter and explained my circumstances. He was gracious, and said that if you didn't show, he'd gladly refund my money. If that had happened, I intended to wait until you got here, and make plans then."

"Mighty smart of you, ma'am," Ned said.

Reluctantly Thal had to agree. His sister had shown remarkable common sense. "But still," he said, "this is no place for a woman alone, and the Black Hills are less so."

"That's why I have you four to protect me," Ursula said gaily.

"With my dyin' breath," Jesse Lee said.

Thal refused to let it rest. "Do you realize how bad it is up in those Hills? Some of the minin' camps and towns are nothin' but nests of thieves and swindlers, and worse."

"Didn't you hear me a minute ago? I know just how it is up there, thank you very much."

"Then I'd think you'd take my advice and go home."

Ursula drummed her fingers on the table. "Consarn it all, Thal. Do you really expect me to sit on my hands and dither when our brother might need us? He and I were always close. You know that."

"Your brothers are lucky to have a fine sister like you," Ned said.

"My own sisters ain't nearly as devoted as you are, Miss Christie," Jesse Lee said. "I'd be proud to be your brother."

"I need a drink," Crawford said.

Ursula surprised Thal by placing both of her hands on his. "Let's quit this squabbling, shall we? All that matters is Myles. We find him or die trying."

"That's the problem," Thal said. "The dying part."

"We know what we're getting into. We're going in with our eyes open, and if we don't get careless, if we keep our wits about us, we should be all right. I promise I won't take unnecessary risks. And I can be of help. I have one thing in my favor that none of you do."

"Oh?" Thal said. He was thinking of their mother, and her comment about Sodom and Gomorrah.

"I'm female. People are more likely to open up to me than they are to you. They won't take offense if I ask questions."

"She's right about that," Ned said. "A pretty gal like her, I'd answer anything she

156

asked me."

"What will it be?" Ursula said, squeezing Thal's hand. "I don't want you mad at me the whole time, so I'll leave it up to you. Do I go, or don't I? I'll return home if you insist, but it will crush my heart that you have so little faith in me."

Thal squirmed inside. She was doing it again. Every fiber of his being screamed at him to tell her no, but as if he were two people, he heard himself say, "You can come."

Squealing in delight, Ursula pecked him on the cheek. "Thank you. You won't regret it. And don't worry. I won't come to any harm."

"I hope to God you don't," Thal said.

CHAPTER 14

Thal had never met anyone famous before. It upset him considerably that when he finally did, he was tongue-tied.

The expedition got under way the next day, as advertised. Wild Bill Hickok rode at the head with the Utter brothers and a man named Pie, and didn't mingle much. The brothers did, especially Charley, who proved to the most dandified man Thal ever set eyes on. From his washed and curried hair to the tips of his beaded moccasins, Charley Utter was a testament to human flowery. It spoke volumes about the man that his most prized possession was his bathtub, which had a roost of honor on his wagon.

Wild Bill Hickok's prized possession, on the other hand — besides his pistols — was a five-gallon keg of whiskey.

Their first stop was to be Fort Laramie. It would take some days to get there. Along about the third morning out, they came to a ranch and Hickok called a halt so he could visit with the owner, an old friend of his.

Thal and his sister and the rest were waiting their turn at the outdoor pump to refill their canteens when who should come strolling up but Charley Utter and Wild Bill himself?

"Say, Bill," Charley Utter said, stopping. "This here is that pretty gal I was telling you about. Miss Ursula Christie."

Thal couldn't get over how big Hickok was. The famous shootist dwarfed Utter.

Hickok wore a frock coat and a wide-brimmed hat. Around his waist was a red sash, and from it poked the butts of his twin Colts. "How do you do, ma'am?" he said in a surprisingly small voice. "Charley informs me you are on a hunt for your brother."

"That we are," Ursula said demurely. She seemed to be in awe that the great man had spoken to her. "This is my other brother, Thalis, and these are his friends."

"Thalis, is it?" Hickok said, offering his hand. "Don't hear that handle much."

Thalis shook, and couldn't think of anything to say.

Hickok wasn't offended. He studied Ned and Jesse Lee and Crawford, and turned back to Ursula. "A word to the wise, Miss Christie. The Black Hills aren't for amateurs. They are infested with vermin. Wherever you are bound, it won't be like anyplace you've ever been."

"My pard is right, ma'am," Charley Utter said. "You must always be on your guard."

"That reminds me," Ursula said. "Perhaps you gentlemen can be of help. We're bound for someplace called American City. Have you heard of it?"

"My God," Charley Utter said. "Not there."

"I beg your pardon?"

"You know of the place, Charley?" Wild Bill said.

"I do, Bill," Charley said, nodding, "and it's not anywhere decent folk should visit. It's one of the worst of the camps, if not *the* worst." He gave Ursula a worried look. "Are you sure that's where you have to go?"

"It's where my brother was heard from last," Ursula said. "But I can't seem to find anyone who knows where it is."

"That's not surprising. There are dozens of camps. Some last longer than others and turn into towns. Others wither and fade away." Charley paused. "The one you want is in Blood Gulch, as they call it."

"My word," Ursula said. "Why do they call it that?"

"Gulches are named after a lot of things,"

160

Charley said. "Deadwood Gulch, for instance, because of all the dead trees. Blood Gulch is where five prospectors were ambushed and killed. Their throats were slit and their scalps were lifted —"

"Charley," Wild Bill said in reproach.

Ursula had blanched slightly, and put a hand to her throat.

"Sorry, ma'am," Charley said. "Everyone says Injuns were to blame, but there's been talk that they weren't. Anyway, on account of all the blood, they call it Blood Gulch."

"And why American City?" Ursula asked.

"I can't help you there. You'd have to ask the man who runs it. His name is Trevor Galt. Each camp has its wolves and its sheep, and he's the top wolf in American City. You and these others would be well advised to steer clear of him."

"We thank you for your advice," Ursula said.

"Be careful, miss," Wild Bill said. "Should you get into any difficulties, feel free to look Charley and me up in Deadwood. We will help you if we can." Smiling, he touched his hat brim to her and the pair strolled off.

"Wild Bill Hickok, by God," Ned exclaimed. "Talkin' to the likes of us."

"You never opened your mouth," Crawford said.

"I didn't hear any of you say anything either," Ned said. "My pard looked like he'd swallowed his tongue."

"I did not," Thal said.

"I was admirin' those pistols of his," Jesse Lee said. "They're the latest Colts. Did you see his ivory handles? They're just like mine."

"Now you're comparin' yourself to Wild Bill?" Ned said. "You have to go a ways yet before bad men will tremble in fear of you like they tremble in fear of him."

"I'm young," Jesse Lee said. "Give me time."

Ursula was looking at them as if she was annoyed. "I can't believe your only interest is in Mr. Hickok when there's my brother to worry about. Didn't you hear what Mr. Utter said about American City?"

"I did," Thal said.

"Why would Myles go to such a place?" Ursula said. "Ma and Pa raised him better than that."

"We'll find out when we find him." Thal almost added, "If we do."

The days became a monotony of travel. They were up at the crack of dawn, ate a hasty breakfast while the teams were hitched, and were under way as the sun cleared the horizon. They always stopped when it was directly overhead for their nooning, as it was called. Sometimes they'd rest for an hour, sometimes more.

Thal chafed at every delay. It didn't help his disposition that a lot of the talk among the expedition members was about how dangerous the Black Hills were, and the many perils they might encounter.

Finally they reached Fort Laramie. Started as a trading post over forty years ago, it was situated on the Laramie River about a mile or so from where the Laramie joined the North Platte. Initially only a stockade, it was now a sprawling encampment. The soldiers had the unenviable task of protecting emigrants using the Oregon Trail from depredations by the Sioux and other tribes.

Thal hoped they wouldn't stay longer than a day. He hadn't counted on the Utter and Hickok train being joined by almost thirty more wagons. A few were transporting mine machinery. Half a dozen contained supplies and merchandise. The rest were gold seekers, eager to reap their fortune. The mere mention of the Black Hills brought flashes of greed to their hungry eyes.

There was a notable exception, a wagon that became the most popular whenever the train stopped. That was because it contained brightly dressed ladies who, for a price, would be as friendly to a man as a man could ever want a woman to be.

"Why, they're prostitutes!" Ursula gasped as she watched the women parading about, parasols on their shoulders, flirting and teasing every male they met.

"They're not nearly as pretty as you." Ned sought to compliment her.

"Did you really just compare me to whores?" Ursula demanded bluntly.

"For shame, for shame," Jesse Lee said to Ned. "How could you?"

Ned defended himself. "I didn't do any such thing. I was only sayin' that Miss Christie is so pretty she could make a lot more money at it than those ladies do."

"Sell my body?" Ursula said, horrified. "What manner of woman do you think I am?"

"Ned, how could you?" Jesse Lee said, as if he were shocked.

"You're puttin' words in my mouth," Ned complained, and turned to Thal. "Pard, help me out here."

"Keep me out of your nonsense," Thal said.

"Me too," Crawford said. "There's only so much stupid I can abide."

That evening Charley Utter stood up and introduced the fallen doves to the entire

164

train. Thal had to bite his lip to keep from laughing when Utter revealed that one of the women was called Sizzling Kate and another Dirty Emma. "And this fine gal on my right," Utter continued with a bow to a heavyset woman with a head like a pumpkin, "is Tid Bit."

"Well, I never," Ursula said. "I'd be ashamed to run around in public with a name like that."

Just then an officer and a sergeant approached, along with a pair of enlisted men. Between them was someone in buckskins. At first Thal thought it was a scout. Then whispering broke out, and an emigrant near them declared, "I don't believe it. That there is Martha Jane Canary."

"Calamity Jane?" another said.

"The very same," the man confirmed. "I saw her over to Cheyenne once when she got drunk and caused a ruckus in a saloon."

"She looks like a man," Ursula said.

Now that his sister mentioned it, Thal reflected, Calamity Jane did. Her hair was cut short and her baggy buckskins hid whatever curves and other female attributes she might have.

"You're definitely prettier than her, Miss Christie," Ned spoke up. "No one would ever mistake you for a man unless they were addlepated."

"There's a lot of that goin' around," Jesse Lee said drily.

The officer and Charley Utter conversed. Utter kept shaking his head until finally the officer motioned at the sergeant and the sergeant motioned at the pair of enlisted men and they brought Calamity Jane up and left her standing beside Wild Bill, who ignored the fawning looks Jane gave him.

"What do you reckon that's all about?" Ned said.

"Looks to me as if the army is passin' her off to the expedition," Crawford said, "and our leaders don't want any part of her."

"The rest of this trip should be interestin'," Ned said.

Charley Utter had been elected train captain and did a superb job of riding up and down the line and keeping everyone on their toes against a possible Indian attack. Some thought it unlikely the Sioux would try anything, not when their party numbered over one hundred and thirty. Thal remembered Custer and the Seventh Calvary, and wasn't so sure.

They came to another ranch at Sage Creek, and some excitement was generated when it was discovered that Buffalo Billy Cody and some others had stopped there as well. Thal would have liked to meet the famous scout, but Cody spent all his time with Hickok and Utter and their entourage.

Thal was more excited by something he witnessed the day before they were to enter the Black Hills proper. When the wagon train nooned, Wild Bill and a younger man known as White-Eye Anderson moved off a ways and Anderson commenced to set up empty bottles and other targets.

Jesse Lee nudged Thal. "Let's go have a look."

"Butt into Wild Bill Hickok's business?" Thal said. "Are you loco?"

"He's only shootin'," Jesse Lee said. "I'd like to see."

"So would I," Ned said. "We could sort of drift over without makin' nuisances of ourselves."

Others from the train were venturing near, so Thal gave in.

Hickok didn't pay any of them any mind. He appeared to be giving White-Eye Anderson instruction on how to shoot. Then it happened. Hickok faced the targets. His hands blurred, and he drew both pistols simultaneously. He preferred the reverse draw, or flip draw as some called it, and there was no one slicker.

His Colts cracking, he fired without aiming. Bottles shattered and cans went flying. When he was done, applause broke out.

Jesse Lee clapped the loudest. "Did you see?" he marveled. "Did you see how quick and sure he is?"

"You're quick too," Crawford said.

"I'm no Wild Bill," Jesse Lee said.

Ursula had folded her arms and was tapping her foot. "So he can squeeze a trigger and hits what he aims at? I'll never understand why men make such a fuss over shooters."

"We do it for the same reason you females make a fuss over a handsome fella," Crawford said.

Ursula snickered. "Because you think shootists are handsome and you'd like to marry one someday?"

Crawford turned a wonderful shade of red. "I never suggested any such thing, Miss Christie."

"Not all shootists are equal," Ned said. "The best ones earn our respect because they're so good at it. That's all it is."

"Oh, pshaw," Ursula teased. "Jesse Lee here practically worships Wild Bill Hickok."

"Not true, ma'am," Jesse Lee said, sounding hurt. "The only one I worship is the Almighty."

"Let's hope he's watchin' over us," Ned

said. "Tomorrow we reach the Black Hills, and we'll need all the help we can get."

"Amen to that," Thal said.

Chapter 15

The Black Hills.

From a distance they did indeed appear to be black, the result, Thal learned, of the heavy timber that covered their slopes. Word had it that the hills in their entirety encompassed some five thousand square miles. That was a lot of territory.

Steve Utter mentioned to Thal that the highest of the hills was about seven thousand feet. The average was much less.

To Thal they had a sinister air, but he told himself it was probably just his imagination.

The Sioux had long claimed the Black Hills as their own. Not that long ago, the government had signed a treaty with them that had agreed, formally assigning the hills as Sioux territory. Whites under no circumstances were supposed to settle there.

Barely eight years later, a Custer expedition found gold. No sooner did word get out than a horde of gold seekers swarmed in, so many that the army couldn't possibly keep them all out, and gave up trying.

The Sioux saw their sacred hills overrun, and didn't like it one bit.

There was irony in the fact that George Armstrong Custer, who in a sense brought about the ruination of the treaty, was slain by the Sioux and warriors from other tribes in the massacre at the Little Bighorn.

For the Sioux, it was too little, too late. The Black Hills had been overrun. Dozens of camps and towns sprang up, and there was no stopping the influx of whites.

The army went from protecting the Sioux from whites, to protecting the steady stream of inpouring hordes from the Sioux.

From a legal perspective, though, the Black Hills were still Sioux territory. This meant that they weren't part of the United States. They weren't under the rule of common law. Or any law whatsoever. Which explained why the hills had become synonymous with lawlessness.

Greed seldom brought out the best in people. Those flocking to the hills weren't what churchgoers would call respectable. The prospectors and miners only cared about their precious yellow ore. The saloon owners and gamblers and doves who followed were out to take the gold that the prospectors found and the miners dug out of the ground, and make it their own.

Thal's mother had been right when she compared the Black Hills to Sodom and Gomorrah. Anything went, as the saying had it. Thievery, shootings, and knifings were commonplace. No one trusted anyone else, with good reason.

All of this was on Thal's mind as the wagon train lumbered deeper into the haunts of the godless.

From a prospector, Thal and his friends learned that American City was in the north part of the hills, to the west of Deadwood, which was where the Utters and Wild Bill Hickok were bound.

A lot of people and wagons left the train at Custer City. That was as far as they were going.

Since the train arrived late in the day, Utter informed those going on that they would rest the night and head out early the next morning. He warned everyone to keep their purses and pokes close, and whatever they did, to not become drunk, or they might never leave.

"That fella sure does exaggerate," Ned said as the meeting broke up.

"Do we stay with the wagons or do we take in the sights?" Crawford asked. "Me, I could go with a drink or three."

Thal wouldn't mind at least one himself. But there was Ursula to think of. "You boys go ahead. I'll stay here with my sister."

"Like Hades you will," Ursula said. "I won't be the cause of spoiling your fun. If you want to go, go. I'll be perfectly fine. I'll visit with a few of the ladies and turn in early."

"I don't know," Thal said uncertainly. The notion of leaving her alone worried him.

"Mr. Utter has posted a guard over the wagons," Ursula mentioned, with a nod at a man with a rifle. "No one will bother me here, I assure you."

"I have an idea," Crawford said. "Hold on a minute." He turned and went to their horses.

"What's he up to?" Ned wondered.

"With him it will be somethin' practical," Jesse Lee said. "That's how he is."

The older puncher reappeared carrying the Henry he'd taken from the family of cutthroats on the prairie. Smiling, he held it out to Ursula. "For you," he said.

"You're lending me your rifle? I doubt I'll need it."

"It's not mine," Crawford said. "And I'm givin' it to you, as a gift. I trust you can shoot? Or didn't you ever learn?"

173

"Pa taught me when I was knee-high to a calf," Ursula said. "But I can't take it."

"You'd refuse a present?" Crawford said, and shoved it into her hands. "It's loaded. Anyone tries to trifle with you, show him that and he'll make himself scarce."

"But, Mr. Soames —"

"I won't take no for an answer. Thal, help me out here. Tell your sister she shouldn't be unarmed. If I had a spare revolver I'd give her that, but I don't."

"Listen to him, sis. It can't hurt to have it handy."

"What will the other women think? You don't see any of them carrying guns," Ursula argued.

"Don't fool yourself," Crawford said. "A lot of doves carry derringers or pocket pistols. Those that don't usually have knives. You need protection, and there's nothin' better than a gun when it comes to discouragin' a bad man."

"That's settled, then," Ned said, even though it wasn't. He nudged Jesse Lee, and the Southerner walked off with him but gave Ursula a look of regret. Crawford tagged along.

"I'll be right there," Thal said to them, and touched his sister's arm. "Be careful, you hear? Don't leave the wagons, no mat-

174

ter what. We won't be more than a couple of hours."

"Go have your fun," Ursula said.

Thal hesitated. That tiny voice was at work again, warning him not to. He silenced it and hastened to catch up to his friends.

"Quit chewin' on your lip," Ned said. "She'll be fine."

The sun had set, and lamps and lanterns were being lit all over Custer City. The first town to be formed in the hills, it didn't have the reputation others did for thievery and bloodletting. Its main street was unique in that when they laid out the town, they made the street wide enough for a wagon with a full team to wheel completely around. Most of the buildings were wooden frame affairs, with false fronts and boardwalks, and there were a lot of log cabins.

But precious few people.

Thal had noticed on the way in that not many folks were out and about, and figured it was because it was the supper hour. But now the first saloon they came to was practically empty. An old man sat at a table playing solitaire, and that was it. They ambled to the bar and ordered drinks, and as the bearded bartender poured, Thal cleared his throat.

"Where is everybody?"

"You gents must be from that train that pulled in not long ago," the barman said.

"If we are, what about it?" Jesse Lee drawled.

"It explains why you don't know where everyone got to." The barman finished filling their glasses and poured one for himself. "My name's Jim, by the way."

"Did they all come down sick?" Ned joked.

Jim shook his head. "A couple of months ago there were pretty near ten thousand people here, if you can believe it."

"I can't," Ned said.

"Then they found gold up to Deadwood Gulch, and by the end of the week there weren't twenty men and women left in all of Custer," Jim related. "We've built back up some, since. Even got a school going. But we're still short on citizens."

"That many left all at once?" Crawford said.

"You had to be here to believe it," Jim said. "They couldn't pull up stakes fast enough. All they cared about was the gold. They left their cabins, their businesses, some of them. It was a stampede, I tell you."

"All because of the gold?" Ned said.

"Mister, to most of these folks, gold is their god. It's all they think about. All they dream about. They want to be rich, and they'll do whatever they have to in order to make that come true. They'll lie. They'll cheat. They'll kill."

Crawford chuckled. "Pardon my sayin' so, but you don't seem to have a very high opinion of your fellow man."

"Not high at all," Jim replied. "Not after the things I've seen, and heard about." He patted the bar and fondly gazed about the saloon. "I'm just glad I ended up here and not in some of the other camps and towns. Compared to places like Deadwood and American City, Custer City is tame."

Thal's interest perked up. "American City? That's where we're bound. The four of us and my sister."

"Tell me it ain't so," the barman said.

"We have to go," Thal said.

"And you're taking your own sister? Don't you care for her? You might as well put a gun to her head and squeeze the trigger. You'd be doing her a kindness."

"Here, now," Ned said. "There's no call for harsh talk like that."

"Harsh?" Jim said, and uttered a bark of a laugh. "Let me set you gents straight." He paused. "American City is the worst place in these hills. All that greed I was telling you about? American City is rabid with it.

The few good folks who have gone in never came out again. I should know. I had a friend who went there thinking to start his own saloon. The next time I saw him, he showed up here, a beaten man."

"I'd like to hear about it," Thal said. The more he learned, the better he could protect his sister, and the sooner he might find his brother.

"In American City it's every man for himself. It's run by a man who used to ride with William Quantrill, the Confederate guerilla."

"You don't say," Jesse Lee said.

"So I've been told. But I'm not about to go up to the man and ask if it's true. Trevor Galt surrounds himself with men as hard as he is. Nothing goes on in American City without his say-so. My friend who wanted his own saloon? When he first got there, Galt was friendly and cordial. He even helped my friend find the workers to build it. Then, when the saloon was ready to open, Galt told my friend he wanted fifty percent of the earnings. My friend refused, and Trevor had him beaten and thrown out of American City. When I saw him, his face was still swollen, his eyes were black and blue, and his nose had been broken. I offered to have him work for me, but he was so scared of Galt he was leaving the Black Hills and never coming back."

Thal mulled the information. "If this Trevor Galt is so terrible, why does anyone go there?"

"Most don't know how he is. They think American City isn't any different or worse than any other camp. He's clever, and doesn't lord it over them where anyone can see, but he lords it just the same."

"I gather it's not a safe place for women," Thal said.

"Haven't you been listening? It's not safe for anyone. If she was my sister, I wouldn't take her anywhere near there."

Thal had a lot to ponder. Foremost was how to persuade Ursula not to go. She'd undoubtedly refuse to stay behind. He was still contemplating all that when they left the saloon and headed up the overly wide street.

"You've been awful quiet for a while now, pard," Ned mentioned.

"My sister," Thal said. "I don't know what to do."

"We're goin' on to Deadwood, aren't we?" Crawford said. "Why not put her up at a hotel or a boardinghouse, and the rest of us will go find your brother?"

"I refuse to leave her by herself."

179

"Then one of us should stay with her," Crawford said. "Problem solved."

"It would have to be me who stays," Thal said, "and I'm the only one of us who knows my brother on sight."

"Why you?" Ned said. "You don't trust your own friends?"

"We'd never hurt Ursula," Jesse Lee said. "Not in a million years."

"Flip a coin to decide which of us it will be," Crawford proposed. "Another problem solved."

"I see what Jesse Lee means about you," Thal said. He liked the older cowhands' idea. Now all he had to do was convince Ursula.

As if Crawford were reading his thoughts, he said, "It'll take us a couple of days to get there. We'll have more than enough time to convince her if all of us work on her together."

"That's hardly fair," Jesse Lee said.

"Not even when it's for her own good?" Crawford said. "Which would you rather have? Her breathin'? Or six feet under?"

"Breathin' it is," Thal said. "Whether she likes it or not."

CHAPTER 16

Deadwood Gulch swarmed with human ants. No sooner had word spread about the gold that was found than the gulch was inundated in a flood of greed-spawned industry.

Deadwood itself was a riotous confusion of growth that made Cheyenne seem tame by comparison. Tents and cabins were everywhere, while buildings sprouted right and left in a frenzy of construction.

The Utter-Hickok expedition had no sooner arrived than it disbanded. Charley Utter and Wild Bill decided to take up residence in one of the sprawling tent cities, with Utter giving a parting wave as their wagon rolled off.

"Well, here we are," Ned declared, uneasily gazing about. They had reined to one side of the main street to be out of the traffic, and were sitting their horses. "We made it in one piece."

"I feel like a minnow in a big pond," Crawford said.

Thal shared the sentiment.

The flow of humanity, the seething activity, was breathtaking. Townsmen, prospectors, miners, and more scurried here and there as if they couldn't reach their destinations fast enough. The prosperous wore expensive hats and suits and gold watches. Those less so wore store-bought apparel. A contingent of Chinese were setting up laundries and shops. Scores of freight wagons and Conestogas lumbered to and fro, or were being loaded or unloaded. Weary mules and teams of oxen lay in the dust to rest.

Thal stared up and down the chaotic street, and realized something. "Any of you see any punchers anywhere?"

"How's that?" Ned said.

"Cowhands like us," Thal said. "Do you see any?"

Ned and Crawford and Jesse Lee glanced every which way, and looked at each other in surprise.

"Can't say as I do," Jesse Lee said.

"Not a single one except us," Crawford said.

"There have to be more cowhands somewhere," Ned said. "We can't be the only ones."

"You see any cows either?" Crawford said.

Ned looked and said, "Well, damn."

Thal turned to Ursula. "You're awful quiet."

"And you know why," she said archly.

"We've been all through that, sis," Thal said. "It's for the best."

"Says you."

Thal sighed. He'd spent the better part of the past two days trying to convince her that it was best she stay in Deadwood, at least until they determined whether American City was the vile pit of wickedness it was rumored to be. Ursula, as he'd predicted, was against the idea. She nearly argued herself hoarse, saying that Myles was her brother as well as his, and she had as much right as Thal did to go on to American City. She was incensed that they were treating her with kid gloves just because she was female, and warned that she would hold it against him the rest of her days if he didn't let her go.

Thal stood by his guns. He cared for her too much, he'd explained, to let anything happen to her. He thought that would soothe her ruffled feathers, but he was wrong.

"I love you just as much as you love me," Ursula had replied, "but you don't see me asking you not to go."

"You're bein' hardheaded," Thal had told her, which only made her madder.

Now here they were, in Deadwood, and Ursula hadn't stopped simmering. All she needed was an excuse to give them a tongue-lashing.

Thal was doing his best not to give her one.

Then Ned spoke up. "You'll thank us for leavin' you here later, Miss Christie. We're coddlin' you for your own good."

"Is that so?" Ursula said, each syllable as icy as a winter's frost.

Ned still didn't catch on. Nodding, he said, "It's natural for a man to want to protect the weaker gender."

"Is that what I am?"

"You're female, ain't you?"

"Ned —" Thal tried to cut him off.

Ned gestured. "I can speak for myself, pard." He smiled cheerfully at Ursula. "Needin' protection is nothin' to be ashamed of. It's not your fault you were born a woman. Or that us men are stronger, and can endure more hardship."

Ursula snorted. "I'd like to see a man give birth."

"You're bein' silly. Men have enough to do without that too. God gave the job to women because you're the ones who cook and sew and such. Motherin' comes naturally."

"I thank you for enlightening me," Ursula said in a tone that made Thal wince. He'd only ever heard that tone a few times, and always right before a storm that put the one out on the prairie to shame.

"Think nothin' of it."

"No," Ursula said. "I'd rather think nothing of you."

"Beg your pardon?"

"Pardon you?" Ursula said, and leaning over, she poked him in the arm. "You mealymouthed, pompous, arrogant so-and-so." She poked him again, her dander rising. "So men are superior, are they?" Another poke. "So women need protecting, do they?" Yet another poke. "It's a wonder you can dress yourself, you're so ignorant."

"What did I do?" Ned said in bewilderment.

"You insulted womanhood. You insulted me. You insulted every man who ever lived. And you insulted yourself."

"I did all that?"

"You will refrain from addressing me until I simmer down or I might just slap you."

"Where did all this come from?" Ned said. "If you ask me, you're bein' mighty childish."

Ursula actually hissed.

"Do you hear that?" Crawford said.

"Her hissin' at me?" Ned said.

"That was the sound of the last nail bein' driven into your coffin. One of these days we should sit down and I'll give you pointers on how to talk to females. If there's anyone worse at it, they haven't been born yet."

"I'm not dead yet," Ned said. "Why are you talkin' about coffins?"

"Sad," Crawford said, and shook his head.

"What is?" Ned said.

To forestall more argument, Thal clucked to his chestnut. "Let's go find a boardinghouse." He took it for granted the others would follow and was relieved when they did.

Poor Ned looked worried sick. He'd finally realized he was on thin ice with Ursula.

Thal concentrated on reading the signs. It took considerable effort, given his condition. He managed to read a banner that announced the Oyster Bay Restaurant and Lunch Counter, and wondered what lunatic would name a restaurant that, since there wasn't a bay to be had for a thousand miles. "Let me know if any of you spot a boarding-house," he said.

Ned, perhaps to take his mind off his debacle with Ursula, commenced to read the signs out loud.

There was Harrmann and Trebor, Wholesale Liquor Dealers. There was the Big Horn Store, the Tin Shop. Dozens of saloons, half as many eateries. There was already a newspaper, the *Black Hills Times.* The Progressive Hall, the City Market, the Senate. Books and Stationery.

Thal came to a smaller gulch that branched off Deadwood. Tents and buildings were spreading up this one too, although not nearly as many yet. It was a lot quieter. On a whim he reined up it and hadn't gone a hundred yards when Ned pointed and hollered.

"Lookee there!"

Thal wrestled with the words on yet another sign and hadn't quite figured them out when Ned saved him the trouble.

" 'Miss Primrose's Boardinghouse,' " Ned read. " 'Ladies Only.' "

"Wouldn't you know it?" Ursula said, scowling. "I was hoping there wasn't one so you'd have to take me with you."

"You'll be safer here," Thal said for the

hundredth time.

"So long as I don't step outside after dark and never go anywhere without an escort." Ursula recited his instructions. "Which reminds me. You said that one of you has to stay to nursemaid me. Who gets that job?"

Thal reined broadside to his friends. "Let's find out. We'll flip a coin. I'll call heads or tails for each of you until only one of you is left."

"Why go to all that bother?" Ursula said. "We already know you have to go because you can identify Myles. And Ned has to go because I'm never speaking to him again."

"What?" Ned bleated in dismay.

"That leaves Mr. Soames and Mr. Hardesty," Ursula continued. "Since Mr. Soames is the oldest, he should be the one to stay behind and serve as my protector." She said the last word sarcastically.

"You want Crawford to be the one?" Thal said in mild surprise.

"It's the proper thing to do," Ursula said, not sounding at all enthusiastic at the prospect.

"Hold on," Crawford said. "If it's protectin' you need, ma'am, then my pard is a heap better at it than me. I'm not ashamed to admit that he can outdraw and outshoot me any day of the week."

"I can draw and shoot," Ned said.

"I don't know about this," Thal said. Jesse Lee had made it plain he was smitten with Ursula. To leave them alone might be asking for trouble. "I'd still like to flip a coin."

"Flip it, then," Jesse Lee said. "I call tails."

Thal took a twenty-cent piece from his pocket, tossed the coin high, caught it, and slapped it down on the back of his other hand. Fate had thwarted him. "Tails it is."

"I stay, then," Jesse Lee said quietly. He didn't look at Ursula.

"I can draw and shoot," Ned said again.

"Give it up, pard." Thal slid the coin back into his pocket. "Let's get you a room, sis, and we'll all go eat."

For the first time in two days, Ursula smiled. She swung down and walked by his side onto a small porch. Jesse Lee, Crawford, and a muttering Ned stayed on their horses.

"Smell the fresh paint?" Ursula said.

A small bell hung on a hook. Thal rang it and remembered to doff his hat. He heard shoes clomp, and the door was opened by a broad woman with hair as white as snow, done up in a bun.

"Yes? I'm Mrs. Peal. How may I help you?"

"How do you do, ma'am?" Thal said. "I'd

like to put my sister up for a spell, if you don't mind."

"Sister?" Mrs. Peal appraised them, and nodded. "Yes. I can see the resemblance. Where do you intend to stay, young man? I only take on female boarders."

"I realize that, ma'am," Thal said, trying to impress her with his politeness. "Some of my friends and me" — and he motioned at the others — "have to go on to American City."

"I've heard only bad things about that place," Mrs. Peal said.

"So have I," Thal said. "Which is why I'd rather my sister stays with you."

"I see." Mrs. Peal gave Ursula another scrutiny. "How about you, young lady? Cat got your tongue?"

"I want to go with them, but they won't let me," Ursula said.

"I call that smart."

"I call it bossy."

A twinkle came into Mrs. Peal's blue eyes. "I see. Very well, Mr. . . . ?"

"Christie," Thal said. "Where are my manners? I'm Thal, and this is Ursula."

"Well, it's a dollar a day for a room and two meals, breakfast and supper. My rules are simple. There's to be no liquor. No smoking. No cussing. No carrying on whatsoever. And no men, which goes without saying. If you can abide by all that, Miss Christie, I have one room left and it's yours if you want it."

"She does," Thal said.

"I'd like to hear that from her."

"Since I have no choice," Ursula said, "I do."

Mrs. Peal grinned. "You have a lot of spunk, young lady. I admire that. Bring your bag in and I'll show you to your room." She paused. "I almost forgot. There's another rule. Each day is to be paid in advance." She held out her hand.

"My sister is paying," Thal said.

"Better and better," Ursula said.

"We'll fetch her carpetbag and be right back," Thal said. Taking his sister's elbow, he led her toward their horses. "Will you behave? For all we know, this is the only boardinghouse in all of Deadwood. We were lucky."

"You were," Ursula said. She brightened, though, and said to Jesse Lee, "I have a place to stay, Mr. Hardesty. What about you?"

"I can sleep anywhere," Jesse Lee said, and indicated an empty lot with trees and brush, across the street. "There will do. If you need me, I'll be handy."

"I'll give a holler if I do," Ursula said.

"You shouldn't need him for anything except to escort you about during the day," Thal said. "At night you're to stay in your room. You hear me?"

"Yes, master."

"I mean it, sis. None of your ornery shenanigans. You're to be on your best behavior."

"You can count on me," Ursula said.

CHAPTER 17

Thal didn't aim to let any grass grow under him. He wanted to get his hunt for his brother over with, collect his sister, and return, safe and sound, to the family farm.

So it was that when he parted company with Ursula, Thal bent his steps to Main Street, heading for a freight outfit he'd noticed earlier. If anyone knew how to get to American City, it would be a company that delivered all over the Black Hills.

On their way there, Ned voiced a complaint. "At times you surprise me, pard," was how he began.

"What did I do?" Thal said.

"You left a coyote to guard the chicken coop."

"Don't you mean a fox?"

"Foxes and coyotes both eat chickens. And now your sister is in the care of one."

"I knew that's where this was headed."

Crawford had been listening. "My pard is

no coyote," he said to Ned. "He'll watch over Thal's sis as if she were his own."

"Who are you kiddin'?" Ned said. "With me out of the way, he'll have her all to himself. He can court her silly before we get back."

"I trust my sister not to let things go too far," Thal said.

"You should protect her better, is what I'm sayin'," Ned said gloomily.

"By *better*," Thal said, "you mean I should have left you with her instead of him."

"That would be a start."

"Jesse Lee won the coin toss fair and square," Thal said. "And he's our friend, besides. I trust him."

"Thank you," Crawford said.

"I never said Jesse Lee was worthless," Ned said. "But this is romance we're talkin' about. It can sneak up on you if you're not careful."

"The important thing is that she stays safe," Thal said.

"So that's it," Ned said. "You prefer him because he's bucked more gents out in gore than I have."

"You haven't bucked any," Thal said. "But you not guardin' her was her idea, if you'll recall. You have only yourself to thank, what with all that jabber about men bein' better

194

than women."

"She's in good hands," Crawford said. "My pard will watch over her like a hawk."

"That's what I'm afraid of," Ned said.

The freight office was busy. Wagons laden with goods were about to depart, and the man who ran the place was going from wagon to wagon, making sure of his inventory.

Thal waited under an overhang, impatiently shifting his weight from one foot to the other.

Crawford gazed the length of the street and pushed his hat back. "Look at them all. I ain't ever seen the like."

"Gold fever," Thal said.

"It's any kind of rich," Crawford said. "A lot of folks hanker after a lot of money. I've never been that way, but that's just me."

"Me neither," Thal said. So long as he had enough to get by, he was happy. Occasionally he'd wonder if there might be something wrong with him. Other people loved money so much, why was it he didn't? Did that make him peculiar? He'd finally decided the answer was no. To each his own, as the saying went.

"Here he comes," Ned said.

Thal looked up.

The freight manager was a burly specimen with a drooping mustache and large jowls. He had papers in his hand, inventory lists, it looked like, and was running a finger down one of them.

"Excuse me, mister," Thal said. "Can I ask you a question?"

The freighter glanced up, blinked as if surprised, and stopped. "By God, cowhands, unless I'm mistaken."

"You're not," Thal said.

"If you're looking for cows, I'm plumb out," the man said, and chuckled at his joke.

"What we're lookin' for," Thal said, "is American City, and I was hopin' you could point the way."

The man's face darkened. "Not that it's any of my business, but why there, of all places? In case you haven't heard, it's hell on earth. A lot who go there don't make it back."

"I have a brother to find," Thal informed him.

"If you want my advice, you'll leave your brother to the demons."

"Demons?" Ned said.

"It can't be as bad as all that," Crawford said, "or no one would go there at all."

"Listen, cowpoke," the freighter said. "I've been all over the West. I've seen my share of bad places. Some of the cow towns, for instance, when the herds are in. There are shootings and stabbings all the time, and worse."

"What could be worse?" Ned said.

"I have it to do," Thal said, "and I'd be obliged for directions."

"It's your funeral," the freighter said. Turning, he motioned at Main Street. "Follow this out of the gulch until you come to a road to the west. In about ten miles it will branch. You want the branch to the northwest, not the southwest. Follow that, oh, another ten miles or a little more and you'll come to Blood Gulch, and American City. And may God help you."

"How come they didn't call it Blood City?" Ned asked. "They named Deadwood after Deadwood Gulch."

The freighter shrugged. "I wasn't there, so I can't rightly say. From what I hear, it was Trevor Galt's doing."

"Maybe he's patriotic," Ned said.

"Mister, the only thing in this world Trevor Galt cares about is Trevor Galt."

"You've met him?" Thal said.

"Once, and that was enough. I had to make a delivery. I never went back. Anyone comes to me and wants me to take freight to American City, I tell them to use another freight company."

"You pass up work?"

"I know. It sounds crazy. But I'm more fond of breathing than I am of turning a profit."

"What happened there that you won't go back?" Thal asked.

"What happened," the freighter replied, "is Trevor Galt. Now if you'll excuse me, I'm a busy man, and I've given you more of my time than I can afford." He hustled into his office.

"Well, now," Ned said.

"The more I hear," Crawford said, "the more I wish we'd never left Texas."

"If it was your brother, you'd do the same," Thal said.

Mounting, they headed north, and before long the buildings and the bustle were behind them.

Thal willed himself to not look back. It would make him think of Ursula. He hated leaving her, but it had to be done. He mused that Ned had been right in one regard. The romance issue aside, Jesse Lee *was* a better protector.

The road to the west proved to be a rutted track not much wider than a wagon. A mile from Deadwood it climbed into higher hills thick with forest.

"You notice anything?" Ned said.

"I saw a jay yonder," Thal said.

"We haven't seen another rider. Or any wagons."

"Haven't you been payin' attention?" Crawford said. "These hills are crawlin' with Sioux. Most whites don't go anywhere unless it's in large groups."

"Maybe we should have waited and found some others headin' to American City," Ned said.

"We'll be all right if we don't get careless," Thal said with more confidence than he felt. He disliked putting his friends as risk, but it couldn't be helped.

"That's probably what General Custer thought," Ned said.

His hand on his Colt, Thal pricked his ears for the sounds out of the woods. Everything seemed ordinary enough. Warblers sang and squirrels scampered, and once a chipmunk chittered at them. Later, several does fled with their tails high. Still, Thal grew increasingly uneasy. He blamed it on all the tales of scalped whites, and accounts of how the Sioux could strike out of nowhere, like ghosts.

Dark clouds scuttled in, and for a while he thought it might rain. The wind increased and the shadows lengthened until the forest was cast in a preternatural twilight.

"Listen," Ned said.

The birds and other wildlife had fallen silent.

Thal figured the weather was to blame. Then he rounded a bend and spied another doe about fifty yards off. She was looking the other way, her ears up, standing as if poised for flight. Suddenly she bolted into the trees. Something around the next bend had spooked her.

Thal could never say what made him do what he did next. "Quick," he said, and reined into the woods. He went a short way and turned the chestnut so he could see the road.

Ned and Crawford had followed without question, but now Ned said, "What is it? Why are we hidin'?"

"Hush." Thal was glued to that far bend. His skin prickled when riders appeared.

Strung out in single file, there were six, in all. Their long black hair was parted in the middle, with braids on either side. They all carried rifles, and they were all painted for war. One wore a cavalry hat, another a cavalry shirt, and a third the pants, the garments no doubt taken from a slain trooper.

Sioux, or the Lakotas, as they were called. Thal knew the tribe was made up of different bands but didn't know how to tell one band from the other. The important thing was that the entire tribe wanted to drive the white man from their territory, and would kill any white-eye they found.

The six sat their mounts with a natural ease. It was said that the Sioux were born on horseback. An exaggeration, but they were considered some of the finest horsemen on the plains. General Custer had found out the hard way exactly how fine when they rallied to the defense of a sprawling village on the Little Bighorn and wiped Custer and his command out.

Thal held himself still as the war party went past. He prayed the chestnut wouldn't whinny. He saw Ned's animal raise its head and braced for the worst, but the horse didn't do anything, thank God.

The Sioux went around a turn to the east, and the clomp of hooves faded.

Ned let out a long breath. "Land sakes," he whispered. "I thought for a second we were goners."

"More of that luck we've been havin'," Crawford said.

"They've got gall, comin' so close to Deadwood," Ned said.

"Lookin' for whites to kill, most likely," Crawford said.

"What if there are more?"

201

Thal worried about that very thing. The six might be part of a large war party. "We can't turn back. We'd run into them."

"Then let's stay right here until the sun goes down," Ned suggested. "We'll only ride at night when the Sioux can't see us."

"And we can't see them." Thal shook his head. "We'll go on as we are."

"Lord help us," Ned said.

Stiff with dread, Thal resumed their trek. It rattled his nerves, never knowing when the shriek of a war whoop might shatter the air. It reminded him of the time Comanches raided a neighboring ranch, and for weeks the Crescent H's hands had worried that the terrors of Texas would pay them a visit.

Presently the dark clouds scuttled off and the sun shone anew, but not for long. Sunset wasn't far off.

Thal pushed on until the last vestige of light faded. Sheltered in the trees, they ate cold beans for supper. Ned wanted to start a fire, but Thal and Crawford were against it.

Along about ten o'clock they turned in. Thal didn't bother spreading out his blankets. He sat with his back to an oak and his rifle across his lap.

Ned, lying on his back with his head propped in his hands, remarked, "I hope

202

this brother of yours is still alive. I'd hate to think we've gone to all this bother for nothin'."

"Another day or two and we'll find out," Crawford said.

"Provided we get there."

"That's what I like about you, Ned," Crawford said. "You always look at the bright side."

"Don't I, though?" Ned said.

"No," Crawford said.

"Thal, tell him," Ned said. "Don't I have the sunniest disposition you've ever come across?"

"You're about as sunny as the dark side of the moon," Thal said.

Crawford laughed.

"Nuts to both of you," Ned said.

Thal would have laughed except that, once again, Ned had a point. They'd be lucky to make it out of the Black Hills alive.

CHAPTER 18

Ursula Christie had never stayed at a boardinghouse before. It amazed her no end that the room Mrs. Peal led her to was more finely furnished than her own bedroom back in Kansas. For starters, the bed was larger and softer and covered with a gorgeous quilt. The chest of drawers was larger too and lustrous with polish, whereas hers had so many scratches and scuffs it looked as if her cat has used it to sharpen its claws. There was a chair, which she didn't have in her bedroom, and a lamp decorated with a flowery design. Embroidered curtains covered the window.

Once she was alone, Ursula plopped on the bed and tried to take a nap. It was pointless. Her mind was racing. Not with worry for her brother, Myles. Or with concern for Thalis. No, she had someone else very much in her thoughts.

Rising, Ursula checked her reflection in

the mirror on the chest of drawers. Her hair needed brushing and her clothes were dusty. A brush took care of the first, a few slaps of her hand the other.

Amused at how bold she was being, Ursula left the boardinghouse and crossed the street to the empty lot. The object of her thoughts was seated on the ground in a small clearing in the trees, absently chewing on a blade of grass. His horse was behind him, still saddled. She coughed to get his attention.

Jesse Lee pushed to his feet as if fired from a cannon. "Miss Christie!" he exclaimed. "What are you doin' here?"

"You're my protector, aren't you?" Ursula said.

"You bet I am. I gave my word to your brother to look after you."

"I was there, remember?" Ursula said, grinning. "As to why I'm here, I could go for an early supper. How about you?"

"I go where you go," Jesse Lee said.

"That's no answer. Are you hungry or not?"

"I am if you are."

Ursula held out her elbow. "Then you can escort me and we'll become better acquainted."

"We were travelin' together for more than

two weeks," Jesse Lee said. "I'd say we already are."

"Posh and poppycock," Ursula said. "We hardly got to talk to each other, what with my brother always around, and Ned."

"He's powerful interested in you."

"Did I ask him to be?" Ursula waggled her arm. "Are you escorting me or not?"

A broad smile split Jesse Lee's face. "I'd be plumb delighted." He took her arm, then reached back with his other hand and snatched the reins to his palomino.

"I'd rather walk," Ursula said.

"So would I," Jesse Lee said. "But it wouldn't be smart to leave my horse unattended."

"No," Ursula realized. "Not here, it wouldn't."

As they strolled along, she contrived to swing her hips more than she normally would, and avoided looking at him for fear she might blush.

"You surprised me, showin' up like you did," Jesse Lee mentioned as they came to Main Street.

"Who else do I know?" Ursula justified her brazenness. "I didn't care to stay cooped up in my room, my brother notwithstanding."

Jesse Lee surprised her by coming to

Thal's defense. "He has your best interests at heart."

"Correction. What Thal thinks are my best, which might not be the same as what I think is best."

"You're a strong-willed gal, and that's no lie."

"I'll take that a compliment," Ursula said, then had a troubling thought. "Do you mind strong-willed women? Some men don't, I've heard tell. They like their females to be sheep."

"My ma was a strong lady," Jesse Lee said. "When she wanted to do somethin', she did it, come hell or high water." He caught himself. "Pardon my language, ma'am."

"Call me Ursula," she said. "I've heard worse. One time my pa banged his shin on a grain bin in our barn and cussed fit to burn my ears off. I told Ma and she said I should forgive him, that that's how men are. Do you cuss a lot?"

"I never much got into the habit, no," Jesse Lee said. "My ma might have helped. When I was little, she'd wash my mouth out with lye soap if I used bad language."

"Our ma ingrained in us from the time we were old enough to waddle that if we cussed, we'd be turned over to Pa, and his switch. Thal and me hardly ever paid the woodshed a visit, but Myles was sent there all the time. He couldn't behave if his life depended on it."

"You don't say."

"Don't get me wrong," Ursula amended quickly. "Myles wasn't a troublemaker. He just did what he wanted, when he wanted. For instance, when he was supposed to out in the fields, planting, instead he'd go into town. He did things like that all the time and didn't seem to care."

"And here we are, tryin' to rescue him."

"He's my brother," Ursula said. "What else can I do?"

"No need to apologize. Where I'm from, kin counts for everything."

The street was jammed, but Ursula hardly noticed. She only had eyes for her escort. He struck her as being just about the handsomest thing in britches there ever was. The feel of his hand on her arm made her tingle. Her ma would say she was being a hussy, but how else was she to learn all she could about him?

It was early yet, and they had the Black Hills Restaurant almost to themselves. She chose a corner table where they would have some privacy, but Jesse Lee mentioned that he'd like to sit where he could keep an eye on his horse, so she picked a table near the front window. She liked that he held out the chair for her, liked that he took off his hat. He had beautiful hair. Not that she'd tell him so to his face. It was her understanding that men weren't fond of being called beautiful.

Ursula had to work on him to get his tongue to loosen. She had a hundred questions about his life in North Carolina. What were his folks like? Why'd he leave the hills? Did he ever miss it or want to go back?

His answers: his folks were nice as could be, he'd left the hills to see something of the world, and yes, he had moments when he missed them, but not enough to regret his decision.

Did he like Texas? Did he aim to live there the rest of his life? And to be a cowboy forever?

Texas fit him like a glove, Jesse Lee said. He hadn't seen anywhere he liked better, so it wouldn't surprise him if he stayed until he was ready to be put out to pasture. As for cowboy work, he liked it more than anything else he'd tried.

Ursula was pleased at how honest he was being. "I'd like to see Texas someday. That is, if I had someone to show me around." She was sure she blushed.

"I'd be happy to, ma'am."

"It's Ursula, please. Remember?" She was enjoying herself so much that she asked without thinking, "And how many men have you killed with that fancy pistol of yours?"

His sat back as if she'd struck him.

"I'm sorry," Ursula said in alarm. "That was rude. I overstepped myself, and I apologize."

Jesse Lee poked at his steak with his fork, then set the fork down.

Appalled by her blunder, Ursula tried to make amends. "Forget I asked. It's none of my business."

"Seven," Jesse Lee said softly.

"My word," Ursula said, shocked. Her brother had intimated that Jesse Lee had killed, but she'd never have suspected so many. "Seven men?"

"Six," Jesse Lee said. "One wasn't."

"Oh." Ursula wrestled with the revelation. Shooting a man was one thing. "A woman?" she said breathlessly. "For real?"

"She was holdin' a shotgun on me and your brother and Craw and Ned. She planned to kill us and help herself to our valuables." Jesse Lee touched his fingertips to his brow. "It was the worst deed I've ever done, but if I hadn't, I wouldn't be sittin' here."

Ursula was silent awhile. She been raised

her whole life according to the commandment Thou Shalt Not Kill. For someone to have shot so many, and a woman, besides, went against the Bible and her own beliefs. "I've killed a few mice. And a snake, once."

"Was that supposed to be funny?" Jesse Lee asked.

"Mercy no," Ursula said. "I'm trying to fathom the enormity of it. We wring the necks of chickens for the supper pot, and butcher a hog from time to time. But that's normal."

"Ah," Jesse Lee said, rather sadly. "You're sayin' I'm not."

"Don't put words in my mouth," Ursula upbraided him. "From chickens and hogs to men is a big step. I don't know as I could. Not even if my life was at stake."

"May you never be put to the test."

Ursula was deeply sorry she'd brought it up. She tried to lighten his mood by saying, "I doubt I ever will. Kansas is pretty tame. There's not that much call for female gun hands."

"Women have more sense," Jesse Lee said.

Taking a sip of water to wet her throat, Ursula decided to find out more. "Do you regret those you've shot?"

"It was them or me."

"That's no answer."

Jesse Lee sat back. "Do I lose sleep over it? No. Do I break into tears now and again? No. Do I fall on my knees and beg forgiveness? No."

"My ma would call that blasphemy."

"I should take you back to the boardin' house," Jesse Lee said unexpectedly.

Startled, Ursula blurted, "I'm not done eating."

"When you're done, then." Shifting in his chair, Jesse Lee stared out the window.

Ursula was bewildered. He didn't act angry. Yet she had hurt his feelings, somehow. Their first day together had gotten off on the wrong foot, and she was to blame. She forked a piece of carrot into her mouth and deliberately chewed slowly. She had a lot of food left. Enough to stall for fifteen to twenty minutes. She spent five of them mulling over how to get back in his good graces, and finally tried with "You do remember I'm a farm girl, don't you?"

Jesse Lee crooked an eyebrow at her. "Meanin'?"

"I'm not very versed in the ways of the world. I've never been anywhere except Salina, and Topeka once. My life is the farm, and trips to the general store now and then, and church on Sunday."

"It sounds like a good life."

"You're missing my point." Ursula set down her fork to give him her undivided attention. "I'm young yet, and I'm the first to admit I don't know a lot about a lot of things. How to dress like fancy ladies do. How to act in public sometimes."

"You act just fine."

"Not with you, I haven't, and that upsets me. I like you, Jesse Lee. And I don't want you to not like me."

"You'd have to go a considerable ways to do that."

"I just did. By bringing up something I shouldn't. Now I don't know how to make amends so we can be friends again." Ursula was pleased by how she phrased that.

"We still are," Jesse Lee said. "It's not you. It's me. My heroes are men like Wild Bill. Shootists. Because I like to shoot myself. I told you it was always me or the other fella. But I didn't have to fill my hand. I could have backed down. Or run. But tucking tail's not in me. I couldn't live with myself, after. If we're not true to who we are, then what good are we?"

Ursula was about to reply when she realized he didn't really want her to. He'd already gone on.

"Some folks would say I have too much

pride. Maybe they're right. I like to think of it not as pride, though, but grit. Cowards tuck trail. Yellow curs back down. I'm not boastin' when I say I'm neither."

"I admire a man with grit," Ursula said.

"Even when it's put to a use others frown on? A lot of folks won't have any truck with quick-trigger artists. They brand us as snake-mean, and as too prone to violence. I'm none of those things. I'm a man who won't be trifled with or abused."

"I admire that too." To prove her point, Ursula reached across the table and placed her hand on his. "Fact is, I admire a whole lot about you."

A flush spread from Jesse Lee's collar to his hair. "I admire a lot about you too."

"Is that so?" Ursula said, and gave him her most charming smile. "What do you suppose we should do about that?"

CHAPTER 19

The directions they had been given proved reliable, but it took two days longer than Thal reckoned it would to reach American City.

The Sioux were to blame.

Twice more, Thal and his friends spied Indians. Once on a ridge about half a mile off, moving away from them, thankfully. The second time they were descending a slope and spotted ten Sioux in a valley below. They quickly sought cover in some timber and had to wait six hours for the Sioux to move on.

It seemed the closer they grew to American City, the more Sioux there were. It forced them to go slow, to always be alert, their nerves on pins and needles.

Once they heard a horse whinny not far off. They drew rein and waited over an hour, but no one appeared.

Eventually the rutted track brought them

215

to the mouth of a gulch. A bend hid what-ever lay beyond.

"Do you see what I see?" Ned said.

A sign on a post had been sunk in the ground. Several arrows stuck out of it, courtesy of the Sioux, and the post had been hacked by tomahawks but still stood.

"Those Injuns have a sense of humor," Crawford said.

"What's so funny about usin' a sign for target practice?" Ned said.

Thal led them over to it.

" 'Blood City,' " Ned read. " 'The Paris of the Black Hills.' "

"They think they're that city in France," Crawford said. "The one where everybody dresses tony, and they put on airs."

"I bet they don't have Injuns there," Ned said.

"To the best of my recollection," Crawford said, "they don't have Injuns anywhere in their whole country."

"Must be nice," Ned said. "Do they have saloons?"

"I don't rightly know," Crawford said. "I have heard they're more partial to wine than whiskey, so maybe not."

"They like grape juice more than red-eye? Those French must not have any taste buds."

"Ain't you comical?" a new voice said, startling them, and a pair of men came out of the shadows carrying rifles. They wore grubby clothes and were grubby themselves.

Thal distrusted them on sight. His hand was on his Colt, but since they weren't pointing their rifles, he didn't draw. "Who might you be?"

"We're keepin' watch for the Sioux," the shortest said.

"Guard duty," the second said.

"You look more like prospectors," Ned remarked.

"We are," the short one said. "But everyone takes a turn. It's one of Mr. Galt's rules."

Feigning ignorance, Thal asked, "Who might he be?"

"Trevor Galt," the short man said. "He runs Blood Gulch."

"He's the mayor," the other guard said, "although there ain't been an election."

"We've got law and order too," the short one said, "thanks to him and his deputies. Leastwise, that's what they call it."

"I hope there's not too much law," Ned said. "I was hopin' to have me a wild and woolly time."

The short man grinned. "Don't worry, mister. The law here ain't like any law you've ever seen."

"It does the opposite of the law you're used to," the other guard said.

"I don't savvy," Ned said.

"You will," the short man said, and the pair looked at each other and both chuckled.

"Can we go on in?" Thal asked.

"That's the easy part," the short man replied.

"It's gettin' out again that's hard," the other man said.

The pair moved aside and motioned for them to proceed.

"If you're smart," the short guard said, "you'll turn around and go, but no one ever does."

"Some guards you are," Ned said.

"We're friendly anyway," the other man said.

"I have to go in," Thal said, enlightening them. "I'm lookin' for someone." He thought to add, "Maybe you've heard of him. His name is Myles Christie."

Both men gave starts.

"The hell you say," the short one said.

"What's he to you?" the other one asked.

"My brother," Thal said.

"The hell you say," the short one said a second time.

"We heard he was shot and I came to find

out if he's all right."

The other prospector was shaking his head as if he couldn't believe what he'd just heard. "Are you the same as he is?"

"Hold on, Hiram," the short one said, giving Thal and his friends another scrutiny. "They look like cowpokes to me."

"We are," Ned said, "and proud of it."

"You are well off your range," Hiram said. "You should have stayed there."

"Is my brother alive?" Thal asked.

"And kickin'," the short man said. "But just so you know, no one hereabouts calls him Myles. It's either Mr. Christie or his nickname."

"What would that be?"

"Shotgun."

Ned laughed. "What kind of nickname is that? He's a farmer, for cryin' out loud. Like Thal here used to be, and their pa."

"Cowboy," Hiram said, "maybe Shotgun grew crops once, but he's taken up a whole new line of work."

"The kind where buckshot means buryin'," the short man said.

Thal didn't like the sound of that. "Tell me more."

"I don't believe we will," Hiram said. "Shotgun might not like it. The mayor neither. We get them mad at us, we're goners. Go on in and find out for yourselves."

"And may God have pity on your souls," the short man said.

They moved back into the shadows.

Troubled, Thal gigged his chestnut.

"Now, what do you reckon that was all about?" Ned said. "And how come you never mentioned that your brother is fond of shotguns?"

Thal stared at him.

"Why do you keep givin' me those kinds of looks?"

Blood Gulch was narrower than Deadwood Gulch. High cliffs towered on both sides, and a small stream that flowed down the middle was lined with tents and a few cabins.

The actual town didn't appear until they were farther in. Thal's first thought was that American City was Deadwood all over again. As they came closer, he saw that it was different. There were a lot more saloons, for one thing, and a lot of gambling halls and even a dance hall or two. The people were packed like pickles in a barrel.

"Why, look at all the females," Ned exclaimed.

Thal had already noticed. A large number of those jamming the street wore dresses and carried parasols. Not homespun dresses either, like ones his mother wore, but the bright, gaudy kind popular with doves and ladies of the night.

"Why, there must be a hundred or more," Ned said. "We've done died and gone to female heaven."

"It's peculiar," Crawford said.

Ned laughed. "No, *you're* peculiar. Look at all those gals. It's enough to tingle a man's toes."

"You simpleton," Crawford said. "There are more women here than we've seen anywhere."

"Lucky us," Ned said.

"This from the man who claimed he wanted to court my sister," Thal mentioned drily.

"I've just sayin' they're a sight for manly eyes," Ned said.

"But why *here*?" Crawford persisted. "Out of all the places we've been. Salina. Cheyenne. Custer City. Deadwood. Why are there more women *here* than anywhere else?"

Thal realized what he was getting at. The women wouldn't have drifted here on their own. Not this many. "They had to have been brought in," he suspected.

"To what end?" Ned said.

"Why do you think?" Crawford retorted.

"What's the one thing women do better than anything?"

"Smell nice?" Ned said.

"No."

"Sashay around?"

"No."

"Talk your ears off?"

Crawford looked at Thal. "Tell me again why you have him for a pard? Did you get hit on the head when you were a sprout?"

"What did I do?" Ned said.

"The one thing women do," Crawford said, "is the same as the one thing honey does."

"They taste good?" Ned said.

Crawford bowed his chin and sighed. "I could just hit you." Shaking his head, he said, "No. Women draw men like honey draws bears."

"Oh," Ned said, and gazed at the bustling street they were about to enter. "You're sayin' all these females are here to draw men to this place?"

"Finally," Crawford said.

Thal had noticed another sign, larger than the one at the mouth of Blood Gulch. The letters, to his eyes, were jumbled. "Someone read that to me," he requested.

"Let me," Crawford offered. "If your pard does it, we'll be here forever."

"I don't read that slow," Ned said sulkily.

"No slower than molasses." Crawford turned to the sign. " 'Welcome to American City, where anything goes. . . .' "

"It says that?" Ned said.

Crawford ignored him. " '. . . Visitors welcome, although we prefer that you stay —' "

"What kind of sign says a thing like that?" Ned said.

" '. . . The Honorable Trevor Galt, Mayor. Population: We stopped countin' at three thousand, two hundred and ten.' "

"That sign is a marvel," Ned said.

Thal was absorbing the feel of the place. It was a beehive, like Deadwood, but where Deadwood had some semblance of order, American City impressed him as being darkly more sinister. It was a seething cauldron of greed and lust that catered to all the vices known to man. ANYTHING GOES, the sign had read, and he could believe it.

Suddenly, deeper in, a gun boomed. It was answered by another, several times.

No one appeared to take notice. A few raised their heads, but most went on about their business without so much as a break in their stride.

"Why, look at that," Ned said. "Anyone

with common sense would hunt cover when shootin' commences."

"Unless you're so used to it," Crawford said, "it doesn't bother you."

"Who could get used to bein' shot at?" Ned said.

"I miss Jesse Lee," Crawford said.

"How come?" Ned said.

Thal stayed to one side of the street to avoid the wagons moving up and down the middle. A sea of sound swamped him: shouts, the hubbub of constant voices, the peal of laughter, curses. Two women on a corner gave him saucy looks, and one wriggled her hips. Others smiled invitingly. The men weren't nearly as friendly. Most eyed them like wolves sizing up prey. Even Ned noticed that something wasn't right.

"Except for the females, I don't think I like this place."

"There's hope for you yet," Crawford said.

A half-empty hitch rail drew Thal over. Dismounting, he stretched, then tied the reins. The strong smell of liquor tingled his nose. Yet another sign announced that they had found the Devil's Due Saloon. Only a few of the letters didn't look right, so he was able to read it.

"Can you imagine your brother comin' here?" Ned said as he swung down. "What was he thinkin'?"

"Probably the same thing everyone else is," Crawford said. "That he wanted to get rich."

"Give me cows and I'm content," Ned said.

Crawford grunted. "I like you again."

"When did you not?"

Thal turned to the batwings and was about to enter when they parted and out lumbered a huge man with a bristly beard that hung to his waist. He had a revolver on one hip and a bowie on the other. His beady eyes fixed on them, and he drew up short. "What do we have here?"

"Uh-oh," Ned said.

CHAPTER 20

The past couple of days had been some of the most wonderful of Ursula's life.

She was smitten. She admitted it. But she didn't let on when she was out and about with the object of her yearning. Anymore than she could help anyway. Proper ladies didn't do that. Proper ladies, as her ma had impressed on her over and over, never threw themselves at a man. Which was too bad, because she very much wanted to throw herself at Jesse Lee.

Since their meal at the restaurant that first night, they'd spent most of their waking hours together. He'd come and call for her in the morning and they'd wander about Deadwood, taking in the sights. Not that there were a lot of places for a single woman — a respectable single woman — to visit. Saloons were out of the question. So were the sporting houses and dance halls.

The best entertainment to be had was at

Deadwood's theaters. She and Jesse Lee visited the Langrishe Theater the second night, and the Gem Theater the next. Ursula liked the Langrishe. Built by a noted comedian, it featured his act, as well as variety and musical acts. The Gem's productions made her blush. Most had to do with skimpily clad ladies flirting and flaunting their skimpily clad bodies. The audience, mainly men, ate it up with a spoon. Many were half-drunk, and their applause was raucous and sometimes dangerous, as when an overexcited patron fired his revolver at the ceiling.

It was as they were coming out of the Gem that Ursula learned how violent Deadwood could be. She'd heard about the many shootings and knifings from Mrs. Peal, who'd warned her to always be on her guard.

"Womanly virtue isn't as respected as it should be," her landlady mentioned the second morning over breakfast. "We have the doves and tarts to thank. Since they share their charms for money, men get to thinking all women are the same, when we're not."

"No has dared to bother me," Ursula assured her. With Jesse Lee always at her elbow, she doubted anyone would.

Then came the Gem Theater. They'd merged with the crowd flowing out the exit. The night air had a tendency to be chill, even in the summer, and Ursula paused to pull her shawl tighter around her shoulders.

Two men hove out of the night in front of her. They reeked of liquor, and other odors. Both were big and thick-boned, the one with a red beard and the other with a red nose. Each had a revolver tucked under his belt rather than in a holster. Their eyes glittering, they looked her up and down.

"Well, take a gander, Kincaid," the man with the red beard said. "We've found us a right pretty filly."

"That she is, Jack," Kincaid said, and reached out as if to stroke Ursula's hair.

"Don't you dare," she said, swatting at his arm.

"Be nice, missy," Kincaid said.

"You don't want to rile us," Jack warned.

It amazed Ursula that they paid no attention to Jesse Lee whatsoever. Not until Jesse Lee growled, "Leave the lady alone."

Kincaid blinked watery eyes, focusing on him. "Stay out of this, boy."

"It has nothin' to do with you," Jack said.

"It sure does," Jesse Lee said. "You can see she's with me. Back off, and I don't mean tomorrow."

Kincaid nudged Jack and both laughed.

"Listen to you," Jack said. "A boy pretendin' to be a man."

"Maybe you ain't heard of us," Kincaid said. "We kilt a man not long ago."

Jack, swaying slightly, nodded. "Folks talk about us in the same way they do Wild Bill or Jim Levy or Charlie Storms."

The only name Ursula was familiar with was Hickok. The others, she assumed, must be famous shootists, as he was.

"The only place anyone has heard of you two," Jesse Lee said, "is in your dreams."

"We've just been insulted, Jack," Kincaid said.

"By a kid, no less," Jack said.

Kincaid pointed at Jesse Lee's ivory-handled Colt. "Look at you. Totin' a man's gun when you're green behind the ears."

"A nice-lookin' gun too," Jack said. "I believe I'll help myself to it and give him mine."

Jesse Lee's face grew hard. He placed his left hand on Ursula's arm and moved her to one side, saying, "So you don't take a stray slug."

"What are you doing?"

"Tendin' to these coyotes," Jesse Lee said. Hooking his thumbs in his gun belt, he stared at the pair in contempt. "Now, where were we? Oh. That's right. You were about to help yourselves to my hardware." He smiled. "Please. By all means. Try."

Kincaid chortled. "You're actin' like you're somebody when you're not."

"That's the trouble with kids," Jack said. "You have to take them down a peg or three to make them respect their betters."

"The day you are better than me," Jesse Lee said, "is the day cows fly."

Sensing that blood was in the air, other theater patrons had stopped to watch.

"We're going to witness a shooting, by God," a man in a suit exclaimed excitedly.

Only then did it dawn on Ursula that it might come to that. She kept expecting the drunks to come to their senses and leave. Instead the pair sidled apart, and the amused glitter in their eyes became angry gleams.

"You'd best tuck tail while you can, boy," Kincaid said flatly.

"If you don't," Jack said, "there will be a new grave on Boot Hill come mornin'."

"No," Jesse Lee said. "There will be two."

"He's so young," Kincaid said to Jack, "we should pound him with our fists."

"You heard him," Jack said. "He wants to be treated like a full-growed man. Fine. We'll treat him like one and shoot him like we would anybody else."

"Show me how dumb you are," Jesse Lee said. "Either of you."

"Don't kill them, Jesse." Ursula anxiously broke her silence. "For my sake if for no other."

"Ain't she cute?" Jack said to Kincaid. "She thinks he stands a chance."

"Do you want to learn him to mind his betters, or should I?" Kincaid asked. His right hand was close to the revolver under his belt.

"You did the last one," Jack said. "Let me do this pup."

"Be my guest," Kincaid said, grinning. He gestured at Jesse Lee. "He'll be easy as sin."

"I think so too," Jack said, and grabbed for his six-shooter.

Jesse Lee drew. His hand flashed and his Colt boomed, and Jack was jarred back a step. Crying out, he clutched at his shoulder and gaped at the wound.

"Why, he done shot you," Kincaid said.

Jack tried to talk, but no sounds came out.

"We can't let that pass," Kincaid said. "Folks will think we're weak sisters. I'll have to do him my own self."

"Do this," Jesse Lee said, and springing, he slammed his Colt against the bigger man's temple. Kincaid, caught flat-footed,

231

staggered and clutched at his six-gun. Jesse Lee went after him, pistol-whipping him again and again and again. About the seventh or eighth thud, Kincaid's knees buckled. Another blow, and Kincaid's legs gave out; he collapsed with a loud groan.

Ursula had never seen Jesse look so fierce. For a few seconds she thought he would shoot them. His whole body quivered with a cold rage. Instead he violently wiped his barrel on his pant leg, then twirled his Colt and shoved it into his holster.

"There," he snapped at her.

"What. . . . ?" Ursula said, and realized he'd done as she'd asked and hadn't killed them. For her. Just for her.

"Pick up your pard and scat," Jesse Lee said to Jack.

"My shoulder's hurt."

"So will a lot more if you don't get out of my sight."

"Kid, you've got a lot of bark on you."

"Call me that one more time. I dare you."

Something in Jesse Lee tone galvanized Jack into stooping and sliding his good arm under Kincaid. He had to strain to lift him, and went on straining as he plodded away with his burden.

"Mister, that was something," a townsman said, addressing Jesse.

Others nodded in appreciation.

"It was nothin'," Jesse Lee said. Angrily taking Ursula's arm, he headed up the street, people parting to give him a wide berth.

"You were wonderful, how you handled that," Ursula praised him.

"I don't want to talk about it."

"Why not?"

Jesse Lee stopped abruptly and turned to face her. "You tied rope around my wrists and act like it's nothin'?"

"I did no such thing," Ursula said in astonishment.

" 'Don't kill them,' you told me," Jesse Lee repeated. "You might as well have tied my hands. You made it plumb easy for them to put windows in our skulls, and then where would we be?"

"You're making more out of it than there is."

"More out of you," Jesse Lee said. He resumed walking, moving so fast she had to take two steps to each of his.

"Slow down, will you, so we can talk this out?"

"Not here," Jesse Lee said. "I won't be a spectacle."

Ursula was aware of dozens of pale faces awash in the light from windows and lamps.

Unaccustomed to being the center of so much attention, she bowed her own face in embarrassment.

Jesse Lee turned into a side street and slowed. Not as brightly lit, it was quiet enough to hear their own footsteps. He came to a closed butcher shop and pulled her into a recessed doorway. "This will do."

They were so close Ursula felt his breath on her cheek. She had to cough to say, "I'm sorry if I upset you back there."

"You cut me off at the knees, askin' what you did."

"I was worried."

"So you made it easier for them to buck me out in gore? That makes no kind of sense."

"Explain to me how I did that. I must have missed that part."

"You hampered me," Jesse Lee said, his voice crackling. "They were out to shoot me and you made me fight with one hand tied behind my back."

"All I did was ask you to let them live. How is that hampering?"

"Don't you see?" Jesse Lee said. "You made it so I couldn't just draw and shoot them dead. I had to choose where to put my lead so they'd live. It slowed me. And it left them able to gun me down." He paused.

"If there's one thing I learned from my pa, it's to never wound an animal or a man. The wounded ones are always more dangerous."

Ursula had heard something to that effect, but she still wasn't convinced she had done wrong. "I had every confidence in you. From what Thal told me, you're almost as good a shootist as Wild Bill."

"No one is in his class," Jesse Lee said. "And that's not the point. The best pistoleer can have holes blown in him if he goes into a shootin' affray with his hands tied."

"There you go again. But you did fine, despite me." Ursula sniffed. "You ask me, I have an apology coming."

Jesse Lee tapped his belt buckle. "Do you want me to take this off, is that it? Do you want me to give up wearin' a six-shooter for the rest of my born days?"

Ursula felt he was exaggerating again. "No, I don't. But would it be so bad if you did? Hardly anyone in Salina goes around wearing a sidearm."

"Deadwood ain't a farmin' town. Every killer in the territory is in these hills, and a lot of them are right here."

"What if I promise to never do anything like that ever again?" Ursula sought to end their spat. "Will you forgive me so we can go do something fun?"

"You just don't see," Jesse Lee said.

"Must we talk about it now? The night's still young. I don't have to be back at Mrs. Peal's for an hour yet."

"Sure," Jesse Lee said without much enthusiasm. He made for Main Street, his face mired in shadow.

Worried, Ursula asked, "What's going through that head of yours? Please. I'd very much like to know."

"I'm thinkin'," Jesse Lee said, "that this won't work."

"What won't?"

"You and me."

Ursula was both elated and devastated. Elated, because this was the first time he'd hinted that there *was* a him and her. And devastated because he was having second thoughts. "You don't mean that."

"I never meant anything more," Jesse Lee said.

CHAPTER 21

Thal was taken aback by the man's size. He didn't reply but waited for the bearded giant to move aside.

"Who are you and what are you doin' here, mister?" the giant demanded.

"We're goin' into the saloon," Thal informed him.

"You're not goin' anywhere just yet." The man puffed out his already enormous chest. "I'm Bull."

"So?" Thal said.

"I'm one of Mr. Galt's special deputies," Bull said as if he were making a grand announcement.

"I don't see no badge," Ned said, stepping to Thal's side.

"Me neither," Crawford chimed in, moving to Thal's other side. "And law dogs always tote tin."

"Not here, they don't," Bull said. "Mr. Galt says it's so we don't stand out and can mingle better." He jabbed a thick finger at them. "Now answer my damn question. You're new in town, and Mr. Galt likes to know about newcomers."

"You mention him a lot," Thal said.

"He runs things," Bull said. "Lock, stock, and barrel." As an afterthought he added, "Mr. Galt is the mayor and gets to do as he pleases."

"We've heard he's the mayor," Crawford said. "But that there wasn't an election."

"Who needs one?" Bull said. "Mr. Galt just sort of made himself the mayor and that was that. Now back to you. Those hats and those clothes and those spurs. You're cow-pokes, by God. Am I right?"

"You are," Thal acknowledged, wondering where this was leading.

Bull bobbed his bristly beard. "Thought so. We don't see a lot of punchers here-abouts. I used to live in New Mexico and saw them all the time."

"You're a long way from there," Thal said.

"Came for the gold, like everybody else," Bull said. "Then I killed a man and met Mr. Galt and he hired me. That's how he picks who works for him. They have to be killers."

Thal thought of his brother. "All of you deputies have killed your man?"

The beard bobbed again. "Mr. Galt says he knows he can count on us not to flinch when push comes to shove. He talks like that. He also says no one is to be bothered in what he calls their pursuits of sin. Isn't that a pretty way of puttin' it?"

Thal wondered if the giant was all right in the head. He hedged by saying, "If you say so."

"I don't say it. Mr. Galt does." Bull put his hands on his hips. "So let me welcome you. You might have heard that anything goes . . ."

"We read the sign," Crawford said.

"— and it means what is writ. Anything does go, so long as you don't cause so much trouble that Mr. Galt has to get involved. If that happens, he brings the eight of us special deputies with him and we settle matters, permanent."

"When you say 'anything,'" Ned said, "what exactly does that mean?"

"It means anything," Bull said, looking at Ned as if he were a dunce. "Drink all you want, whore all you want, gamble all you want. Robbin' and killin' we allow too, so long as you don't get carried away."

"Hold on," Crawford said. "It's legal to take somebody's poke? Or to kill someone?"

"Take all the pokes you want if you think

you can get away with it. As for the killin', it can't be willy-nilly."

"How do we tell the difference?" Ned said.

"You're slow, ain't you?" Bull said, smirking. "If someone tries to take your poke and you kill him, that's fine by Mr. Galt. But if you start shootin' at everybody you see, that won't do, and we'll bury you faster than you can spit."

"Why, this town is wide-open," Crawford said.

"Ain't it, though?" Bull gazed happily about them. "It's the most openest town there ever was, and it's all thanks to Mr. Galt." He turned to go. "Have a good time, gents."

"Wait," Thal said. "I'm lookin' for my brother. Maybe you've heard of him. We were told he goes by the handle of Shotgun Christie."

"Shotgun is your brother?" Bull said, and surprised Thal by bursting out in laughter and clapping him on the arm. "Don't that beat all? Him and me are friends."

"You are?"

"He's a special deputy too, just like me," Bull said. "Wait until he hears you're here. I didn't even know he had a brother."

"Where could I find him?" Thal asked.

Bull motioned at the thronged street. "He

240

could be anywhere. Us deputies move around a lot." He scratched his beard, and his eyebrows puckered. "Tell you what. Stay right here in this saloon. I'll mosey around and try to get word to him. Let him know where to find you."

"I'm obliged."

"Your brother saved my bacon once. I owe him."

"Saved it how?"

"A drunk got mad and stabbed a few people. He was wavin' an Arkansas toothpick around and threatenin' to stab more when I got there. I made him drop the knife by breakin' his arm. He had a partner I didn't know about, and the no-account was goin' to shoot me in the back when your brother blew his head clean off."

"My brother did?" Thal said.

"Us special deputies look out for each other," Bull said. "Watch each other's back."

"My brother is a killer."

"Didn't you hear me? He did it to save my life. All those he's killed except the first were in the line of his work."

Thal felt a strange sort of emptiness inside. Myles had always had a restless streak, but he'd never shown the least inclination to hurt another human being. "His first?" he repeated.

"A miner assaulted a gal over to the Lace House. Broke her nose, and was poundin' on her when Myles told him to stop. The miner drew a six-shooter, and your brother cut loose on him with both barrels."

Thal remembered how gentle his brother had been, growing up. Like the time Myles nursed a kitten that had lost its mother. And another instance when Myles took a shine to a calf and treated it like his pet.

"Have a good time, gents," Bull was saying. "Wish me luck findin' him." He smiled and lumbered away.

"I ain't ever heard the like," Crawford said.

"What have we gotten ourselves into?" Ned said.

Thal was awash in more childhood memories. Of Myles and him, collecting butterflies in nets their ma made. Of the two of them at their favorite fishing hole. Of catching tadpoles with their hands. Growing up together had been fun. Simple. Peaceful.

"Didn't you hear me?" Ned said.

"This is no place for an honest cowpoke," Crawford remarked.

"We stick together and we'll be all right," Thal said.

Another shot sounded down the street, and a man screamed his death wail.

"You sure about that?" Crawford said.

"They named this town wrong," Ned said. "It shouldn't be called American City. It should be Hell on Earth."

Thal entered the Devil's Due. The place was packed. It was elbow to elbow at the bar. Poker, faro, and roulette were being played. Liquor flowed like water, and cigar smoke hung thick below the rafters.

"There's somethin' different," Crawford said.

"A saloon is a saloon," Ned said.

"No. Look closer."

Thal had noticed too. The babble of voices was louder than usual, the laughter more shrill. The faces were harder too, many aglow with greed or lust. It was an assembly of two-legged wolves out to howl, indulging in every vice known to man. He shuddered slightly, and was annoyed at himself.

"I miss Texas," Ned said.

Hooking his thumb close to his revolver, Thal shouldered toward the bar. The looks he was given weren't exactly friendly. Not until a vision in pink blocked his way, with golden curls cascading past her shoulders.

"Hold on there, handsome. Lookin' for a good time?"

The woman had too much rouge on her cheeks. Her eyelids were colored blue. She reeked of whiskey, not perfume, and her dress had seen a lot of wear but not nearly as much as she had.

"We're just here to drink," Thal said.

"Nonsense." She giggled and ran a finger over his ear. "For five dollars I'll take you to the moon and back." She plucked at his shirt. "Buy me a drink first, and then we'll have us some fun."

"No, thanks, lady," Thal said.

"What's wrong with you?" she said, sounding hurt. "Ain't I good enough? Ask anyone and they'll tell you that Sagebrush Sally gives you your money's worth."

"I'm sure you do," Thal said patiently, "but I'm here to wait for my brother. Nothin' more."

"Fine, then," Sally said grumpily. "It's your loss." Tilting her nose in the air, she sashayed off.

"Pushy dove," Ned said, chuckling. "You're lucky she didn't rip your clothes off right there."

Thal wasn't as amused. He spied an open space at the far end of the bar and made for it before someone else did. Two bartenders were filling glasses as fast as they could, and were hard pressed to keep up. Thal had to shout twice to get the attention of the nearest. The whiskey, when it came, had been watered.

"I'd have to drink ten gallons of this to get drunk," Ned griped after taking a gulp.

"It's probably for the best," Crawford said. "We need our wits about us."

Thal agreed. American City was the last place in the world to become booze-blind. They were liable to wake up with their pokes gone, if they woke up at all.

"What do you make of your brother bein' a killer?" Ned asked.

"You would bring that up."

"I'm here with you, ain't I?" Ned replied. "It affects me as much as it does you. Will your brother be friendly or not?"

"He should," Thal said. Although, now that he thought about it, it had been years since he saw Myles last, and apparently his brother had changed a lot in that time. An awful lot.

"It's too bad Jesse Lee ain't here," Crawford said. "We're in a nest of sidewinders, and he's good at stompin' snakes."

"At least Thal's sis is safe," Ned said.

An altercation broke out over at the roulette wheel. There was pushing and shoving and a lot of cursing, but the hotheads were prevailed on to calm down.

Down the bar, a drinker jostled another, by accident, spilling his drink. A knife was flourished and threats uttered, and the first man offered to pay for a refill.

"Bloodthirsty bunch," Ned said.

Thal leaned on his elbows and wearily bowed his head. They had been in the saddle all day and he was bone-tired. To say nothing of being hungry enough to eat a buffalo. He was imagining a thick slab of steak, dripping with fat juice, when he heard Ned address someone.

"What do you two want?"

Thal looked up.

A pair of hard cases had come around the bar. They were dirty and unkempt, and heeled. Their beards were matted from neglect; their hair was greasy.

The foremost had the build of a bulldog. Pugnaciously thrusting out his jaw, he pointed at Thal. "I'm here to talk to him."

"Me?" Thal said in surprise, straightening.

"We hear you're rude."

"Me?"

Sagebrush Sally stepped from behind the pair, her hands on her wide hips. "Yes, you."

Thal's temper flared. "The hell I was."

"Don't be talkin' to her like that," the bulldog said. "Our friend Sal says you turned her down, and that was rude."

The other man nodded. "You owe her five dollars."

Thal should have known. The dove wanted her money, one way or the other. "I'm not payin' her a cent."

"You're not listenin', mister," the bulldog said. "You don't have a choice. Pay Sal the money you owe or we'll take it out of your hide."

"There are three of us," Ned said, "and only two of you."

"Two is enough," the bulldog said, and hitched at his belt.

CHAPTER 22

Mrs. Peal was in her parlor, knitting, when Ursula returned to the boardinghouse. Ursula greeted her and went to walk on by.

"Troubles, dearie?" the older woman said.

Ursula hesitated. Her landlady had shown a kindly nature, and she could use an ear to bend. "Mind if join you?"

"Not at all," Mrs. Peal said, her needles clacking. "I usually turn in earlier, but I couldn't sleep tonight."

"I doubt I will much either," Ursula said, claiming a chair close to the settee.

"Is it your gentleman friend?" Mrs. Peal asked, and smiled. "I've seen how you look at him when he comes calling. You wear your heart on your sleeve, if you don't mind my saying. But he's a handsome one, I'll give you that."

"Oh," was all Ursula could think of to say.

"I was your age once," Mrs. Peal said. "I know how we are when we're head over heels. At one time, my Claude was all I could think about. He's gone now, and I miss him terribly. Between you and me, I can't wait to join him. But the Good Lord is taking his sweet time about calling me to my reward."

"Did Claude and you ever spat?" Ursula made bold to ask.

"Did we ever!" Mrs. Peal said with a grin. "In our younger days we were at each other's throats now and again. Oh, he never struck me or anything like that. Claude was decent as the year is long. But we did argue. About finances. About where we should live. Those sorts of things."

"You ever argue about killing?"

Mrs. Peal's needles froze in her hands. "I beg your pardon?"

"Jesse Lee — that's his name — shot a man tonight. Only wounded him, but he might have done more if I hadn't asked him not to." Ursula gnawed her lower lip. "He didn't like that. Said I was tying his wrists."

Setting her knitting in her lap, Mrs. Peal clasped her hands. "What did the man do that your Jesse Lee shot him?"

"He and a friend were trying to impose themselves on me, and Jesse stopped them."

"I see," Mrs. Peal said slowly. "There's a lot of that goes on. Men imposing on women, I mean. You were fortunate to have someone to defend you."

"I'm thankful for that," Ursula agreed. She was loath to think what might have happened had Jesse not been there.

"This Jesse Lee of yours. I couldn't help noticing his sidearm. Ivory handles say a lot about a man."

"He's awful quick on the shoot," Ursula said. "He didn't like me butting in, though. He thinks it's an obstacle to us getting along."

"Your butting in?"

"No, that I didn't want him to kill."

"Oh," Mrs. Peal said, and sat back. "The butting in I can understand. My mother used to say that the worst thing a wife can do is make a nuisance of herself by nagging her man about everything under the sun. Some women go so far as to insist everything be done their way, and if the man doesn't, they nitpick him to death."

"That's not me," Ursula said.

"Good for you. It's a terrible habit. I had to work hard at keeping in mind that Claude had his own way of doing some things, and that didn't make him wrong."

"Did Claude ever kill?"

"I should say not."

"Jesse Lee has. Seven times."

"That many?" Mrs. Peal said, and coughed. "It's a wonder he's not behind bars."

"He's not a bad man," Ursula explained. "He doesn't ever start his fights, but he sure finishes them."

"I see. What are his intentions regarding you?"

"I was hoping they were to court me," Ursula confessed. "But tonight he got mad at me. He said maybe he and me weren't meant to be."

"What do you think?"

Ursula had been wrestling with her feelings since the incident outside the Gem. She was of two minds. Part of her was appalled at the notion of a man who resorted to a six-shooter to settle a scrape. But that was her head talking. Her heart yearned for Jesse Lee to fold her in his arms. "I'm confused."

"About how you feel about him?"

"No. I like him, Mrs. Peal. A lot. When I'm with him I get all warm inside. He makes me happy in a way no one ever has. I don't quite know how to explain it."

"There's nothing *to* explain," Mrs. Peal said. "It's called love."

"I wouldn't go that far," Ursula said. To her, love implied wanting him to get down on bended knee. But then again, she hadn't thought that far ahead.

"Perhaps not," Mrs. Peal said with another grin. "But you might want to consider that often we don't see what's right in front of our face. Be that as it may, you've admitted you're smitten. You want to spend more time with him. Get to know him better. Maybe work out if he's the one for you."

"That's it exactly."

"Then you need to have a talk with yourself about whether to accept him as he is or bend him to your will."

"It's not that simple."

"On the contrary, young lady, that's the issue you face. Will he or will he not unbuckle his gun belt and never strap it on again if you asked him?"

"I couldn't ask that."

"But would he if you did? In your best estimation?"

Ursula thought about it. Jesse Lee had told her his heroes were men like Wild Bill Hickok. Did his heroes count for more than she did? she wondered. Which was silly of her, she reckoned, since neither of them had made a commitment yet. "I honestly can't say. We've only just begun to become acquainted. Although I doubt it."

"Ah," Mrs. Peal said. "Then let's say you

keep on getting acquainted, and down the road a piece, when you've been together awhile and matrimony is in the air, what then? Would he, you think?"

"You ask hard questions."

"A woman has to if she wants to stand on her own two feet and not work in a saloon or a sporting house. I learned that from my mother too. Pick the right man and you'll have a good life. Pick the wrong one and you'll be miserable most of your days."

"How do you know if a man is right or not?"

"That's easy. Will he stand by you? Does he ask your opinion and not decide everything for himself? Does he only think you're good for cleaning and cooking or does he regard you as a person?"

"I wouldn't know any of that about Jesse Lee."

"It's worth finding out," Mrs. Peal said. "Especially if you aim to spend your whole life with him. Take it slow, is my advice. Find out what makes him tick. And if you like what you find, throw your loop, as the cowboys say."

Ursula laughed.

"As for the other, that's on your shoulders. You said yourself that your Jesse Lee isn't a bad man. Then he must be a good man who stands up for his principles. Men like that won't be abused. They won't be put upon, or insulted. And they'll back it up with their six-guns if they have to."

"That's not wrong, you don't think? The six-gun part?"

"Without men of principle, where would we be? Men who stand up for themselves and for others are the backbone of society. They become lawmen, or soldiers. They're willing to lay down their lives for what they believe, and not everybody can say that."

"I don't know what Jesse Lee aims to become."

"Come right out and ask him," Mrs. Peal advised. "If he's half the man you think he is, he'll come clean."

"I don't know," Ursula said uncertainly. She might find out that Jesse Lee was only interested in acquiring a reputation like Hickok's. "I might not like what I learn."

"There are no guarantees when it comes to love," Mrs. Peal said.

That night, Ursula slept fitfully. She had a nightmare in which she chased after Jesse across a terrifying landscape where the trees were red and orange, not green, and bizarre shapes were everywhere. She finally caught up to him and placed her hand on his shoulder, only to have him shrug it off, climb onto a horse, and leave her standing in the dust. Her mother liked to say that dreams were an omen, and if so, this one wasn't to her liking.

At breakfast with the other boarders, she hardly said ten words. Afterward, she stepped out into the bright sunshine of the new day, and her heart sank. The past couple of days, Jesse Lee had been on the porch waiting for her. Not this morning.

Worried, Ursula crossed the street to the empty lot. She was relieved to see his horse. Not that she could imagine him deserting her. She went around a pine and stopped.

Hunkered by his fire, Jesse Lee was putting his coffeepot on. "Mornin', ma'am," he said without looking up.

"Are you still mad at me?" Ursula asked.

"No, ma'am."

Ursula didn't buy it. Something was wrong. "If not, then what's the matter? You're not yourself this morning."

"I'm the same gent I've been since you met me." Jesse took the lid off the pot, peered inside, and placed the lid back. Slowly unfurling, he said, "I'd offer you a chair if I had one."

"Posh," Ursula said, and going over, she sat across from him, her legs tucked under her. "We need to clear the air."

"It's clear for me," Jesse Lee said.

"I might have given you the wrong impression last night," Ursula said. "I don't hold it against you, shooting that man."

Squatting, Jesse Lee said, "You didn't like it, though."

"Well, of course not. A man was shot, after all."

"And there you go." Jesse Lee turned his attention to the coffeepot.

Stung and perplexed, Ursula composed herself before trying her next sally. "I have a hard time following you sometimes. There what goes?"

"It became obvious last night, Miss Christie," Jesse Lee said, his Southern drawl more pronounced than usual, "that you don't cotton to shootists."

"I cotton to you," Ursula said brazenly.

"But not my pistol. And you can't have one without the other."

Ursula recalled her talk in the parlor with Mrs. Peal. "Let me ask you something, if you would be so kind."

"Anything," Jesse Lee said.

"Were I to ask you to give up your gun, to set it aside and never strap it on again as long as you lived, what would you say?"

"Good-bye."

"You would choose your pistol over me?"

"No. You'd do the choosin'. It's both or none."

"How can you be so attached to a gun? Don't human beings count for more than metal and ivory?"

"Who could answer that any way but yes? But the thing is, ma'am —"

"If you don't call me Ursula, I'll scream."

"The thing is, Ursula, there are a lot of human beings runnin' around who don't give a rat's whisker about other human beings. Hostiles. Killers, you name it. They will do you in if they think they can get away with it."

"Ah," Ursula said. "You'd rather not be done in, so you wear that Colt for protection."

Jesse Lee looked at her in shock. "How can you think so poorly of me?"

"What did I do now?"

"Only a coward wears a six-gun for that reason. And I ain't ever been afraid of any man."

"I believe you. Then why —"

He didn't let her finish. "This Colt," he said, patting his, "is a tool. It's only as good, or bad, as the gent who uses it. I wear it because sometimes I run into fools like those two last night. Not because I'm afraid to run into them. But so when I do, I can

257

use my Colt to keep them from buryin' me, or anyone else."

He pondered for a few moments, then said, "It's the principle of the thing."

Mrs. Peal, Ursula reflected, had used the very same word. "You wear a gun because you won't be imposed on by those who do wrong."

Jesse Lee smiled. "You have it at last. I wouldn't go anywhere without my Colt. I'd feel undressed. So if you want to be in my company, you have to accept both of us."

Ursula had a sense that she was about to make one of the most important decisions of her life. "If I say I do, can we go to the theater again tonight?"

"If I have to shoot somebody, it won't upset you?"

"So long as you are in the right, no, not ever."

Jesse Lee smiled. "What is it folks say? You must be a glutton for punishment."

Ursula looked him in the eye, and that warm feeling came over her. "I'm a glutton for something," she said.

CHAPTER 23

Thal had never drawn his revolver on anyone in his life. He'd never wanted to. He wasn't Jesse Lee. When confronted, he preferred to find a peaceable solution. It was just his nature. Now, as the angry bulldog glaring at him stood ready to draw on him, he braced himself.

Ned took half a step and thrust a finger at Sagebrush Sally's belligerent friend. "Leave my pard be. We're not payin' that gal a penny. She didn't do anything to deserve it."

"She offered to, but you threw it in her face," the bulldog snarled. "A lady should be treated with more respect."

Ned didn't help matters by laughing and saying, "A *lady*? Mister, have you looked at her lately? Wearin' a dress doesn't make a woman a lady. It's what's inside the dress, and inside that dress is nothin' but a whore."

"Did he just insult her?" Sally's other

defender said.

"I believe he did," the bulldog declared.

"I never did like cowboys," the other man said.

"Me neither," bulldog said.

"Hurt them for me, Zant," Sagebrush Sally said, placing her hand on the bulldog's arm. "Hurt them bad." She grinned with glee at the prospect.

"I believe I will," Zant said, and held his hand with his fingers spread wide close to his six-shooter.

Crawford had edged closer to Thal and Ned. "If he goes for his, all three of us jerk our Colts at the same time," he advised. "He can't get all three of us."

"The two of us can," the other man said.

"You ready, Simpson?" Zant said.

"Born ready," the other man said.

Thal couldn't quite believe it was happening. He'd known that American City was wide-open, but he hadn't really expected to be braced by any of its wilder element.

"Any last words before you meet your Maker?" Zant taunted. He was enjoying this, like a bulldog worrying a bone.

From behind them someone said, "I have a few."

Only then did Thal realize the saloon had fallen completely quiet. He figured it was

260

because of the gun affray about to take place, but he was wrong.

Bull had returned, and he wasn't alone.

The newcomer looked a lot like Thal, only his hair was darker and he was considerably thinner. His eyes were a piercing blue, his chin a spear-point. He wore a tailored suit and polished boots and a flat-crowned black hat with a short brim. A slight bulge under his left arm betrayed a shoulder holster. But it was the object he held in his right hand that drew the most attention: a double-barreled, English-made shotgun with a walnut stock. The barrels had been filed off so that they were barely a dozen inches long, while the stock had been sawed and rounded so it fit the man's hand like the handles of a pistol. Both hammers were cocked.

"Shotgun!" Zant blurted, and straightened.

Simpson took a step to one side, as taken aback as his partner. "We weren't doin' nothin'," he said.

"Looked like it to me," the man they'd called Shotgun said. "Looked to me like you were about to shoot him." He flicked a finger at Thal.

"The cowpoke and his friends insulted Sally," Gant said. "We were only standin' up for her."

"It's nothin' for you to be bothered over," Simpson said.

The thin man's smile was pure ice. "I shouldn't be bothered that you two were about to shoot my brother?"

"Bro . . . ?" Zant said, and was too shocked to finish.

"The hell you say," Simpson said, more than a touch of fear in his voice. He took another step to the side.

The thin man looked at Thal, and the ice was replaced by genuine warmth. "Thalis," he said.

Thal had been struck dumb by his brother's timely appearance. Everything about him was different, from the fancy clothes to his sinister manner. "Myles," he said, and managed to smile.

"It's been a while."

"It surely has," Thal said. "We heard you got shot, and the whole family was so worried they sent me to find you."

"Save that," Myles said. He turned back to the hard cases, and the ice returned to his steely blue eyes. "Now, where were we?"

"Nowhere," Simpson said. "Zant and me will back off and leave these three be. We didn't know he was your brother. Honest to God, we didn't."

"That's true," Zant said. "We were only standin' up for Sal here."

"So you've said." Myles fixed his gaze on her. "You put them up to gunnin' him." It was a statement, not a question.

"Now, hold on," Sagebrush Sally said, trying hard to show she wasn't afraid. "It's not like any of us gals haven't done this before. Anything goes, remember?"

"My own brother," Myles said.

"It's all right," Thal said, thinking to end it. "No harm was done."

"Only because Bull happened to find me in time."

"Look here," Sagebrush Sally said, placing her hand on Myles's jacket. "Like your brother says, no harm was done. Mr. Galt would say the same."

"You're thinkin' for him now, are you?"

Sagebrush Sally swallowed and licked her lips. "Sheathe your claws and I'll buy drinks for everybody and we can all be friends."

"Now you're tellin' me what to do."

"Oh God," Simpson said.

"Shotgun, please," Sally said. "Quit being a bastard about this."

Myles clubbed her. He slammed the scattergun against her temple and she folded at his feet without so much as a whimper. It happened so fast, she was on the floor before anyone could blink.

"Myles?" Thal said.

"Oh God, oh God," Simpson said. He extended both hands, palms out. "We're sorry, you hear? We didn't know and we're sorry. Let us go. We're not about to try and draw on you. Look. My hands are empty."

"Mine aren't," Myles said, and shot him. The boom of the scattergun was like a cannon in the confines of the saloon. At the blast, the top of Simpson's head exploded and his hat went flying. The body toppled with a thud, and Myles turned to Zant. "That leaves you."

Zant was staring at his dead partner. Anger was taking hold, and he growled, "You had no call to do that."

"You brace my brother, you answer to me."

"We didn't know!" Zant roared, and coiled. "You and the airs you put on. Like you're God Almighty with that shotgun."

"I'm givin' you your chance, aren't I?"

To Zant's credit, he didn't flinch. "I'll be damned if I'll cower to you like Simpson did."

"Good for you," Myles said.

Everyone in the saloon had frozen, one man in the act of laying a card on a table, another with a glass halfway to his mouth.

Not so much as a muscle twitched.

"I'm waitin'," Myles said.

"Someone should fetch Mr. Galt," Zant said. "Let him decide whether you're in the right or not."

"Right has nothin' to do with it," Myles said. "You know that better than anyone. Quit stallin' and get to it."

"Bull, what do you say?" Zant called out, grasping at a straw.

"No, you don't," Bull replied. "You're not draggin' me into this. It's between you and him."

"I'll count to three," Myles said.

"Hold on," Zant said. His anger had faded and he was staring at the scattergun as if it were a snake that was about to bite him. "How about I pay you to let me leave?" An idea seemed to occur to him, and he brightened. "Or better yet, how about I pay your brother for the inconvenience I caused?"

"Is that what you call it?"

"That's fair, ain't it?" Zant said. "I have pretty near sixty dollars on me. It's all his if you'll let me go."

Thal felt he had to say something. "I don't need his money. This is over as far as I'm concerned."

"Me too," Zant said eagerly.

"There's more involved than you, big

brother," Myles said. "This is about re-spect."

"I respect you, Shotgun," Zant said quickly. "I truly do."

"But you see," Myles said with deceptive calm, "if folks hear you braced my brother and I didn't do anything, *they* won't respect me. And I can't have that. I can't have that at all."

"Don't make me beg."

"You disappoint me, Zant," Myles said. "I thought you were tougher. But I reckon you're one of those who's only tough when he's pickin' on those who aren't."

Thal realized his brother was referring to him.

"I'll count to three and we'll get this over with," Myles said. Then, in a staccato rush, "One, two, three."

Zant tried. He clawed for his revolver, a Smith & Wesson, and almost jerked it clear.

Myles shot him square in the chest.

At that range, the twelve-gauge lifted Zant off his feet and flung him like a rag doll. He crashed into the wall, and opened his mouth as if to scream. His limbs thrashing spas-modically, he sank into a crumpled heap, leaving a scarlet smear in his wake.

"And that's that," Myles said, breaking open the scattergun to reload.

Thal, like everyone else, scarcely breathed. His brother — his very own brother — had just murdered two men, and clubbed a woman besides. It didn't seem real.

Myles turned to the onlookers. "What are you gapin' at? Get on with what you were doin'."

As if a cord had been cut, movement resumed, and the buzz of conversation, more subdued than before, filled the air.

"Nice goin'," Bull said to Myles, and chortled. "I never did care for Zant much. He acted too big for his britches."

"Would you see to the bodies so I can talk to my brother?"

"Be glad to," Bull said.

Myles, smiling, offered his hand to Thal. "I can't tell you how happy this makes me. You comin' all this way on my account."

It felt odd to Thal, shaking his own brother's hand. He smothered an urge to hug him, as he had sometimes done when they were kids. "Ma and sis were awful worried."

"Hold on a minute," Myles said, and turned so his back was to the wall and he could see everyone in the saloon. Extracting the spent shells, he slid a new shell from an inside pocket and inserted it. He did the same with a second shell, snapped the shotgun closed, and fondly ran his hand along the twin barrels.

"When did you take up a shotgun?" Thal asked.

"I've taken up a lot of things," Myles said. He patted the scattergun. "I'm partial to slugs. Buckshot spreads too much."

Thinking that Myles did it to spare bystanders from being wounded or killed, Thal remarked, "It's good you're so considerate."

"Considerate, nothin'," Myles said. "A slug weighs a lot more than buckshot. Hit a man with an ounce of lead and he goes down. You should remember that from when we used to go huntin' together."

"We shot birds and other game," Thal said, and looked at the two bodies. "We never shot people."

"That was then," Myles said.

Several doves were helping Sagebrush Sally to stand. She was woozy, and would have fallen without their support. As they led her off she glared at Myles but had the presence of mind not to say anything.

"Bitch," Myles said.

"You've changed, brother," Thal said.

"It's called growin' up," Myle replied. "We all do it." He cradled his scattergun. "Why don't you introduce me to your friends and I'll treat the three of you to drinks?"

Thal went through the motions mechanically. He was more than a little bewildered by the turn of events. The brother he remembered wasn't the same as this man standing in front of him. The brother he remembered would never have done what Myles just did.

"We have a lot of catchin' up to do," Myles was saying. "How about if I see you to a hotel and then we take in the sights?"

"I'm obliged," Thal said, "but we're sort of short on funds."

"It will be on me."

"You're doin' that well, are you?"

"Big brother," Myles said, "I'm doing more than well." He gave a light laugh. "I'm the terror of this town, and I love it."

CHAPTER 24

Thal's brother wasn't exaggerating.

It was soon apparent that a lot of people were in fear of him. Those who got in Myles's way were quick to get out of it. Fingers were pointed, tongues wagged. At first Thal thought it might be because Bull had tagged along, and Bull's size was enough to draw attention. But no, he soon realized his brother was the attraction. The notorious Shotgun was as famous in American City as, say, Wild Bill Hickok was everywhere else.

Myles was in a jovial mood. He asked after their ma and their pa, and talked about the old days growing up on the farm.

For a while, Thal almost forgot that his brother had bucked two men out in gore. Almost.

Ned was uncommonly quiet. He hung back with Crawford, and only spoke if Thal addressed him.

Five blocks from the Devil's Due Saloon stood the Manor House Hotel. Decked out in Eastern finery, it boasted a chandelier and a rare cleanliness in that neck of the world. The desk clerk and the rest of the staff wore uniforms with a lot of gold braid.

Myles led them to the front desk. "I need three rooms," he announced.

The clerk was scribbling on a paper and didn't look up. An older man with gray around the ears and a salt-and-pepper mustache, he answered, "Sorry, but we're fill up."

"You'd better think again, Conner," Myles said.

The desk clerk snapped upright and the whites of his eyes showed. "Mr. Christie! I didn't know it was you."

"Three rooms," Myles said, and indicated Thal and his companions. "One for my brother and each of these others."

Conner coughed and consulted the hotel ledger. "There are a couple of drummers who checked in this evening that I can throw out. I'll claim there was a mix-up and their rooms had already been reserved."

"Whatever you have to," Myles said.

"Let me see," Conner said, running a finger down a page. "I don't know who else I can evict without them raising a fuss."

271

"No need for that," Thal said. "Ned and me will take one room, and Crawford can have the other."

"Are you sure?" Conner said.

"When I said three," Myles said, "I didn't mean two."

Conner colored and coughed and bent to the ledger again. "There's that actress who is so fond of herself. She can stay at the Ruby Theater. I know for a fact they have rooms at the back."

"That's settled, then," Myles said. "We'll be back in a couple of hours. Have the rooms cleared by then."

"Yes, sir."

As they emerged from the hotel, Bull chortled. "I like how you put that old fussbudget in his place. I wish folks were as scared of me as they are of you."

"Kill a few more and they will be," Myles said.

Half afraid that his brother wasn't joking, Thal asked, "How many have you put slugs into with that cannon of yours?"

Myles shrugged. "I don't count anymore. Mr. Galt tells me to shoot someone, and I shoot them."

"You're an assassin?"

"I'm a special deputy," Myles said. "So is Bull. There are six others like us who uphold the law."

"Is that were you were doin' at the saloon?"

"Don't start on me, Thalis," Myles said. "I'm not little anymore. I'm a grown man, and I live as I like."

"I can see that," Thal said. "And it worries me."

"It shouldn't." Myles clapped him on the shoulder. "Quit bein' so serious. We should celebrate bein' together again. We'll go to the Gold Nugget. That's our headquarters."

"Your what?"

"It's where Mr. Galt hangs his hat, so to speak. He owns it, and runs the whole town from his office. There's not another saloon like it anywhere in the Black Hills."

Once again, it wasn't an exaggeration. Three stories high and made of stone taken from a nearby quarry, the Gold Nugget was a monument to opulence. From the brass doors to the paneling and paintings and a bar a hundred feet long, it was a sight to behold. The poker tables were covered in felt, the chairs all had high backs. Variety acts played on a stage trimmed with velvet. Balconies with curtains overlooked everything.

A host of women in tight dresses mingled with the customers, laughing and flirting and enticing everyone to have a grand time. The women were all young and pretty. Not an old dove among them.

"My word," Ned blurted when a redhead sashayed by and winked at him. "It's like we've died and gone to heaven."

"More likely hell," Crawford said.

At the back was a door with large gold letters that read MAYOR TREVOR GALT. FOUNDER OF AMERICAN CITY.

"I hope he's in. I'd like you to meet him," Myles said, and knocked. When someone hollered to enter, he opened the door and motioned for Thal and the others to precede him.

The office was fit for royalty. Seated in a chair that could double as a throne, behind a mahogany desk, was American City's lord and master.

Thal didn't know what he was expecting, but it wasn't the man who rose to greet them.

Trevor Galt was even thinner than Myles. He wasn't all that tall either, not much over five feet. He was so pale as to almost be an albino. His hair was white, but he couldn't be much over forty years old. His eyes were a piercing green with peculiar yellow flecks, his eyebrows formed arches, and his forehead was higher than most. His suit, down

274

to his cravat with its diamond stickpin, was immaculate. A gold watch chain decorated his vest, and rings adorned every finger. "Shotgun. Just the gentleman I was about to send for. I have a job for you," he said with a British accent.

At least, Thal reckoned it was British. He wasn't much good at telling one accent from another unless it was German. Germans clipped their words, as if they bit them as the words came out of their mouths.

"Mr. Galt," Myles said. "I'd like you meet my brother and his friends."

Trevor Galt came around the desk to shake their hands. "Your brother, you say? From Kansas, isn't it?"

"Texas." Thal set him straight.

"Even further away," Galt said. "What brings you to our fair city, if you don't mind my asking?"

"They'd heard I was shot," Myles said.

"Do tell?" Galt was suddenly all interest. "Clear down to Texas? How did that miracle occur?"

Thal caught on to a few things right away. Trevor Galt was a polished customer, as suave as they came, with an excess of manners and charm. But there was something else, something about Galt's cold eyes and expression that hinted at darker currents. "I heard it from our sister."

"And where did she hear it from?"

"I've been wonderin' that my own self," Myles said.

Thal didn't see any harm in telling them. "She got a letter from a Mr. Tweed."

"Tweed?" Galt said, and his features hardened.

"That dang newspaperman," Myles said. "Always pokin' his nose in."

"I don't see what's wrong about it," Thal said. "Ursula wrote to you care of the marshal, and this Tweed was kind enough to write back."

"We don't have a marshal here," Myles said. "Just us special deputies."

"Well, no harm was done," Trevor Galt said. "And you must be pleased to have your brother visit."

"I truly am," Myles declared.

"I'd have brought Ursula along," Thal mentioned, "but we'd heard so many tales about American City, I didn't think it was safe. So we left her at a boardinghouse in Deadwood."

Myles gave a start. "Hold on. Our sis is here in the hills?"

"In Deadwood," Thal said again.

Myles appeared astonished. "Ursula . . . in the Black Hills?" He shook his head in amazement, then swore and bunched his fist. "Are you addlepated? Bringin' Ursula to the hills? *Her,* of all people?"

"What's the matter?" Trevor Galt said.

"My sister," Myles said angrily, "is as sweet a gal as ever was born, and as innocent as can be. And my big brother, my big, dumb lump of a brother, brings her *here*!"

Thal resented his tone. "You have no call to talk to me like that."

"And you left her in Deadwood all by her lonesome?" Myles's whole body shook, he was so mad. "If you weren't my brother, I'd shoot you where you stand."

"Calm down, Shotgun," Trevor Galt said. "I'm sure your brother didn't mean any harm to come to her."

"It better not," Myles snarled.

Thal was about to explain, but Ned chose that moment to step forward and jab a finger at Myles.

"Now, just you hold on, mister. I don't care if you are Thal's brother. He's my pard, and you don't get to talk to him like that. He came all this way to see if you were all right, didn't he? As for your sister, he didn't bring her. He left her in Kansas with your folks. But she went and snuck off, and the next we knew, we ran into her in Cheyenne.

So don't be callin' him dumb and threatenin' to snuff his wick."

For a few anxious moments, Thal thought
Myles might hit him.

"Snuck off, you say?" his brother finally
said. "That sounds like somethin' she'd do.
Damn her anyhow. Let me guess. She
wouldn't go back, no matter what you said?
You either had to bring her or she'd have
come on her own?"

"You know your sis all right," Ned said.

"We left her with another friend," Thal
informed him.

"My pard," Crawford said.

"Another cowpoke?" Myles said.

"What's wrong with that?" Thal said.
"We're not infants. He won't let anyone
harm her." No, the real danger, if you could
call it that, was from the two of them
becoming better acquainted.

"I still don't like it," Myles said. "You
haven't been in these hills as long as me.
They are no place for a gal like her. You and
me should go fetch her. I'll put Ursula up
at the hotel so we can keep our own eyes on
her."

"There's no need for that." Now that Thal
knew his brother was alive — and had seen
how much he'd changed — he didn't aim
to stick around that long.

"The blazes there isn't," Myles declared.

"Permit me to have a say," Trevor Galt interceded. "I agree with Shotgun. Deadwood is a nest of pimps, confidence men, and worse. Your sister will be much safer here than there. Especially as she will be under my personal protection. I'll assign a special deputy to guard her room day and night if that is what it will take to convince you."

"You'd do that for me?" Myles said.

"For any of my deputies," Galt said.

Thal hesitated. This was the last thing he wanted. He didn't trust Trevor Galt any further than he could toss Bull. "I didn't intend to stay all that long."

"Nonsense," Myles said. "You and her came all this way. We should spend more time together than that."

"Certainly," Galt said. "While you two become reacquainted, I'll send Bull and a couple of others to fetch your sister."

"I'll need to go along," Thal said. "She might not come otherwise."

To his dismay, Ned said, "Why not let me go? I don't mind. She knows me, so Jesse Lee and her won't think it's a trick of some kind."

"Jesse Lee?" Myles said.

"My pard," Crawford said.

Trevor Galt smiled. "Good. Then it's settled. Your sister can stay in the guest suite at the Manor House. At no charge to any of you, I might add, so don't worry on that score."

"Mr. Galt," Myles said, "you beat everyone I ever knew, all hollow. My brother and me are grateful."

Although he didn't feel the same, Thal nodded.

"Why don't you take your brother and his friends out and treat them to drinks?" Galt said to Myles. "On me."

"What was that about a job you had for me?" Myles said.

"Forget about that. Bull and Mateo will take care of the problem. You need to be with your brother."

Galt ushered them to the door, bade them to have a good time, and closed it behind them.

"Did you hear him?" Myles said. "Drinks, and sis's room, on him. Isn't he just about the finest gent on God's green earth?"

"He's somethin'," Thal said.

CHAPTER 25

They were the greatest, most wonderful, most glorious days of Ursula's life.

Now that they had worked things out, all was right with the world.

She spent every waking moment with Jesse Lee. Always an early riser, she was washed and dressed by breakfast in the boarding-house, and as soon as she was done eating, she thanked Mrs. Peal and excused herself.

Jesse Lee would be waiting on the porch, and off they'd go to explore Deadwood. They tried different restaurants. They visited every store. They attended all the theaters. In between, they walked and talked. Ursula had never talked so much. About her life on the farm. About everything that had ever happened to her that might be interesting or make him grin. She opened her heart and poured out its contents.

For Jesse Lee's part, he wasn't quite as forthcoming. Ursula figured that was because he wasn't naturally gabby. He had a reticence about him, but with a little prying, she got him to talk about things in his own past.

It was strange. Deadwood thronged with people. Thousands upon thousands. Yet it was as if she and Jesse Lee were the only two there. They hardly noticed anyone else. Even stranger, everyone else hardly noticed them. They'd stroll down a busy street with eyes only for each other, and it was if no one else was there.

To be sure, Jesse Lee was pointed at now and again. The shooting was to blame. He had acquired a reputation. A small one, but a reputation nonetheless. He paid the fawners no mind.

Before, she would have been bothered by it, but now she wasn't. She understood him, understood why he wore his ivory-handled Colt.

He had said it was part of him, and that made no sense until she realized that it wasn't like an arm or a leg, it was part of the inner him. Jesse Lee, deep down, was a good man. A man who didn't do wrong, and who wouldn't countenance wrong being done to others. He would stand up to the wrongdoers, using his Colt only if he had to. It was his tool for right, as it were.

And it wasn't just Jesse Lee. Others lived by the same creed, she came to understand. Wild Bill Hickok, for instance. It was claimed Hickok had killed over forty men, which Ursula suspected was an exaggeration. However many it was, Hickok never shot anyone except those as deserved it. With nearly all those he'd killed, he'd been wearing a badge at the time. Hickok's fancy Colts were his own tools for right.

Speaking of Hickok, as they were strolling along Main Street one evening, who should approach from the other way but the famous gunfighter, as folks were taking to calling men like him? As tall as he was, and with those broad shoulders and narrow waist, Hickok would have stood out in any crowd.

Doubly so with his flowing hair and sombrero, his Prince Albert frock coat, his red sash, and those silver-mounted pistols.

People parted before him like commoners for a king. They gaped. They whispered.

James Butler Hickok was more than famous. He was a legend in his own time.

As the famous man came toward them, Ursula moved to one side as everyone else was doing. Since she and Jesse Lee had taken to going everywhere arm in arm, Jesse Lee moved with her. She smiled, wondering if the Prince of the Pistoleers, as he was called, would remember them.

Hickok stopped, bestowed a warm smile on them, and doffed his sombrero. "Well, look who it is. Miss Christie, wasn't it?"

"Mr. Hickok," Ursula said, and felt herself blush.

Hickok's eyes roved over Jesse Lee. "And you were with her brother, as I recollect. I don't recall ever being introduced."

"This is Jesse Lee Hardesty," Ursula said. "He and I have been taking in the sights."

"And more, I hear," Hickok said, and addressed Jesse Lee. "Were you the one involved in an affray the other night with Jack Wilson?"

"Was that his whole name?" Jesse Lee said.

"Wilson is a bad one," Hickok said. "He and his partner, Kincaid, go about like they are cocks of the walk. You shot him in the shoulder, I hear."

Jesse Lee nodded.

"What were you thinking?"

Jesse Lee glanced at Ursula and didn't say anything.

"Take my advice, young fellow," Hickok said. "When you have to shoot, it is you or them. Going for the shoulder, or trying to shoot their revolver from their hand, as a lawman once told me he did, is misplaced charity. It will get you killed. I usually go

284

for the guts. The shock stops a fight as quick as anything except a shot to the head."

"I know," Jesse Lee said.

"He did it on my account, Mr. Hickok," Ursula felt compelled to say. "Because I'd asked him not to kill anyone."

Hickok regarded her thoughtfully while nipping at his mustache. "That's decent of you, ma'am. But if you care for this young gentlemen, you might want to change your outlook. When a man goes into a shooting halfhearted, he comes out in a pine box."

"I understand that now," Ursula said.

"Then your young gentleman is lucky." Hickok placed his sombrero back on. "In more ways than one." He gazed wistfully about. "I find myself missing my wife, Agnes. It would please me if she were here, and I might send for her yet."

"You should," Ursula said. "A wife deserves to be with her husband."

As if he were talking to himself and not to her, Hickok said, "I need to get settled first. I need luck at the tables so I can buy her that home she wants. She's a gracious lady, and should have that much." He blinked, and shook himself, and smiled. "Well, listen to me. I won't detain you any longer. Much luck to both of you."

Ursula watched that broad back move off.

"He sure is nice."

"Somethin' is botherin' him," Jesse Lee said.

"How can you tell?"

"You could see it in his eyes."

"I hope he's reunited with his wife soon." Ursula gave Jesse Lee's arm a playful squeeze. "Now what about us? Where would you like to go next?"

"How about to my camp?" Jesse Lee added quickly, "For the peace and quiet."

Nothing would please Ursula more. They had taken to ending their evenings around his fire. Or, rather, beside it, since she often sat with her head on his shoulder. She kept hoping that he would kiss her, but so far he'd been, much to her regret, a perfect gentleman.

It was nice to leave Main Street behind. Jesse Lee rekindled his fire and they sat arm in arm, not saying much, content to be together. She wondered what he was thinking about, and presently found out.

"Wild Bill Hickok has a wife," Jesse Lee said out of the blue.

"A lot of men do," Ursula said, and giggled.

"A lot of men aren't Wild Bill. They're not pistoleros, like he is. Yet he took a wife."

"Why does that surprise you so much?"

"A man like him. All the enemies he's made. All those who would buck him out for the glory. Never knowin' when he might be back-shot. Yet he took a wife the same as any other man."

"Imagine that," Ursula teased.

"If he can, maybe I can too."

"Why couldn't you?"

Jesse Lee picked up a stick and added it to the fire. "I was thinkin' it wouldn't be fair to the gal to hitch myself to her when I might not live long enough to make anything of the marriage."

"Oh, Jesse Lee."

"Well, that's reasonable, ain't it? A man doesn't want to do wrong by the woman he cares for. Look at Wild Bill. Hopin' to get a house for his Agnes. If he can do it, anyone can."

"Of course they can, silly." Ursula laughed. Men came up with the silliest notions.

Jesse Lee shifted and looked at her. Not a normal look, but a deep, penetrating gaze, as if he were trying to see into her soul. "Do you like me as much as I like you?"

"More silliness," Ursula said. "If I haven't made that plain by now, I don't know how else I can."

"What would you say to bein' my gal?"

"I already am." Ursula pecked him on the cheek. "Where have you been that you haven't noticed?"

"No," Jesse Lee said, and gently taking her hand, he raised it to his mouth and kissed it.

Ursula sat up. Her heart was twittering and her lungs didn't seem to want to work. "What are you saying?"

"I'd like to court you, formal-like. And if things go on as they have been, with us gettin' along so well, and you cottonin' to me as I cotton to you, then I'd like for us to stand before a parson and I'll put a ring on your finger."

"Are you proposing?" Ursula asked, the words nearly catching in her throat.

"I reckon I am," Jesse Lee said. "Sort of."

"Then I say yes. Yes. And yes again."

"I know this is kind of sudden. Are you sure?"

"Don't spoil it." Ursula was regaining some composure. She'd grown as hot as the fire, though, and was afraid she'd break out in a sweat.

"Then it's settled," Jesse Lee said, and grinned. "What do we do next?"

"You kiss me, you fool."

Jesse Lee bent, his lips touched hers, and Ursula felt as if a bolt of lightning cleaved her from head to toe. She melted against him as the kiss went on and on. When they finally parted, she was panting.

"Goodness," Jesse Lee said.

"What?"

"Are all our kisses goin' to be like that?"

"Let's find out. Kiss me again."

They kissed, and kissed some more, and after a while, Ursula rested her cheek on his chest and felt more content than she had her whole life long.

Jesse Lee stroked her hair.

"So this is love," Ursula said. "No wonder folks like it so much."

"You're my woman?"

"And you're my man."

"You're not goin' to change your mind?"

"I very much doubt it."

"But you don't know for sure?"

Ursula turned her face up to his. "There you go again. Who can predict? We take it a day at a time and see what happens. The way I feel right now, I'll be yours forever." To shut him up, she kissed him, which led to more kisses. Gradually he relaxed, and once again she rested with her cheek on his chest, his fingers in her hair.

"This is nice," Jesse Lee said.

"Isn't it, though?" Ursula would be happy to sit there forever, just the two of them and the fire. She had never been so happy.

"What do you reckon your folks will say?"

"I don't know and I don't care," Ursula replied. "You're not courtin' them. You're courtin' me."

Jesse laughed. "I admire how you stand up for yourself. How you didn't let your brother force you to go home."

"I love Thalis dearly, but sometimes he treats me as if I'm ten years old," Ursula said. "I'm a grown woman."

"I noticed."

Grinning, Ursula snuggled against him. "When he comes back we'll break the news. I hope it gives him a conniption."

"Poor Crawford," Jesse Lee said.

"Why poor?"

"He'll need to find a new pard."

"I'm your partner now," Ursula said. "And if you don't think I am, go marry him instead of me."

Jesse Lee kissed the top of her head. "You make me grin."

"Good."

The next half hour seemed an eternity. When they rose and Jesse Lee escorted her to the boardinghouse, Ursula clung to his arm as if for dear life.

"I hate being parted from you, but I suppose it has to be until we're man and wife.

Then we won't have to ever be parted again."

"We'll be like Wild Bill and his Agnes."

Ursula stopped and took his chin in her hand. "Promise me something," she said solemnly.

"Anything."

"Promise me that if anyone or anything tries to come between us, you won't let them."

"You can count on that," Jesse Lee said.

CHAPTER 26

Ursula awoke the next morning with a smile on her face. She lay in bed a few minutes, enjoying memories of the night before. Their stroll through Deadwood. All those kisses. Their talk with Wild Bill Hickok. All those kisses. Jesse Lee proposing. And all those kisses.

Springing out of bed, she hummed as she washed, hummed as she dressed, hummed as she floated down the stairs and took a chair at the kitchen table.

She was halfway through her oatmeal when Mrs. Peal remarked, "You look positively radiant today, my dear."

"Do I?" Ursula said, feigning ignorance, when in truth she was so happy she felt lighter than air.

"Be careful you don't split your lips, smiling that much."

Ursula laughed. She would tell Mrs. Peal about Jesse Lee's proposal later, when they were alone. She finished eating, skipped down the hall to the front door, and stepped out to the greet the man she loved.

Jesse Lee was waiting.

So were others.

Ned Leslie was leaning against the rail, and three other men were lounging by their horses out at the street. Ned straightened and brightened and took off his hat. "Miss Christie. It's marvelous to see you again."

"What's this?" Ursula said.

"They showed up about an hour before daybreak," Jesse Lee said, not sounding pleased. "Thal sent them."

"That's right," Ned said, nodding. "We're to fetch you to American City to join him."

Ursula was stunned. She'd looked forward to another delightful day with Jesse. "I thought he wanted me to stay here."

"He found Myles," Ned said, "and Myles wants to see you. But he can't come here, so Thal sent me to take you to them."

Ursula glanced at Jesse Lee. "I don't know," she said.

"You don't want to go?" Ned said. "I thought the whole reason you came to the Black Hills was to find Myles."

"It was," Ursula said. But she still didn't want to. Not and spoil her happiness.

"I don't savvy," Ned said. "What's stoppin' you?"

"It's too sudden," Ursula said. "Give me a minute to talk to Jesse Lee while I make up my mind."

Looking thoroughly confounded, and not a little crestfallen, Ned placed his hat back on. "I'll be over by the horses. Take as long as you need." He went down the steps.

Ursula stepped to Jesse Lee. "What do you think?"

"They're your brothers," Jesse Lee said.

Ursula frowned.

"You came all this way because you were worried about Myles."

"I know, I know."

"If you don't go, then what?" Jesse Lee said. "You wait here for Thal to collect you on his way back to Texas?"

"Quit being so logical," Ursula said, and held his hand where the others couldn't see. "It's you that matters now. I care about Myles, sure, but I care about you more."

"I'm yours and you're mine," Jesse Lee said.

"Forever," Ursula said. She stared over his shoulder at Ned and the strangers. "I suppose I better go. Thalis and Myles will hold it against me if I don't. But you're to be by me the whole way. We don't go anywhere without each other from now on."

"You took the words right out of my mouth."

Ursula grinned, then sobered. "One thing, though. I want Thalis and Myles to hear about your proposal from me. Not from Ned or anyone else. Let's keep it our secret until we get to American City."

"Fine by me," Jesse Lee said, "but I'd love to kiss you right now."

"I'd love to let you." Ursula laughed, and released his hand. She saw that both Jesse Lee's palomino and her sorrel had been saddled and were waiting. "You got ready to go before you even talked to me?"

"I reckoned you'd want them, them bein' your brothers, and all."

"Let me go collect my things. Tell Ned I'll be out in about ten minutes."

Mrs. Peal took the news with a scowl. "American City, you say? That den of iniquity is no place for a young girl like you. If your brothers had any sense, they would have come here."

"I'll be all right," Ursula assured her. "Thal and Myles are there, and Jesse Lee will always be by my side."

"Still," Mrs. Peal said, "don't stay any longer than you absolutely must. Be shed of that vile pit as soon as you can."

"I intend to."

Ursula gave the older lady a hug and departed.

"There you are," Ned said, beaming, as she approached. "Give me that bag and I'll tie it on for you."

"Jesse Lee will do it," Ursula said. She wanted to show where her loyalties lay so there would be no misunderstandings. "Who are these other gents?"

Disappointed, Ned turned. "They're special deputies. They work for Trevor Galt, the man who runs American City. The big one is called Bull, the Mexican feller is Mateo, and that broom handle is named Rafer."

Ursula didn't like the looks of any of them. Bull had beady eyes, and could use a washing. Mateo had hungry eyes, and not for food. Rafer had bloodshot eyes, and sores on his face.

"So you're their sister," Bull said.

Mateo took off his brown sombrero and bowed. "It is my pleasure to meet you, *señorita*." He wore a pearl-handled Remington on his left hip, rigged for a cross draw. *"Eres muy bonita."*

Ursula didn't know what that meant.

Rafer nodded at her while scratching one of his sores.

"Let's be on our way," Ned said.

Reluctantly Ursula climbed onto the sorrel. She almost changed her mind. She didn't want to go, not at all. But she imagined Thalis and Myles, waiting for her, and with a fond glance at the boardinghouse, she gigged her mount.

Jesse Lee immediately swung his palomino in next to her. He rode with his right hand on his hip, close to his Colt.

Ursula consoled herself with the thought that they could have some long talks along the way. Then Ned brought his roan up on her other side.

"Ain't this somethin'? Together again."

To change the subject, Ursula said, "Tell me about American City and how you found Myles."

The recital was a long one. Ned was trying to impress her, she suspected. She didn't like the part about their near encounter with the Sioux, and she liked even less the incident at the saloon.

"Myles shot those two men dead? My own brother?"

"They don't call him Shotgun for nothin'," Ned said. "Those two weren't his first neither."

"I remember when he was ten and caught a fly and let it go rather than squash it," Ursula said.

"Your brother Myles has changed," Ned

said. "Thal said so his own self."

A sense of dread came over her and, try as Ursula might, she couldn't shake it. She was glad Jesse Lee was there. She could rely on him if things became ugly. On him and his ivory-handled Colt.

She only hoped it wouldn't come to that.

"You keep that up," Crawford said from where he lounged in a chair, reading a news-paper, "you're goin' to wear a hole in the floor."

Thal had been pacing since they got back from supper. He had a lot to ponder, and he did his best pondering when he walked. "It's been three days. They'll be here any time now."

"You regret sendin' for her, don't you?"

"I do," Thal admitted. "I was so glad to see my brother again I wasn't thinkin' straight."

"She should be fine," Crawford said. "She has you and him and the rest of us."

Thal went to the window. He wouldn't admit it, but he didn't share the older puncher's confidence. Not after what he'd seen of American City. To call it lawless didn't do it justice. Deadwood was lawless. American City was a vile pit. Every vice was encouraged. Every lust was met.

The sign at the edge of town had read ANYTHING GOES, and anything did. It was as if all the worst hard cases in the world had gathered in one place, and were free to do as they pleased. If the love of money was the root of all evil, then American City wasn't just a root, it was the whole tree.

Yes, Thal reckoned, "pit" was as good a description as any. He recalled hearing a pastor once warn of the dangers of the Pit down below. American City was the pit up above.

When Thal had sent Ned to fetch Ursula, he'd been under the impression things weren't as bad as everyone had said. He was wrong.

Hell had its Satan, and American City had Trevor Galt. He called himself the mayor, but he was much more. Galt lorded it over all he surveyed. His special deputies lent the illusion that American City had law and order, when in fact they were to maintain disorder.

Thal began to see the light the morning after Ned left for Deadwood. He'd been wakened not much after dawn by a knock on his door to find Myles dressed and holding his scattergun. "A little early for breakfast, ain't it?" Thal had said. "I was hopin' to sleep in a little longer."

"Mr. Galt doesn't like to let grass grow under him," Myles replied. "He wants to pay Tweed a visit and he'd like for you to be there."

"The man who wrote to Ursula?"

"The very same. Get dressed. Mr. Galt doesn't like to be kept waitin' either."

Befuddled from lack of sleep, Thal did as his brother wanted.

Trevor Galt was in the lobby, along with a couple more special deputies. One was a small, muscular man called Tiny who wore two revolvers, strapped low. The other answered to the name Olivant, and had a shock of corn-colored hair, along with a drooping mustache. Olivant favored a Remington in a shoulder holster.

"There you are," Trevor Galt said, rising from a chair. He was as immaculately dressed as the night before. A derby crowned his head, and he carried a cane with a snake's-head handle.

"Hope I didn't keep you waitin'," Thal said.

"Not overly long," Galt said. "Has your brother explained where we're going?"

"Yes, but not why," Thal said.

"I want you there to corroborate me, should the need arise." Twirling his cane, Galt sauntered out into the growing light of the new day. He inhaled and smiled. "I do so like mornings. Starting each day fresh, with a wealth of opportunities."

"If you say so." Thal was partial to sunsets.

"You're not very vigorous early in the day, are you?" Galt said. "But no matter. Come along."

Taking it for granted Thal would follow, Galt headed down the street. Tiny and Olivant flanked him, and Myles came behind.

Thal caught up to his brother. "How are you feelin' after last night?"

"Fine." Myles was watching doorways and windows, his thumb on the hammers of his scattergun.

"You were able to sleep? Those killin's didn't bother you any?"

"I've never lost sleep over a shootin'," Myles said. "What's the use? It's no different than stompin' a snake. You do it and you forget about it."

Two blocks down stood a building with a banner. Thal struggled to make sense of it and finally asked Myles to read it to him.

" 'The *American City Journal.* Published twice weekly. Reasonable advertising rates. Abraham Tweed, Owner and General Manager.' "

Trevor Galt knocked with his cane. He let

a few seconds go by and knocked again, louder.

"Maybe he's not up yet, Mr. Galt," Olivant said.

"Then we will rouse him, or you will kick down this door."

Thal wondered what the newspaperman had done to rile Galt so. It must be something serious, he figured.

Galt knocked again, striking the door so hard it shook in its hinges. "I do so hate to be kept waiting."

Thal thought of how long he'd kept Galt waiting in the lobby.

"Hold on, hold on," someone within shouted. "I'm coming, consarn you."

Galt stepped aside and nodded at Myles, who took his place with the scattergun leveled.

"What are you doin"?" Thal asked in alarm.

"Mr. Tweed," Trevor Galt said, "is in for a surprise."

CHAPTER 27

The man who answered the door was in his fifties, if not older. His brown hair was streaked with gray, as was his thin mustache. His shirt and pants were rumpled, as if he'd slept in them or couldn't be bothered to have them ironed. Thick spectacles were perched on the tip of his nose. They had the effect of making his eyes seem larger than they were, so when they widened in surprise, it made him look like a two-legged owl.

"Mr. Galt!"

"Abraham," Galt said, and when the newspaperman continued to stare, he snapped, "Are you going to stand there with your mouth hanging open or let me in?"

"Of course," Tweed said, and stepped aside. A flicker of fear crossed his face as the special deputies filed in after Galt.

Thal smiled and nodded, but Tweed didn't respond. He wondered if Tweed thought he was another deputy.

Over beyond a railed-off area stood the printing press. Thal had never seen one before. It was bigger than he'd have imagined, and looked complicated to operate. Nearby it was a desk where letters were being sorted. "That's some contraption you've got there, Mr. Tweed."

The newspaperman was staring worriedly at Trevor Galt. "It's a Victory-Kidder rotary press," he said absently.

Galt held his cane with the snake's head on his shoulder and gave the printing press a look that suggested he'd like to take the cane to it and bust it to pieces. "Permit me to introduce Mr. Christie. Thalis Christie. Does his name ring a bell?"

"No," Tweed said, his Adam's apple bobbing.

"I should think it would," Galt said. "Given that you wrote to his sister."

"I did?" Tweed seemed truly confused.

"You've forgotten? But don't take my word for it." Galt pointed his cane at Thal. "Relate the circumstances as you told them to me, Mr. Christie, if you would be so kind."

Thal told how Ursula had written to Myles, care of American City's marshal's office, and about the letter she'd received from Tweed.

"Now do you remember?" Galt said.

"Oh, that." Tweed nodded. "I did the young lady a favor. She was worried about her brother."

"How considerate of you," Galt said sourly. "But I'm a bit puzzled by something, and I'd like you to clear it up for me."

"Certainly," Tweed said. "I'm always happy to help you in any way I can."

"How kind of you," Galt said. Stepping over to the newspaperman, he lightly touched the tip of his cane to Tweed's chest. "Let's start with how you ended up with the letter. It was addressed to the marshal, was it not?"

"We don't have a marshal. We only have your special deputies." Tweed flicked Myles, Olivant, and Tiny a nervous glance.

"You're missing my point, Abraham," Galt said. "How is it that *you* ended up with her letter?"

"Oh. The postmaster gave it to me."

"Mr. Edgerton? Why should he do a thing like that?"

Tweed's face twitched. "I often answer general inquiries about the town."

"Do you, now?" Galt arched an eyebrow. "This is news to me. How long has it been going on?"

305

"Since shortly after I arrived," Tweed said. "Someone has to answer general inquiries, don't they? And since I run the only newspaper —"

"You assumed it might as well be you."

"Well, yes," Tweed said. "I mean, why should you have to bother with something so trivial?"

"Suppose I decide what's trivial and what isn't?" Galt hefted his cane as if he were contemplating using it. "How many general delivery letters have you answered?"

"Not more than a dozen," Tweed said. "We don't receive all that many."

"How fortunate for you."

"Sorry?"

"It seems to me," Galt said slowly, "that Mr. Edgerton and you have taken over a responsibility which wasn't yours to take. I'm the head of our city government. By rights, all correspondence addressed to any office in the city should go through me."

"Every single one?"

"Must I repeat myself?"

"No," Tweed said quickly. "I apologize for overstepping. We didn't think we were doing any wrong."

"I'm not pleased, Abraham," Galt said.

"Please," Tweed said. "I answered Mr.

Christie's sister out of kindness, nothing more."

"I'm sure you did," Galt said. "Which brings me to my second puzzlement."

"You have another?" Tweed said bleakly.

"It strikes me as strange that you didn't pass her letter on to Myles here. He's the one she was worried about."

Myles had been glaring at the newspaperman the whole while, and now he moved closer and pointed his scattergun. "I don't like that you didn't give me her letter, mister. I don't like it even a little bit."

"Now, hold on," Tweed said, his voice quavering. "You were laid up. You'd been shot, remember?"

"I'm not likely to forget a thing like that."

Galt glanced at Myles. "He doesn't seem to comprehend. Perhaps words aren't enough. Why don't you show Mr. Tweed exactly how you feel?"

Before Thal could think to stop him, Myles rammed the scattergun's twin muzzles into the newspaperman's stomach. Tweed cried out, doubled over, and clutched himself.

"Myles, no," Thal said.

Ignoring him, Myles raised the scattergun as if to club Tweed over the head. Instantly Thal sprang and grabbed his brother's arm.

"No! What do you think you're doin'?"

Myles went rigid with resentment. "Let go of me."

"He did you a favor and you beat on him?" Thal said.

"I won't tell you twice."

Thal released his hold but was set to grab Myles again if he had to. "Sis and me wouldn't be here if not for this gent. You owe him your thanks. Not to treat him like this."

Trevor Galt appeared amused. "That's all right, Myles. You've made your point. As for you, Thalis, it would be wise if you don't meddle in matters which you don't fully understand." Galt turned to Tweed, who was gasping and grimacing in pain. "Which brings us to you. I'll have a talk with the postmaster. Effectively immediately, all general delivery letters are to be forwarded to my office and not to the newspaper. Am I clear?"

Tweed nodded.

"Have I mentioned how fortunate you are? Because, to be honest," Galt said, cupping Tweed's chin, "I suspect there's more involved here. I'm well aware of your sentiments toward me. You feel I've usurped power, as it were, and don't agree with my methods. Is that not so?"

"Please. All I do is run the newspaper."

Galt let go and stepped back. "And you can go on doing so provided you don't meddle in matters that don't concern you." He paused. "Take that editorial you wrote a while ago. About the need to hold elections."

"All towns have them," Tweed gasped.

"And American City will, eventually," Galt said. "When I decide the time is right. Until then, it's up to me to wrest order from the chaos."

"A chaos you encourage."

Galt frowned. "I encourage a certain laxity, yes. But I do so in the town's best interests. We're the most remote town in the Black Hills. No one would come here without incentive to do so. All our saloons and the ladies I've brought in? They are as big a lure as gold, if not more so."

"Some would say they bring in the wrong element."

"Wrong in whose eyes? Yours? If you don't like how American City is run, you'd be well advised to set up shop somewhere else."

"I like it here," Tweed said. "I think this town has great potential."

"Finally something we agree on," Trevor Galt said, and made a *tsk-tsk* sound. "I must say, Abraham, I'm disappointed in you. But

I'm also optimistic that the two of us can come to a meeting of the minds and work together to make our dream for American City come true."

"I very much doubt your dream is the same as mine."

"There you go again. Don't force me to pay you another visit, Abraham. The next time will be the last, if you catch my drift." Galt started to turn. "Oh. And if word of our little talk should get out, I'll know who's to blame, and that next visit will come sooner rather than later." He smiled and sauntered from the premises.

Myles and the other two followed, but Thal lingered. "I'm sorry," he said. "My sister and me are obliged that you wrote her."

"If that accounts for your being here," Tweed said, "I wish I hadn't. You strike me as a decent sort, Mr. Christie, and there's no place for decency in the hell Trevor Galt has created. Leave American City as soon and as fast as you can."

"I'm stuck here awhile yet," Thal said. "My sister is on her way."

"God in heaven!" Tweed blurted. "I never meant for that to happen. The moment she arrives, turn her around and flee."

"Mr. Galt has promised to look after us,

as a favor to my brother," Thal mentioned. "We should be all right for a day or two."

Tweed glanced at the front door and lowered his voice. "You're a fool to trust that man. Mark my words. If you care for your sister, you won't let her stay more than five minutes."

Thal wanted to talk longer, but Myles filled the doorway.

"Are you comin', brother?"

With a nod to Tweed, Thal joined his sibling. "I was thankin' him for lettin' us know about you."

"The damn meddler."

They headed for the hotel.

"You shouldn't have hit him, Myles," Thal brought up. "It was uncalled-for."

Myles was swaggering along as if he owned the boardwalk. "You don't get to tell me what to do anymore. I'm all grown up."

"Do you like how you've become?"

"What's not to like?" Myles said. "I have it good here. I work for the man who rules the roost. I make good money. I get drinks for free, and if I want, a different painted cat scratches my back every night."

"You pay for it?" Thal said.

"Don't look so shocked. Men do all the time. Don't tell me you haven't."

"Afraid not," Thal said.

"Not even once?"

"Ma and Pa raised us better than that."

"They raised us to be like them," Myles said. "But I'm not, and never have been. All those Sunday school lessons? I hated goin'. I hated the hogwash they fed us."

"You never let on."

"Damn right I didn't," Myles said. "I knew if I did, Pa would take a switch to me and Ma would blister my ears."

"But all this," Thal said, gesturing at the bustling heart of American City. "It's a nest of sidewinders."

"And I'm one of the top snakes," Myles boasted. "People fear me. I'm treated with respect. Not like in Kansas where I was just another farmer."

"You can't go through life havin' folks be afraid of you."

"Why not? I *like* that they're afraid. I like it when I walk into a saloon and the whole place falls quiet. I like it when people point and whisper. I like it that if I tell someone to jump, they ask 'how high.' "

"Oh, Myles."

"Don't 'Oh, Myles' me. I did the same thing you did."

"I'm a cowpoke," Thal said. He almost added, "Not a paid assassin."

"You weren't when you left home. You

312

made yourself into one. Just as I've made myself into how I am."

"I brand cows. You shoot folks."

"Look at it this way," Myles said. "You ride herd on cattle, I ride herd on people. I do what my job calls for, just as you do what your job calls for."

"We'll never see eye to eye on this," Thal said. Not when he could never bring himself to blow another human being apart with a shotgun.

"Do you know why that is?" Myles didn't wait for an answer. "Because you were always the good son. You did whatever Pa and Ma asked. You were polite to others, did your chores without fail, all that."

"You make it sound like a bad thing."

"They controlled you, big brother. They wanted you to think a certain way. To act a certain way."

"What you call control," Thal said, "I call love."

"I'm not sayin' our folks didn't care for us," Myles argued. "I'm sayin' it was wrong for them to force us to be like they are. We have the right to choose. You did, becomin' a cowboy. So don't point your finger at me and say I did wrong."

Thal tried one last time. "It's not the choosing. It's *what* you chose."

313

"More of that good-and-bad business," Myles said. "It's bad to cuss. It's bad to drink. It's bad to go to bed with a whore. It'd bad to snuff somebody's wick. I could go on and on."

"None of that is good," Thal said.

"For you, maybe. For me, it's perfectly fine. I like doin' all that. It suits me down to my boots."

Thal didn't know what to say. This wasn't the brother he remembered. Or was Myles right, and he'd been like this all along?

"I'll live as I like from here on out," Myles informed him. "And neither you nor Ma or Pa or anyone else will make me change. Nothin' will this side of the grave."

"That's what worries me," Thal said.

CHAPTER 28

By the time she reached American City, Ursula had come to a couple of conclusions. The first was that Ned Leslie was as dense as a rock between his ears. It had taken him the entire first day to realize she wasn't interested in him romantically. He'd ridden next to her, prattling up a storm, oblivious of the looks she gave Jesse Lee.

Thankfully Jesse had been amused by Ned's antics, and informed her, when they stopped to rest the horses, that Ned would catch on eventually.

"He's a mite slow but he's not hopeless," was how Jesse Lee put it.

That night, when Ursula sat at the fire holding Jesse Lee's hand, the light finally dawned. Ned noticed, and reacted as if he'd been struck by lightning.

The next day he hardly spoke to her.

Ursula's second conclusion was that the special deputies were unlike any lawmen she ever heard of. They were lechers, and worse. Particularly Bull and Mateo, who constantly undressed her with their eyes. Rafer didn't seem interested in her, but he, like the other two, struck her as a vicious character. They didn't do anything to give her that impression. It was a feeling she had.

That same night around the campfire, Bull too had seen she was holding Jesse Lee's hand, and exclaimed, "Why, lookee there. We've got us a couple of lovebirds."

"I beg your pardon," Ursula had said.

"You heard me, gal." Bull leered at her. "You and the pup have taken a shine to each other."

Jesse Lee was on his feet before Ursula realized he'd let go of her hand. She almost spoke up and asked him not to say or do anything, but changed her mind. Lechers like Bull needed to be put in their place, and she was confident Jesse Lee was the man to do it.

"Pup?" Jesse Lee had said.

"You're young, ain't you?" Bull replied.

"Get up and I'll show you who's a pup."

Bull laughed. "You don't want to prod me, boy. I've done in more than my share." His hand, which had been resting on his knee, slid toward the holster on his hip.

Jesse Lee's own hand blurred, and his Colt

was out and cocked. "Try and you die."

Bull imitated stone.

"Did you see, Mateo?" the one called Rafer exclaimed, and whistled in appreciation.

"I saw, amigo," Mateo said, sounding impressed.

"Wait until Tiny hears there's another as quick as him," Rafer said. "He won't like it any."

"No, he will not," Mateo said.

Jesse Lee was still holding his six-gun on Bull. "Apologize to my dulce for talkin' like you did."

"All I did was say you were lovebirds," Bull said testily. "Where's the harm in that?"

"It wasn't what you said," Jesse Lee replied. "It was how you said it."

Bull looked at Ursula. "Sorry, ma'am." He didn't seem sorry at all. He seemed mad.

Jesse Lee twirled the ivory-handled Colt into his holster and sat back down, all in a fluid motion. Taking hold of Ursula's hand, he stared into the flames as if nothing had happened.

"Let's all be friendly, shall we?" Ned had said. "Jesse, these gents came along to make sure Miss Christie gets to American City safe. I'm sure Bull didn't mean any harm."

"Yes, let's forget it," Ursula urged. "Talk

about something else."

No one had anything to say. In due course they'd turned in, and the next morning, once they were again in the saddle and on the move, Ursula became aware of a change in the special deputies. They weren't as friendly. Their manner was colder. Several times she caught Bull giving Jesse Lee looks that didn't bode well.

Now, on the verge of entering American City, Ursula hoped nothing would come of it.

The sign at the outskirts filled her with trepidation. ANYTHING GOES was an invite to let loose the worst in human behavior, and she soon saw the proof. Drunks lurched about, some clutching half-empty bottles. Painted women in too-tight dresses paraded their fleshly wares. There wasn't a friendly face to be seen. But plenty of hungry looks were cast her way, the looks that wolves might give a doe.

Ursula moved her mount closer to Jesse Lee's. "Don't you stray off on me, you hear? I don't like the looks of this place."

"Makes two of us," Jesse Lee said.

In another block a commotion broke out. Two men were pushing and shoving and calling each other vile names. Suddenly one pulled a pistol and shot the other in the chest.

To Ursula's amazement, no one did anything. Some of the passersby gave the dead man a glance, and that was all. The rest went on their way as if nothing out of the ordinary had occurred. As for the special deputies, they rode past without saying a word.

"Land sakes," Ursula declared to Jesse Lee. "What sort of place is this?"

Bull brought them to the Manor House Hotel. "Wait here," he growled when they drew rein at a hitch rail. Beside it was a sign that said SPECIAL DEPUTIES ONLY. Only one horse was tied there. All the other hitch rails were lined end to end.

Jesse Lee swung down and offered his hand to her.

Ursula didn't need the help, but she let him help her down. "Thank you, kind sir." She liked that he was so attentive.

Ned tied his own horse and came over. "Be careful from here on out," he said. "If it had been up to me, I wouldn't have brought you here."

"Why did you, then?" Jesse Lee said.

"Thal asked me to, and he's my pard," Ned said. "He reckoned his sis wanted to see Myles again."

"I do, very much," Ursula said. "I'm grateful that you came for me."

"I hope you stay grateful," Ned said, and fell silent as Mateo and Rafer swung down.

"What do you think of our fair city, *señorita*?" the former asked.

"It's a bit" — Ursula racked her brain for the right word — "raw."

"Much like bloody meat, you mean?" Mateo said, and laughed. "*Sí, señorita.* Most excellent. That is American City."

"Why do you stay, then?"

"Me, *señorita*?" Mateo chuckled. "I like my meat with lots of blood."

Ursula smothered another rush of dread. She told herself that they wouldn't be there long, that she'd spend a day or so becoming reacquainted with Myles, and head home.

"Are you all right?" Jesse Lee asked.

"Flustered a little, I reckon," Ursula admitted.

Down the street a gun boomed and a man screamed. Once more, hardly anyone broke stride. A few glanced in the direction the shot came from and went on their way.

"What sort of people are these?" Ursula said.

Minutes went by.

Just when Ursula was about to suggest they wait in the lobby instead of out in the street, boots thudded, and Thal was there. "Sis!" he said happily. He embraced her, then held her at arm's length. "No harm has come to you?"

"No," Ursula said.

"And none will," Jesse Lee said.

Thal hugged her a second time and whispered in her ear, "Prepare yourself. He's not like we recollect."

Out of the hotel strode Myles. "Well, look who it is! My little sister came all this way."

Ursula spread her arms and Myles hugged her, but not as warmly as Thalis had. Myles was more reserved, as if, despite his smile, he wasn't as pleased to see her as he let on.

"I was worried after that man wrote to me saying you had been shot," Ursula said.

"That won't ever happen again."

"I beg your pardon?" Ursula couldn't get over the change in him. Thalis was right. Myles dressed differently, carried himself differently. Then there was the scattergun, which Myles held against his leg as if to keep her from seeing it.

"We saw to Mr. Abraham Tweed," Myles said enigmatically.

"And what's that?" Ursula asked, nodding at his howitzer.

"This little thing?" Myles brought it up and held it in the crook of his elbow. "I don't go anywhere without it. It's why everyone here calls me Shotgun."

"And you like that?"

"I like havin' men step aside when I walk down the street."

"Oh, Myles," Ursula said.

"That's not all," Myles said.

Thal motioned as if to stop him from going on. "She doesn't want to hear about the men you've shot."

"He has?" Ursula said in horror. Taking another life went against everything their parents had taught them.

"Only when I've had to," Myles said.

"That's not entirely true and you know it," Thal said.

"Don't you judge me, big brother. I've told you before."

"Please," Ursula said. "Let's not argue. Not after we're all together again after so long apart."

Her brothers might have gone on spatting anyway, but just then a man in immaculate clothes, who had emerged unnoticed, leaned on a cane and said, "Gentlemen, gentlemen. I agree with your lovely sister. You shouldn't be at each other's throats."

"We hadn't gone that far," Thal said.

The man ignored him. Coming up to Ursula, he gave a courtly bow. "Trevor Galt, at your service, my dear." Lightly grasping her fingertips, he raised the back of her hand to his lips. "How do you do?"

"Oh my," Ursula exclaimed.

"I happen to be the mayor," Galt continued suavely. "Your brother is one of my special deputies, as are the gentlemen who escorted you here from Deadwood." He gestured at the Manor House. "This hotel? I own it, as I do half a dozen saloons and twice again as many businesses. Between those and my other interests, it's safe to say I'm a man of some importance."

Ursula realized he was trying to impress her. He hadn't let go of her hand so she pulled her fingers free and smiled courteously. "You don't say."

"Yes," Trevor Galt said, gazing up and down Main Street. "American City is my brainchild. I organized the first expedition here, I laid out the town according to how I saw fit, and now I oversee its day-to-day affairs. Nothing happens here without my consent."

Ursula pretended to be awed. "My word. You're a man of considerable importance."

"You have no idea, my dear," Galt said.

"He's lettin' us have rooms for free," Thal revealed, "for as long as we stay."

"Exactly so," Trevor Galt said. "You have

only to express a desire, and I'll see that it comes true."

"Ain't that kind of you?" Jesse Lee said.

"My only desire right now is to eat," Ursula said. "We've spent all the day in the saddle and I'm wore out. Is there a restaurant you'd recommend?"

"There's one I happen to own," Galt said with a grin. "It's down the street a ways. I'll escort you there, personally."

Before Ursula could say that wasn't necessary, Galt had hold of her elbow and was guiding her away. She glanced at Jesse Lee and her brothers. "You're coming too?"

"Count on it," Jesse Lee said.

Ursula knew he was angry, but she couldn't very well refuse their host's hospitality. She told herself that Galt was being courteous, nothing more.

"You truly are striking, my dear," he remarked. "Myles and Thalis gave me no idea."

"Why should they?" Ursula said. "They're my brothers."

"Even a brother can appreciate beauty. I'm not averse to admitting that I appreciate yours."

"Posh," Ursula said. She wasn't used to such compliments. "I'm a farm girl, plain and simple."

"I beg to differ," Galt said. "There's nothing plain about you. Why, a visit to a millinery, and a new dress in the latest fashion, and I daresay you'd turn every head in American City."

"I'm not out to turn heads."

"I am," Trevor Galt said.

CHAPTER 29

The Black Rose Restaurant — which Thal thought a peculiar name — was said to be the most luxurious in American City, and he believed it. From the moment they walked in the door, they were in the lap of luxury. Waiters in purple uniforms waited on them hand and foot. Several chandeliers sparkled on the ceiling. Gleaming brass was everywhere, from the spittoons to the trim on the paneled walls. The tables and chairs were as elegant as everything else; the napkins were tied with purple ribbons.

The manager, a man who ran the place for Trevor Galt, came out to attend to them himself. At Galt's command, several tables were placed in a long row so their entire party could sit together.

Quite a party it was too. There were Galt and the special deputies he'd brought along: Myles, Bull, Mateo, Rafer, Tiny, and Olivant. Two others, Dyson and Carnes, were out making rounds. There was Thal and his pard, and Crawford and Jesse Lee. Lastly there was Ursula, and early on, Thal became worried about her.

Trevor Galt was treating her like his queen. He insisted she sit near him at the head of the tables so they could talk. Ursula gave in, but Thal knew his sister well enough to know that she wasn't happy about the attention Galt was heaping on her.

Someone else was unhappy too, and it showed.

Jesse Lee looked downright mad. Thal had never seen him scowl so much. Jesse kept giving Galt dark looks, and Thal wasn't the only one who noticed. At one point, he saw Mateo nudge Tiny, flick a finger at Jesse Lee, and say something into Tiny's ear that caused the diminutive gunman's dark eyes to narrow and glitter.

Myles was up at the head of the table too. Ursula kept trying to hold a conversation with him, and Galt kept inserting himself.

The mystery of Jesse Lee was cleared up when Ned poked Thal with an elbow and leaned toward him.

"Pard?" he whispered.

"What?" Thal said, watching Galt contrive to place his hand on Ursula's wrist.

"There's somethin' you should know,"

327

Ned whispered. "I found out about it on the way here."

"I'm listenin'," Thal said. He refused to be distracted from his sister. She was in a pickle.

"It's about your sis."

"Can you get to it or will this take a month of Sundays?"

"Why are you snappin' at me?" Ned said. "I'm doin' you a favor by lettin' you know. It surpised me considerably and it will surprise you too."

"Ned, consarn it," Thal said.

Ned bent farther and looked around as if afraid he'd be overheard. "It's about Ursula."

"You already said that."

"She's hitched herself."

"My sister is a horse now?" Thal said impatiently.

"What? No. That's plumb ridiculous. How can a horse hitch itself? Some horses are smart, sure, but I never yet met one that can loop a rein around a hitch rail."

"My sister, Ned."

"What about her?"

"I'm fixin' to hit you."

"Oh. She's hitched herself to the man she wants to spend the rest of her days with."

Thal forgot all about the shenanigans at

the head of the table, and turned. "Who are you talkin' about?"

Ned chuckled. "Are you blind as well as silly? Who else but Jesse Lee Hardesty, yonder?"

Thal stared across at the Southerner, who was at the next table, close to Ursula. Thal had wondered why Crawford and Jesse Lee didn't sit across from him and Ned, and now he knew. It explained the dark looks Jesse Lee was giving Trevor Galt. "No."

"Yes," Ned said. "And it's partly your own doin'. You're the one who left him to look after her. That was sort of like leavin' a wolf to guard a lamb. Now, if I had stayed with her, this wouldn't have happened. Well, unless she fell in love with me like she fell in love with him."

Thal was hardly listening. All he could think of was Ursula and Jesse Lee. He knew his sister. He knew that once she made up her mind about something, it took an act of the Almighty to change it. If she had set her feather on Jesse Lee, then he was the one, and every other man be hanged.

Ned poked him again.

"Eh?" Thal said, wishing his pard would fill his mouth with food.

"What will you do?"

"What can I do?" Thal said. His sister

wouldn't stand for any meddling on his part.

"You're her brother. You ought to do somethin'. Because if things keep on like they are, Jesse Lee is liable to throw down on Galt, and Galt's gunnies ain't about to take that kindly."

"Damnation," Thal said.

Ned wasn't done. "Jesse Lee is quick. Maybe the quickest I've ever seen. I'll give him that. But quick won't help a lot against eight hired guns, if we include your brother." He paused. "Where do you reckon your brother will stand if lead starts to fly? With Galt or with us?"

Thal couldn't begin to guess. Myles had changed so much he was unpredictable.

"You're closer to Crawford than me," Ned whispered. "Why don't you lean over and tell him what's goin' on and have him rein in Jesse Lee if it looks like his pard is about to do somethin'?"

It was a good idea, but Thal would have to lean so far it would be obvious to everyone else, and Trevor Galt might wonder what he was up to.

"Well? What are you waitin' for?"

"Not yet," Thal said. "We'll talk to them both, later."

"It might be too late by then," Ned said. "Jesse Lee has steam comin' out of his ears."

Just then Ursula happened to glance down the row of tables. Thal caught her eye and gave a barely perceptible nod at Jesse Lee to warn her.

Ursula was worried sick. She'd already seen that the man she loved was fuming, and she wanted him to know things were fine, that she couldn't care less about Trevor Galt. But Galt was taking liberties, touching her when she didn't care to be touched. Only her wrist and her arm, but that was more than enough.

The man presumed too much, and she was tempted to slap him. But she was worried about what Jesse might do. Or Thalis and the other cowboys, for that matter. Myles, she was uncertain about. He might take her side, he might not. Then there were all those gun sharks at the other end of the tables. The so-called special deputies. A pack of killers was more like it, to her way of thinking.

The cowboys wouldn't stand a chance.

In a quandary, Ursula wasn't listening to what Trevor Galt was saying, and it annoyed her when he squeezed her wrist to get her attention. "What was that?" she said.

"Aren't you paying attention, my dear?"

Ursula made excuses. "It's been a long

day. I did mention I'm very tired, didn't I?"

"Yes, you did," Galt said. "I was merely saying that it would please me greatly if you would agree to attend the theater with me tomorrow night. It's not as grand as the Gem, over in Deadwood, but the acts are entertaining."

"I don't know," Ursula hedged.

"Why would you refuse?" Galt asked, a slight edge to his tone. "It's only for fun, I assure you."

"If my brother and his friends come along, I suppose."

"If you insist," Galt said, not sounding happy at the prospect.

Ursula smiled sweetly. "My ma always says that a young lady should never go anywhere without a chaperone."

"Does she, now?"

"Otherwise a girl can get a reputation as being loose and free, and I wouldn't want that. I am anything but loose."

Galt was scowling. "Of course you're not."

"So, yes, my brother and his friends will be my chaperones, and we'd be happy to go anywhere you like." Especially since, Ursula reflected, tomorrow night would be their last in American City. They would leave the morning after, and good riddance to the Black Hills.

"You Americans and your quaint cus-
toms," Galt said.

"Where are you from?" Ursula was curious.

"Bristol, England," Galt said. "I was born
and raised there. I suppose my accent gives
me away. Try as I might, I can't seem to
lose it."

"Tell me about it," Ursula said, moving
her arm so his hand no longer touched her.

"Bristol is a port," Galt said distractedly.
"One of the busiest. There are, oh, I don't
know, about a hundred thousand people by
now."

"Goodness, that's a lot. What else?"

"My time there was unremarkable. It's
dull compared to here. My countrymen are
very set in their ways. Stodgy, you might
say. You can't carry firearms. And you
certainly can't shoot anyone and get away
with it."

"Why would you want to do that?"

"I didn't mean myself, personally," Galt
said. "I was talking about America in general. Or the West, at any rate. Shootings take
place all the time. In Kansas, I understand,
the cow towns all have their very own boot
hills where the dear departed are laid to
rest."

"Sad to say," Ursula said.

"You don't approve?"

"Of all the shooting affrays?" Ursula realized Jesse Lee must be listening, and remembered his defense of her in Deadwood. "There are times when it's justified. But there are just as many, if not more, when it's not."

"I wouldn't argue with that," Galt said. "But I must confess, I find the whole concept invigorating."

"Concept?"

"Of a man being able to mold his own destiny by dint of his intelligence and will, and a loaded six-gun."

Ursula gazed down the tables. "Or eight of them? Isn't that how many special deputies you have?"

"Surely you don't hold that against me?" Galt said. "Every town needs law and order."

"Even a town where anything goes?"

Galt laughed. "You're sharp, my dear. That's the lure to bring people here. Why else would they come? The other towns in the hills have as much gold and as many attractions. American City needed something to set it apart. Something special. So I hit on the idea of letting everyone think it was wide-open. That every heart's desire could be fulfilled. But that, as I say, was a lure, and nothing more."

"American City seems pretty wide-open to me," Ursula said.

"Indeed," Galt said. "But within certain limits. Hence, my special deputies. They instill a degree of law and order while giving the impression there isn't any."

"There's still too much violence for my taste." Ursula much preferred the peace and serenity of a place like Salina. "I've heard a lot of shooting since we arrived."

"That's normal. Don't let it sway your opinion," Galt said. "I'm hoping you might be induced to stay around awhile. Spend time with your brother Myles. And in my company as well."

Ursula figured the time had come to tell him that she was spoken for, but as luck would have it, two hard-looking men came hurrying into the restaurant and over to their table.

"Mr. Galt," the taller said. "Sorry to bother you but it's important."

Galt sat back. "Miss Christie, you must pardon me. These are more of my special deputies." He indicated the tall one, who had a hooked nose and a sallow complexion. "This is Mr. Dyson. The other is Mr. Carnes." The latter wore a fur coat, of all things, even though it was summer. Rising, the three moved off a short way.

Ursula looked over at Jesse Lee. "Thank you," she said.

"For what?"

"For not doing what you hankered to do."

Myles, who had hardly uttered a word since they got there, perked up. "What was that?"

"Nothing," Ursula said.

Fortunately Trevor Galt returned to the table. "I have bad news, my dear. I am afraid I must go deal with an issue that has arisen. And my deputies must go with me."

"All of them?"

"I'll leave Bull with the rest of you. But I need Myles to come. I might have need of that shotgun of his."

At the other end of the tables, Bull let out a bellow. "Mr. Galt, there's somethin' I've been meanin' to tell you. Somethin' you should know about —"

Galt gestured sharply. "Not now. You can tell me whatever it is later." He smiled at Ursula, wheeled, and departed with his other special deputies in tow.

Thank goodness, Ursula thought. She went to take a sip of water and caught Thalis giving her the look he did when he was upset with her. "What?"

"We need to talk," her brother said, "and I don't mean tomorrow."

CHAPTER 30

Ursula hardly ever paced. She didn't have a nervous disposition, as some did. A cousin of hers couldn't still if her life depended on it, but now her. Ursula was usually calm about things. Even when life threw a crisis at her, she kept her wits, and her nerves, about her.

Not now. She was waiting for her brother and Jesse Lee to come to her room. They had gone to their own rooms to give Bull the impression that they were turning in for the night. Once Bull left, they'd be right over. Their rooms were just down the hall.

She could guess what Thal wanted to talk about. On the ride from Deadwood she had worked out how she would put it to him, and she was all set.

A commotion out in the street drew her to the window. Parting the curtains, she peered down. She was worried Trevor Galt had returned, but no, a couple of men, their anger fueled by too much liquor, were quarreling. She closed the curtains and continued to pace.

A light knock on her door caused her to jump. Scooting over, Ursula unlocked it and peeked out.

"What are you waitin' for?" Thal asked.

Ursula opened the door wide and he slipped inside.

"Bull went downstairs," Thal let her know.

"Where's Jesse Lee?"

"In his room with Crawford," Thal said, moving to a chair. "Which gives us time to talk before he gets here."

"No."

"I beg your pardon?"

"Whatever you have to say, you can say to the two of us." Ursula informed him.

"It's gone that far?"

Before Ursula could answer, there was another, firmer, knock. She yanked on the door handle and threw herself at Jesse Lee, who acted surprised but embraced her. Rubbing his neck with her nose, she breathed, "Together again at last."

Jesse Lee coughed, glanced over his shoulder, and quickly drew her in and closed the door behind them. Only then did he see her brother. "Thal," he said.

"So Ned was right," Thal said. "I shouldn't

have left you alone with her."

Ursula whirled on him. "Don't you dare. This is as much my doing as his. We fell in love, plain and simple. I was going to break it to you easy, but now easy can be hanged." She gripped Jesse Lee's left hand. Not his right. He'd cautioned her about that in Deadwood.

"Sis!" Thal exclaimed.

"Don't sound so shocked. A woman can cuss as well as a man." Ursula paused. "Jesse and I are getting married. We haven't set a date yet, but he's asked me and I've accepted."

"You've made your choice, then."

Ursula saw no reason to belabor the obvious.

"What about Ma and Pa?"

"What about them?" Ursula rejoined. "They're not marrying him. I am. They can give us their blessing or they can have nothing to do with us. That's entirely up to them."

"You'd turn your back on Ma if she was against it?"

"No, she'd be turning her back on me," Ursula said. "A person has a right to marry who she wants, and I will not let anyone stand in our way. Not her. Not Pa. Not you."

Thal sighed. "Where did this ferocity

come from?"

"It's always been there. Maybe you just didn't notice." Ursula led Jesse Lee to the bed and they perched on the edge. She sat so that their shoulders and legs touched.

"I wish I had known sooner," Thal said.

"What difference would it make?"

"I might have insisted that if Myles wanted to see you, he should go to Deadwood instead of having you brought here."

"I don't care where I see him."

"Do you care if Trevor Galt takes a dislike to your fiancée?"

"Let him," Jesse Lee said.

"Why would he?" Ursula said. "What I do is nothing to him."

"That's where you're wrong," Thal said. "I might not be the sharpest knife in the toolshed, but I can see that Galt has taken a shine to you. It sounded to me as if he wants to wine and dine you, as the fancy folks say."

"He can wine and dine Bull."

Thal laughed, without much mirth. "This is serious. There's no tellin' how Galt will take the news. He might set some of his special deputies on Jesse Lee."

"Let him," Jesse Lee said again.

"No," Ursula said. She was unwilling to put him at risk. "We'll keep it a secret a little longer. I'd rather not, but what can one

341

more day hurt? Then we'll light a shuck for Deadwood." She caressed Jesse's hand. "Does that sit all right with you? Can you control your temper that long?"

"I won't have to."

"You're not fixin' to brace Galt, are you?" Thal said in alarm. "That'd put all of us in danger."

"If it comes to that, I will," Jesse Lee said. "But I won't have to control my temper because the cat will be out of the bag."

"You're going to tell Galt about us?" Ursula said in dismay. Twenty-four hours. That was all they needed, plus a little more, and they'd be shed of American City.

"You're not usin' that noggin of yours," Jesse Lee said. "Who else knows about you and me besides Thalis?"

"Ned does," Ursula said. "He figured it out on the ride from Deadwood."

"He wasn't the only one. Or have you forgotten?"

Ursula sat bolt upright. "Bull and that Mateo and Rafer. They were along too."

"And what was Bull saying to Galt at the restaurant right before Galt went hurryin' off?"

"Oh no," Ursula said. The remembrance brought a rush of fear. "Bull said he had something to tell Galt."

"Guess what it will be."

Thal came out of his chair and began doing what Ursula had done a short while ago: pacing. "This can turn ugly. I've seen how Galt can be when he's mad, and I suspect I haven't seen the worst. The man doesn't like to be bucked. Not by anyone."

"It's not as if I set out to deceive him," Ursula said.

"He might think different," Thal said. "You had all night to tell him you were engaged, but did you? You did not. You let Galt treat you to a meal, and you didn't slap his hand when he fondled your arm."

"He did no such thing," Ursula said angrily.

"Take that back," Jesse Lee said.

"Forget I said it, then," Thal said. "We need to make tracks before Galt comes back. I'll go get Ned and Craw and we can be long gone before Galt shows up."

"What about Myles?" Ursula said. "I've hardly gotten to peak to him."

"Who's more important?" Thal said. "Him or Jesse Lee?"

Ursula saw what he was getting at, and felt a prick of conscience that Jesse Lee mattered more to her than one of her own brothers.

"I hate tuckin' tail," Jesse Lee said.

"Are we agreed or not?" Thal said. "Time's a-wastin'. Every minute counts if we're to make it out of here without any trouble."

"We're agreed," Ursula said. "Hurry and fetch them."

Thal couldn't move fast enough.

Bringing his sister to American City had been a mistake. He'd realized that the moment he saw Trevor Galt set eyes on her.

Thal felt sorry that they wouldn't get to spend more time with Myles, but as Myles kept pointing out, he was a grown man and didn't need them to look after him.

Ned was seated glumly on the bed, fiddling with the fringe on the quilt, when Thal entered. "You're back sooner than I expected."

"Pack your things," Thal said. "We're fannin' the breeze." His saddlebags were on the chest of drawers. The only items he'd taken out were his razor and his hairbrush, which he quickly replaced. When he turned, Ned was still sitting there. "Didn't you hear me?"

Moving much too slowly for Thal's liking, Ned rose. "Where are we headin', if I'm not bein' too nosy?"

"Texas," Thal said. "And what's gotten

into you? You're actin' like you're on your last legs."

"I can't get over that she picked him instead of me."

"Would you rather it was Trevor Galt?"

"Over my dead body," Ned said,

"It might come to that if you don't light a fire under your backside. We're leavin' before Galt comes back. He might not want us to."

"We're grown men. We can do as we please." Ned stepped to the washbasin to collect his effects.

"Let's not push our luck," Thal advised.

"You reckon he'd go that far? Try to stop us?"

"Didn't you see him droolin' over my sister?"

Ned moved faster.

With their saddlebags over their shoulders, and their rifles in hand, they went to the next room down.

Thal knocked.

"Who is it?" Crawford asked from inside.

"Ned and me."

The door opened. Crawford was naked from the waist up, with a towel in his hand. "I wanted to be sure it wasn't your sister. Jesse Lee would think poorly of me if I let her see me with my shirt off."

"We have a bigger problem than your bare ribs," Thal said, and told him about their decision to skedaddle.

"Can't say I'm sorry to hear it," Crawford said. "I've never liked anywhere less than this place."

"Your shirt," Thal said, "and less talk."

"Give me a minute."

Ned was watching the stairs and nervously fingering his saddlebag. "Just so you know, I don't have any hard feelin's toward Jesse Lee. She picked who she picked."

"Good to know you've matured," Thal said.

"When was I ever not?"

A shadow moved on the landing, and into the hall lumbered Bull. For someone so huge, he could move as quietly as an Apache. "Gents," he said, smiling, but it promptly faded. "What are you up to?"

"Nothin'," Thal said.

"Then why the saddlebags?"

"No reason," Ned said.

Bull balled his big hands. "Do you think I'm dumb? You're fixin' to go somewhere, and Mr. Galt might not want you to."

"He doesn't rule us," Ned said.

Bull snorted. "Cowboy, he rules everybody in American City, and don't you think he doesn't. He didn't give me orders about whether you can go anywhere or not, so I'll have to ask you to stay put until he gets back."

"If we refuse?" Ned said.

"I once walloped five men with my fists. They jumped me in a saloon, and I busted their bones." Bull raised a callused fist toward them. "Do you want some of the same?"

Thal figured to reason with him, but Ned didn't know when to keep quiet.

"You can't tell us what to do, you tub of lard. It's a free country, or ain't you heard?"

"You just insulted me."

"I'll do it again if you don't step aside and let us pass," Ned blustered.

Thrusting his jaw out, Bull came toward them. "I'm beginnin' not to like you."

"Hold on," Thal said, moving between them. "How about if my pard and me go back to our room and we forget all about this?"

Crawford chose that moment to step out, fully dressed, with his saddlebags and rifle. "We all set?"

"So I was right," Bull said. "All three of you go in that room and we'll wait for Mr. Galt."

Thal was inclined to do as Bull wanted, but Ned went up to him and poked him in

347

the chest.

"I've had enough of you bossin' us around."

"Mister, I've only started. You forget I'm a special deputy."

"A special jackass is more like it," Ned said.

Bull hit him.

CHAPTER 31

The blow smashed Ned against the wall. He was able to stay on his feet but only because the wall held him up.

Bull drew his fist back to punch him again.

Thal sprang to his pard's defense. He'd only ever been in two fights in his life, both when he was much younger. His natural reaction was to draw his revolver, but a gunshot might bring the desk clerk or someone else to investigate, and word would get to Trevor Galt. Instead he swung his fist with all his strength and slugged Bull squarely on the jaw.

It was like hitting an anvil. Pain exploded up Thal's arm clear to his shoulder. He thought he'd broken his hand but had no time to examine it.

Bull spun and drove his own fist into the pit of Thal's stomach, doubling him over. He heard Crawford curse, and a flurry of movement, and looked up to see the older

349

puncher go down from a blow to the temple. Bull was beating all three of them.

Girding himself, Thal leaped. He landed a couple of punches, though they had no effect, then blocked a looping left that drove him back a couple of steps. Bull was immensely strong. His nickname was well deserved.

"Damn cowboys," Bull growled, and waded in.

All Thal could do was block and sidestep. He succeeded in sparing himself from five or six punches, but then one slipped through and it felt as if his ribs caved in. The world swam, and he staggered. Fingers as thick as railroad spikes gripped his throat, and his breath was choked off.

"I'm goin' to break your bones."

Thal's vision cleared.

Bull towered above him, that huge fist cocked.

There was a silvery flash, and a thud, and the giant grunted. A second flash, and a second thud, caused Bull's grip to weaken. At a third streak of silver, Bull's legs buckled and he oozed to the floor in a giant pile.

Over him stood Jesse Lee, with his ivory-handled Colt. "I should have just shot him."

Ursula was there too, grabbing hold of Thal so he wouldn't fall. "Are you all right?"

"Fine," Thal gasped, although his throat and his ribs were welters of pain.

Crawford was picking himself up from the floor. "That mountain of muscle about stove my face in." His nose was bleeding, and he wiped at it with a sleeve.

Ned had recovered enough to come over and kick Bull in the side. "For two bits I'd stove in his head."

"We have to get out of here," Ursula urged. "Galt could return any minute, and there's no telling how he'll take this."

Thal could guess. The lord of American City wouldn't like having one of his special deputies knocked senseless. Nor would Galt like it that they were intent on lighting a shuck without a by-your-leave.

Jesse Lee twirled his Colt into his holster. "Sometime this year, gents," he said. "We have to get Ursula out of here."

They hurried to the stairs and started down, moving as quietly as they could.

Thal was out in front, his sister and the Southerner holding hands behind him, Ned and Crawford at the rear. He came to the next landing and passed a man in a suit coming the other way. Slowing, Thal smiled and nodded, and the man did the same.

Five or six people were lounging or talking in the lobby. Over at the front desk, the clerk was busy checking someone in.

"Act natural," Thal said over his shoulder. No one paid any attention. He reached the glass-and-brass doors and pushed out into the night.

"So far, so good," Ned said.

"Don't jinx us," Crawford said.

Main Street bustled with activity, as always.

Their horses were at the hitch rail. Ned scooted to his and threw his saddlebags on. "I'm not lettin' any grass grow under me."

Thal couldn't get out of there fast enough either. It had been a mistake, coming all this way to check on a brother who didn't want to be checked on. But then, how was he to know how much Myles had changed? The Kansas farm boy Thal grew up with had turned into a paid assassin.

They shoved their rifles into their saddle scabbards and prepared to mount up and go.

"What's all this?"

Thal nearly jumped at his brother's voice. Plastering a smile on his face, he turned.

Myles had come up unnoticed. He wasn't alone. The deputy called Rafer stood to one side, his thumbs hooked in his gun belt.

"Are all of you goin' somewhere?" Myles said.

Thal hesitated, and looked at the others. They appeared as unsure of what to say as he was.

"Didn't you hear me?"

It was Ursula who recovered her wits first. "We're taking our mounts to the livery stable."

"That's right," Ned said. "We don't want to leave them out in the street if we're goin' to be here a couple more days."

"I'll show you the way," Myles offered.

"You don't need to," Thal said. "We know where it is." Truth was, they weren't stopping until they were well out in the wilds.

"It's no bother, big brother," Myles said.

"What's with them?" Rafer said to him. "They're actin' peculiar."

"We're tired, is all," Ursula said. "We haven't had any rest all day."

"Which is why you should let me have your animals attended to, my dear," declared Trevor Galt, striding up. The rest of his special deputies were all with him: Mateo, Tiny, Olivant, Dyson, and Carnes.

"We don't want to put you to any bother," Ursula said.

"Nonsense," Galt said in that oily way he had. "Haven't I made it plain that you are my special guests?"

Thal was rooted in consternation. To try

to leave now would make Galt suspicious. But what else could they do, with Bull lying upstairs unconscious?

Grasping at a straw, he said, "We're Texans. We see to our own animals."

"You're from Kansas," Galt said in amusement, "and the young one there is from the South."

"Still," Thal said.

"We'd much rather do it ourselves," Ursula said, backing him up.

Galt leaned on his cane, his brow furrowing. "Why are you making such a fuss? I'm doing you a kindness."

"Yes, why are you?" Myles said.

Thal wasn't about to antagonize them. Not when lead might fly, and with his sister there. An inspiration came over him, and he said, "If you really want to, then go ahead and see to our horses. We're goin' back upstairs and turnin' in." Before Galt could object or anyone say anything, he wheeled and pushed on through the double doors. Crossing swiftly to the stairs, he took them two at a time. He must be quick. It might already be too late. A glance showed that the others had followed, and that they were confused.

"What are you doing?" Ursula said, catching up.

"Savin' our hash," Thal replied. "I hope."

Once out of sight of the lobby, Thal ran. He reached the third floor and smiled on seeing that Bull still lay on the floor, out to the world. No one had come across him yet. "Hurry," Thal said. "Haul him into the room Ned and me are usin'."

"You've gone loco," Ned said.

It took all of them, straining and puffing, to drag the huge bulk inside. Once they had done so, Thal turned to his pard.

"Did you leave your saddlebags on your horse?"

"What? Oh. I forgot about them," Ned said.

"Go back down and fetch them. Bring your rope too."

"My rope?"

Thal pushed him toward the door. "Don't ask questions. Go now, before they take the horses away, if they haven't already." He gave Ned a shove and closed the door behind him.

"*That's* what you're up to?" Crawford said.

"It was all I could think of," Thal said.

Ursula looked fit to pull her hair out. "It would be nice if one of you would explain it to me. Why didn't we leave? Just climb on our horses and go? They were right there."

"So were Galt and all his gunnies," Thal said.

Jesse Lee touched Ursula's cheek. "Your brother was worried you'd come to harm."

"I don't like being babied," Ursula said.

"Would you rather be dead?" Thal rejoined.

"We're right back where we started," Ursula said. "With that big lump to deal with."

"We'll tie him and gag him and roll him to the other side of the bed where no one can see," Thal proposed. "Then we'll sit tight and along about the middle of the night, sneak out, collect our animals, and fan the breeze."

"Galt is bound to wonder where Bull got to," Ursula pointed out.

"So what?" Thal said. "If Galt asks, we'll act innocent. We'll say we haven't seen Bull since earlier. That should buy us the time we need."

"Good thinkin'," Crawford complimented him.

"I don't know," Ursula said.

"If you have a better idea, sis, let me hear it," Thal said. It was the best he could come up with, given the circumstances.

Just then Bull groaned.

"He's coming around!" Ursula gasped.

"Not if I can help it," Jesse Lee said, and drawing his Colt, he took off Bull's hat and struck him twice over the head. "That should keep him until Ned gets back."

Suddenly weary, Thal leaned against the chest of drawers. They were taking an awful chance. Galt might overlook a lot but not an attack on one of his special deputies. Granted, Bull had thrown the first punch, but still. He wondered if American City had a jail, or whether the deputies always dealt with troublemakers with hot lead, as his brother had done in the saloon.

Ursula came over. "A penny for your thoughts."

"I wish you'd stayed in Kansas." Thal would never forgive himself if anything happened to her. He should have put his foot down back in Cheyenne and thrown her onto a stage.

"We've been all through that," Ursula said. "I was the one who sent for you, remember? I couldn't let you search for Myles alone."

"Myles," Thal said bitterly.

"He's not the brother we knew, is he? Why do you suppose he changed so much?"

"Maybe he didn't," Thal said. "Maybe he was this way all along."

"Balderdash. He and I were close growing

up. We played together, did things together. There wasn't a violent bone in his body. Now he blows men apart for a living."

"None of us are the same as when we were little. It's how life is."

"I want the old Myles back," Ursula said. "The one who wouldn't harm a fly. The one who laughed a lot and was always playful."

"That Myles is gone."

Ursula frowned. "What a terrible thing to say. There must be some of the old Myles left. If we stuck around long enough, we might help him find himself."

"Wishful thinkin'," Thal said, and motioned at the sprawled form on the floor. "And we can't anyway. So put it from your head."

Jesse Lee came closer. "You and Ned will stand guard over him, I take it?"

"He won't take much guardin'," Thal said. "Craw and you can stay with us too if you want." It was better to stick together, he reflected, in case of trouble.

"Craw can," Jesse Lee said. "I'll be with your sister." He held up a hand when Ursula went to speak. "Whether you want me to or not. It's for your own good. I wouldn't put it past Galt to pay you a visit after he thinks we've turned in."

"I was about to say," Ursula said, "that

I'd be happy to have you with me."

Thal imagined the two of them alone in her room, with the bed for company. "Ned can stay with you too."

"Like blazes he will," Jesse Lee said.

"Crawford, then."

"Oh, Thalis," Ursula said. "Don't you trust me? Are you afraid Jesse Lee will make a wanton woman out of me?"

A light knock spared Thal from having to answer. He opened the door a crack and saw it was Ned. "You must have run all the way down there and back," he said, opening the door wider.

"I have the rope," Ned said as he entered, his saddlebags over his shoulder, "and we have trouble."

"More?" Crawford said.

"Galt is on his way up," Ned informed them. "Him and all his deputies besides."

"Oh hell," Crawford said.

CHAPTER 32

Before Thal could close the door, Trevor Galt appeared on the landing down the hall. "Stay hidden," Thal said to his sister and Jesse Lee, and shouldering Ned aside, planted himself in the doorway. He pulled the door partway shut, enough that Galt couldn't see inside. "Did you come to tuck us in?" he joked as the self-appointed mayor and his pack of gun hands approached.

Galt didn't find it humorous. "I'm looking for Bull," he said, glancing up and down the hall.

"He'd be hard to miss."

"I left him here to make sure you and your friends weren't disturbed."

"By who?" Thal said.

"Drunks and such," Galt said. "You don't know where he got to, do you?"

Thal was worried that Bull might regain consciousness any moment and let out a bellow. "He hung around for a short while after you left. Then I heard him talkin' to someone out here."

"To whom?"

"I didn't look," Thal said. "When we went down to stable our animals, Bull was gone."

"You didn't hear what was said?"

"The only thing I heard was Bull saying, 'All right, I'll come.' To be honest, I wasn't payin' much attention. I was talkin' to my sis."

"How very strange," Galt said, and turned. "Shotgun, you stay here with me. I want the rest of you to go downstairs and ask around. Someone must have seen Bull leave."

"On our way," Rafer said.

Galt rubbed his chin. "It's not like Bull not to do as I tell him. Whatever it was that caused him to leave must have been important."

"No doubt," Thal said.

Galt stared at the door to Ursula's room. "Your sister has already turned in, I take it?"

"She has," Thal said, adding to his lies.

"What a shame. I would have liked to talk to her more."

"There's always tomorrow," Thal said.

"Yes, I suppose there is." Galt smiled and started to turn, but stopped. "I've been meaning to ask. That young friend of yours, Hardesty, I believe his name is. . . ."

"Jesse Lee?" Thal said. "What about him?"

"When we were at the restaurant, he kept giving me dirty looks. What was that all about?"

"You'd have to ask him," Thal said. "I have no idea."

"You might want to talk to him about it," Galt said. "I let it pass but I won't be so charitable if he keeps it up. I won't tolerate disrespect, from him or any other man."

"I don't blame you," Thal managed to say with a straight face.

"I'll send Myles to collect all of you for breakfast. Say, about six o'clock?"

"That early?" Thal said. "My sister was hopin' to sleep in. She's plumb tuckered out."

"How would eight be, then?"

"That would be fine," Thal said. Especially since they would be that much farther from American City when Galt realized they were missing.

"Eight it is." Galt took a couple more steps but stopped again when Myles fell in beside him. "What are you doing?"

"Comin' with you. What else?"

"I should think you'd like to spend some time with your brother," Galt said. "He

362

came all the way from Texas. The two of you must have a lot of catching up to do." With a flourish of his cane, he ambled off.

Myles didn't look happy. "Well?" he said.

"Beats me," Thal replied.

"What is there to say?" Myles said.

"I know one thing," Thal said, since he had been wondering about it himself. "Ma and Pa will want to know when you're comin' home. You don't aim to stay in the Black Hills forever, do you?"

Myles shrugged. "I can't rightly say how long it will be. I like it here. I like that I work for the top rooster, and he only has to crow and folks fall over themselves to do anything he wants."

"You like the power."

"I reckon I do, at that," Myles admitted. "Here, I'm somebody. Back in Kansas I was just another farmer."

"What's wrong with that? Pa's a farmer."

"I don't see you wearin' bib overalls and chewin' on a piece of straw. The farmin' life didn't appeal to you any more than it did to me."

Thal had to concede that Myles had him there. "Even so. There's a big difference between nursemaidin' cattle and unlimberin' that scattergun on someone."

"Not that again."

"I can't get over that you kill people," Thal confessed. "Anything else, I might have accepted."

Myles's jaw muscles twitched. "I don't need your acceptance, big brother. I won't be judged, by you or anyone else. If all we're goin' to talk about is that, you might as well go to bed."

"What else, then? Our years growin' up?"

"What would be the point? I'm not the tender-heart I was as a boy. Fact is, I don't think about those days much."

"I'm sorry to hear that."

"If you ask me, sis and you live too much in the past. People change, Thalis. If I were to go home, I wouldn't enjoy myself. I'd be restless to come back to the life I like."

"Ursula and you were always close," Thal reminded him.

"When we were knee-high to a calf," Myles said. "It was fun playin' in the hay and runnin' through the corn and all the other things we did. But that was then. I don't play in hay anymore, and the only use I have for corn is to eat it."

"You've grown hard, Myles."

Myles shrugged a second time. "I see the world as it is, not as I used to. It's dog-eat-dog, and if you want things in life, you have to be the hardest dog around." He softened a little, and smiled. "Look. It's good that you like bein' a cowpoke. It seems to fit you, just as what I do fits me."

"If you say so."

"There you go again. You think I should be more like you, and won't accept me as me."

"Ursula isn't happy about the change in you either."

"That's too bad. She's always been a good sister. I'm sorry if I hurt her feelin's, but she has to do some growin' up of her own. I'm not the little boy she remembers, and the Black Hills ain't Kansas."

"Some say they're hell on earth," Thal said.

"Then hell's not as terrible as the parsons paint it. It's got all the things I like, and then some. When I die, I hope I end up in hell and not the other place."

"You don't mean that."

Myles sighed. "Do you see how you are? Talkin' to you is pointless." He cradled his scattergun, wheeled, and departed. At the landing he looked back, sadly shook his head, and descended out of sight.

Thal coughed to be rid of a constriction in his throat. When someone touched his elbow, he didn't need to look to know who it was. "You heard him, sis?"

"Every word," Ursula said.

"It was a mistake, us comin' here."

"He's our brother."

"Not anymore."

"Oh, Thalis."

Thal turned. Her eyes were misting, and he hugged her. "It hurts, I know. But it's the truth. Any ties we had aren't there anymore."

"I don't believe that," Ursula said. "Myles would be there for us if we really and truly needed him."

Thal very much doubted it. Their brother was lost to them, in spirit if not in flesh. "He won't shed any tears when we go."

Jesse Lee stepped around the door. "About that. What time do you want to light a shuck?"

"Three or so," Thal said. By then Galt and his special deputies would have turned in, and the streets would be mostly empty.

"My pard and me will wait in her room," Jesse Lee said, taking Ursula's arm. "She needs to get some rest." Beckoning to Crawford, he ushered her to the next door.

Thal went to his bed and sat. He was so tired he wasn't sure he was thinking straight. Tired, and sad. He'd always liked his brother, always liked that they had always gotten along. Until now.

Thal completely forgot that Ned was there until Ned spoke.

"We trussed up the buffalo while you were jawin' with Galt. He won't get loose without help."

Thal slid to the corner of the bed and peered over.

Bull was wrapped from boots to neck in coil after coil of rope. His wrists and ankles were bound, and something blue stuck out of his mouth.

"You gagged him with your dirty bandanna?" Thal realized.

"It was the only thing handy," Ned said.

Thal sank onto his back with his fingers laced behind his head. He should try to get some sleep too, but his mind was galloping like a horse.

"Why do you suppose your sister picked Jesse Lee over me?" Ned asked him.

"Not now," Thal said.

"Is it that he's her age? And easy on the eyes? Or is it that accent of his? I hear ladies are fond of accents."

"Did you also hear about the puncher who shot his pard because his pard didn't know when to hush up?"

"Ha-ha," Ned said. "My heart is broke and you make jokes."

"You'll live," Thal said, "and there will be

other gals."

"Not for me. Your sister was my one and only. I fell head over heels the moment I laid eyes on her."

"Have you looked in the mirror lately?"

"What for?"

"You have brown goo tricklin' out your ears."

"You mock true love?"

"I mock you," Thal said. "Or have you forgotten that filly over to San Antonio? The one you fell in love with. The one you pined after for months. The one who was goin' to be Mrs. Ned Leslie."

"She would have been too, except that someone else asked her first," Ned said.

"You're hopeless."

"I can tell you're in one of your moods." Ned went to the window and gazed out. "I'll be switched."

"Is your filly out there?"

"Olivant and Tiny are. They're across the street, lookin' up at our window."

Thal sat up. "Don't let them see you."

"Too late." Ned made a show of looking up and down the street, then closed the curtains. "Come see for yourself."

"No need," Thal said. It might seem suspicious if he were to look out the window too.

"Do you reckon Galt left them there to

keep watch on us?"

"What else?" Thal said. Which meant Trevor Galt had suspicions of his own. "We'll have to sneak out the back of the hotel when we go."

"The livery is only a couple of blocks away. We should get there with no problem."

Thal didn't share his friend's optimism. "You know," he said, as a troubling thought occurred to him, "none of us went along when Galt had our horses tended to. How do we know he took them to the livery? What if he took them somewhere else to keep us from leavin'?"

"If his brain is as devious as yours, he might have," Ned said.

Thal got up and took to pacing again. Just what he needed. Something else to worry about.

"I've been thinkin'," Ned said.

"We're in trouble."

"I'm serious. Remember when we were out on the range? And I said how I was hankerin' to go gallivantin' around and see more of the world?"

"I do," Thal said.

"I didn't realize how good we had it. There's a lot to be said for havin' a steady job and earnin' decent wages and not havin' someone out to shoot you or knife you or beat on you with their fists."

"So our world tour is off?"

"Go to hell," Ned said, but he grinned as he said it.

"Didn't you hear my brother?" Thal said. "We're already there. The trick will be to make it out alive."

CHAPTER 33

Ursula couldn't sleep no matter how she tried. She'd curled up on the bed while Crawford dozed in the chair and Jesse Lee kept watch at their window. A little while ago he'd whispered that two special deputies were across the street, keeping an eye on the hotel.

That worried her. Escaping from American City might not be as easy as she'd hoped.

She couldn't stop thinking of Trevor Galt, and the man's sheer, unmitigated gall. No man had the right to impose himself on a woman, and that was exactly what Galt was trying to do.

She'd only been in the man's company a short while, but that was enough for her to read the man's character as if he were a book. Trevor Galt was all about Trevor Galt. He saw himself as God Almighty, at least as far as American City was concerned. His interest in her had been sparked by one thing and one thing only: pure and simple lust. She saw it in his eyes.

Ursula felt only revulsion for a man like him. All those times he'd touched her at the restaurant — it made her skin crawl. She'd been tempted to slap him, but that would aggravate matters.

As it was, she had unwittingly placed her brother and his friends in peril.

If she'd stayed in Kansas, none of this would be happening, but what sort of sister would she be if he hadn't wanted to see with her own eyes that Myles was all right?

Myles. Just thinking about him almost brought tears to her eyes. He'd changed so much. He wasn't the nice, friendly boy he'd been on the farm. He'd become twisted somehow, deep inside. He'd shown so little warmth toward her, she had to wonder if any had ever truly been there.

She tried to put everything from her mind so she could rest for the ride ahead, and couldn't. She was too overwrought. For once, her calm demeanor failed her.

Along about one in the morning, she decided enough was enough, and sat up.

Crawford was still asleep in the chair.

Jesse Lee stood to one side of the window, leaning against the wall, his arms folded.

He looked over and smiled. "You look right pretty with your hair mussed like that," he said quietly.

Sliding off the bed, Ursula went to the mirror. In her tossing and turning, she'd made a mess of her hair. "Wonderful," she said. She took her brush from her bag and set to putting herself in order.

Jesse Lee came over, his spurs jingling slightly. "I didn't mean to upset you."

"It's not the hair," Ursula said. "I'm worried about all of us getting out of here in one piece."

"I won't let anything happen to you."

"There are a lot of those special deputies," Ursula mentioned, "and Galt himself."

"He strikes me as the kind who lets others do his killin'."

Ursula stopped stroking, and scowled. "If any of you lost your lives on my account . . ." She didn't finish.

"This is on Myles's shoulders, not yours. He's the one who came here. He's the one who got involved with Galt. He's the one who took to usin' a scattergun for his livin'."

"I know."

Jesse Lee wasn't done. "If Myles was half the brother you thought he was, he'd be mad at Galt for tryin' to force himself on you, and see you safely out of town. A

373

brother should stick with his family above all else."

"I know," Ursula said again.

"Then quit blamin' yourself." Jesse Lee leaned in to plant a kiss on her cheek.

Turning, Ursula kissed him full on the lips instead. She yearned to melt into his arms, but they weren't man and wife yet. So she settled for a lingering kiss and a tender embrace.

"That was nice," Jesse Lee said when she drew back.

"Wasn't it, though?" Ursula said dreamily. "A thing like that could get to be a habit."

Jesse Lee grinned. "A habit like that is one I'd do a lot."

"I certainly hope so." Ursula placed her cheek to his chest and wished she could keep it there forever. For a few moments she forgot about Trevor Galt and American City and Myles and all the rest.

Then there was a soft knock on the door, and she gave a start.

Placing his hand on his Colt, Jesse Lee went over. Poised to draw, he jerked the door open. "You," he said.

Thal slipped inside. "I've changed my mind. We're not goin' to wait until three. We should go while the streets are still fairly crowded. It will be harder for Galt or his deputies to spot us."

"You know about the pair across the street?" Jesse Lee asked.

"I do."

"Has Bull come around?"

"He started to, but Ned hit him over the head again. Two or three times." Thal smiled at Ursula. "Be ready in five minutes." Without waiting for a reply, he slipped back out.

Ursula's gut balled into a knot. They weren't out of the room yet, and she was scared. Not for herself. For Jesse Lee and Thal and the other two.

Jesse Lee had closed the door and gone to the chair. "Pard?" he said, and shook Crawford.

The older puncher mumbled something.

"Craw, consarn it," Jesse Lee said. He glanced at her. "Wakin' him up can be like tryin' to wake Methuselah." He shook harder.

Crawford blinked and sat up and adjusted his hat. "What is it?" he asked sleepily. "I was havin' the pleasantest dream."

"We're leavin' sooner than we thought," Jesse Lee said. "Thal's idea."

"Suits me," Crawford said, stretching. "This place doesn't agree with me. Too many sidewinders."

Jesse Lee grunted. "I never saw anywhere where so many snakes need stompin'. Which is why I have a favor to ask."

"Anything," Crawford said.

"If somethin' happens to me, you're to look after her."

The mere notion of harm coming to Jesse caused Ursula's heart to flutter. She noticed that he'd avoided looking at her as he said it.

"That goes without sayin', pard," Crawford said.

"I'm sayin' it anyhow. See that she gets to her folks. I'm countin' on you, Craw. I don't need to say how much she means to me, do I?"

Crawford shook his head.

"Don't talk like that," Ursula chided.

"It had to be said," Jesse Lee replied. He still didn't look her way.

"I can look after myself," Ursula said. "Give me a gun. I know how to use them."

"That's not what it's about."

"Don't talk about something happening to you." Ursula kept her voice level with an effort. "I don't like it."

"No one can predict," Jesse Lee said.

Going over, Ursula clasped his hand to force him to face her. He did, reluctantly. She could see how moved he was. She swallowed to clear her throat. "We're in this together. From now on, we're in everything together."

"You're more important."

"The blazes I am," Ursula said. "You mean as much to me as I do to you. So, Crawford?"

"Ma'am?" Crawford said uncertainly.

"If he takes a bullet, you're to forget about me and do what you can to get him to his horse and out of town alive. Do you hear me?"

"Oh, Ursula," Jesse Lee said.

"Don't 'Oh, Ursula' me," Ursula said indignantly. "I won't be treated differently than you."

"You have to be."

"Explain to me why."

"You're female."

"Don't give me that baggage. I didn't take you for one of those men who lords it over his woman."

Jesse Lee seemed to choose his next words carefully. "Love ain't lordin'. You're right in that a man who puts his woman first is no different than a woman who puts her man first. But that's the whole point. When you care for someone, you don't want them hurt. You want to protect them. To do whatever it takes to keep them safe. So don't be mad that I'm lookin' out for you. It's what comes naturally. I'd be less of a man if I didn't. Hellfire, I'd be no man at all."

That was quite a speech for him, and Ursula was moved. "Just so you know I feel the same way."

They were ready when Thal's next knock came.

Ned, plainly nervous, nodded in greeting.

The back stairs were narrow, and shadowed. At the bottom a small lamp cast a weak glow. The rear door didn't see much use, and creaked when Thal pushed on it.

"Careful," Jesse Lee said.

Thal looked at him questioningly.

"They might be watchin' the back too,"

Nodding, Thal pushed more slowly. He poked his head out, looked both ways, and whispered, "The coast looks clear."

Ursula was grateful for the cool breeze that washed over her. She hadn't realized she was sweating so much. They were in an alley strewn with old crates and other debris, and the reek was terrible. Jesse had hold of her hand, and she let him lead her. She jumped when a cat meowed and skittered off in fright.

Her brother and the cowboys were somber and grim. All of them had their hands on their six-shooters.

At the end of the alley, Thal stopped and again poked his head out.

Ursula thought she heard something behind them. The cat, she reckoned, and looked over her shoulder. Her breath caught in her throat. Something had moved near the hotel, something much larger than a cat. It was there and it was gone. She thought it might be a trick of the feeble light and shadows. At least, she hoped it was.

"I don't see any of them," Thal said. "We'll turn left and go a couple of blocks and then make for the livery."

"That's the long way around," Ned said.

"It's the safe way," Thal replied. "They'd expect us to make a beeline."

"What if Galt has someone watchin' the livery too?" Ned said.

"They won't stop us," Jesse Lee said.

Ursula had never heard him sound so . . . hard. That he was prepared to kill to spirit her to safety should shock her, but it didn't. The special deputies were bad men, and bad men deserved their just deserts. That she lumped Myles with the other assassins shocked her more. But the truth was the truth.

They hurried down a side street. As late as it was, riders and people on foot were everywhere. Which was to be expected. The saloons and bawdy houses were open twenty-four hours a day. American City, Galt had boasted, never closed its doors to those with money to burn.

Thankfully no one paid them any mind.

Jesse Lee, Ursula noticed, put himself between her and the street, shielding her with his own body. She was so touched she could have kissed him.

Crawford, who was in front of them and to one side, glanced back, and stopped. "Wait."

"What is it?" Thal asked.

"I thought I saw someone come out of the alley."

"You did or you didn't?" Ned said.

"Keep goin'," Jesse Lee said.

Ned was looking all around them. "Why do I have the feelin' that they're closin' in on us?"

Thal gave him a sharp look. "Because you worry too much."

"What are you mad at me for?"

Thal didn't answer.

Her own nerves jangling, Ursula wished their ordeal was over. She wanted out of American City. She wanted to be back in Kansas. She wanted a long, happy life with Jesse Lee. A home and children of their own. Two boys and two girls. She imagined holding a baby in her arms and rocking it to sleep.

Jesse Lee stopped abruptly. "Hold it."

"What?" Thal said.

"Craw was right. It's the one they call Dyson. He's back there. I caught a glimpse of him."

"I knew it," Ned said.

"If there's him, there's others," Crawford said.

Thal looked at Ursula. "Protect her, no matter what."

"Maybe they won't try to stop us," Ursula said. "Maybe they're only wondering what we're up to."

"Wishful thinkin'," Ned said.

"A man like Galt won't take kindly to bein' lied to or havin' one of his deputies knocked out and trussed up," Thal said.

"He'll take it personal," Crawford said.

"But none of that is reason enough to try and kill us," Ursula said.

That was when a revolver boomed.

Chapter 34

It came from behind them, the flash of the muzzle simultaneous with the blast.

Ursula heard something buzz past her ear. It sounded like a hornet, and she realized she'd almost been shot.

With a lightning flick of his hands, Jesse Lee let go of her and drew his Colt. Whirling, he fanned the hammer twice, his six-shooter bucking and thundering.

From the vicinity of the alley came a bellow of pain. A muzzle flashed again, but the shot went wide.

"That sounded like Bull!" Ned said.

"Run!" Thal hollered. He fired at the alley too. "Get my sister out of here!"

Jesse Lee grabbed Ursula's wrist and did as her brother wanted, moving past the others, who fell in behind them.

The man at the alley kept shooting. So did someone else, across the street from him.

Ned and Crawford added to the din, backpedaling as they went.

Ursula had never heard so many guns firing all at once. It was so loud her ears rang.

Up and down the street, people were hunting cover. A few of the men cursed. A few of the women screamed.

Ursula hunched over to make a smaller target. Everyone knew that in a gun battle, bystanders were just as likely to take a slug as those taking part. And a wound — however slight — could prove fatal if infection set in.

In the midst of the confusion and panic, Jesse Lee came to a recessed doorway and pulled her into it. Letting go, he commenced to replacing the spent cartridges in his Colt.

Thal, Ned, and Crawford joined them, her brother looking back the way they came. "I don't think they're after us just yet."

"None of us were hit," Ned declared happily. "If that's not luck, I don't know what is."

"Reload," Jesse Lee said.

Thal groped at his belt. "If that one was Bull, how did he get loose?"

"Who cares?" Crawford said. "He is, and now the entire bunch will be out for our blood."

"I think you hit him," Thal said to Jesse Lee.

"Bull will be madder than ever over that," Ned said.

Ursula wanted them to be quiet so she could listen for pursuit. At least two special deputies were out there, maybe more. "Once you're ready, we run to the stable and don't stop for anything."

"With you in the middle," Jesse Lee said.

"To shield me like you were doing earlier?" Ursula said. She should be grateful, but she wasn't. "I don't need special treatment."

"Yes," Jesse Lee said, "you do."

"Don't argue with him, sis," Thal said.

"We protect you at all costs, ma'am," Crawford said. "All of us, together."

"That goes without sayin'," Ned said.

Ursula looked from one to the other, at their earnest, caring faces, and would have been overcome with emotion, but just then a commotion broke out up the street.

Thal risked a look. "There's two more comin' from the other way. It's that two-gun gent, Tiny, and the one they call Olivant."

"Four to four now," Ned said.

"With more on the way," Jesse Lee said. "We can't waste any more time. I'll take the lead. The rest of you stick to my heels."

"Why you?" Thal said.

"Because I can shoot."

No one disputed him.

Ursula considered leaving her bag there, but it wasn't that heavy. She could run with it without any problem.

"Ready?" Jesse Lee said.

The other three nodded.

Jesse Lee sprang out. Almost immediately a six-gun boomed up the street and he answered in kind. From behind them came another shot, and Jesse spun and fanned his hammer. "Now!"

Thal grabbed Ursula and practically pushed her into Jesse Lee's back. Thal put himself on her right, Ned scampered around to her other side, and Crawford moved in behind her.

"Go!" Thal cried. "Go! Go!"

Jesse Lee moved out, not running, but striding quickly and purposefully, his Colt level at his waist.

Most bystanders had scattered, but a few were still scurrying for cover. They included a man in a buckboard who was trying to turn it around, but his two-horse team balked.

Another side street appeared. Jesse Lee had started past it when suddenly, half a block away, a second-floor window shattered, a rifle barrel was thrust out, and the rifle banged twice.

Instantly Jesse Lee responded, and more glass shattered.

"This way," Thal said, propelling Ursula into the side street and over to the corner of a building that hid them from the rifleman.

Ned and Crawford were quick to follow.

Behind them a pistol banged. A split second later, up the street, so did another.

"Jesse!" Ursula cried.

Jesse Lee darted over to her and once again began to reload. "They have us boxed in."

"Then we go this way," Thal said, gesturing down the new street.

"It will take us back toward the hotel," Ned said.

"Can't be helped," Thal said, and gripped Ursula's wrist. "You set, Jesse?"

"Hold on," Crawford said. "They know this town better than we do. No matter which way we go, they'll cut us off."

"It'll be cat and mouse," Ned said, nodding, "with us the mice."

"It doesn't have to be," Crawford said.

The others looked at the older puncher.

"If you've had a brainstorm, pard, we're listenin'," Jesse Lee said.

"As soon as there are enough of them,

they'll close in on us," Crawford predicted. "If we're smart, we'll find a spot to lie low for a while and throw them off our scent."

"In the middle of the city?" Ned said dubiously.

"No, he's right," Jesse Lee said. "So far they've been cautious, but once they out-number us, the kid gloves will be off."

"I'm against lyin' low," Ned said. "It'll give them time to set up an ambush at the stable."

"They might already have," Crawford said.

Jesse Lee moved ahead of them up the new street, as he had done before. "Stay close."

"Lordy, I hate this," Ned said.

So did Ursula. Everything had happened so fast, it hadn't really sunk in that Trevor Galt's pack of gun sharks were trying to kill them. Now that she had a few moments to think, fear clawed at her. Through sheer force of will she swatted it down and steeled herself for come what may.

Her protectors were looking every which way, never knowing where the next shot would come from.

From the street they had vacated came shouts. The special deputies were yelling back and forth.

Ursula caught some of it. They were

wondering where she and the others had gotten to.

"We need to find a place quick," Ned urged.

They passed a store. They passed a butcher's. A freight office. All closed and dark.

Not quite a block off was a saloon, its front window lit bright. From inside wafted the tinny notes of a piano, and merry laughter. If its patrons had heard the shots, they had gone on with their revels anyway.

"How about the whiskey mill?" Ned said.

"They'd find us easy, as lit up as it is," Thal said.

Jesse Lee stopped and turned. "Look what I found."

Between two of the buildings was an inky gap barely shoulder-wide.

Ursula didn't consider it much of a haven. "So?"

"So in we go," Jesse Lee said, and plunged into the blackness.

"I hate this even more," Ned said.

Ursula didn't like the feeling of being confined. She'd never liked cramped spaces. Not even being in a closet when she was little. A tingle of apprehension rippled down her spine, and she struggled to contain her fright. Thal still had hold of her, and she concentrated on his hand and not on the high walls that loomed so close.

"How much farther?" Ned asked behind her.

"Hush," Thal said.

Ursula had never realized how much Ned Leslie complained. Thank goodness she hadn't been attracted to him. He was liable to be one of those husbands who carped about everything. Men liked to claim that only females griped a lot, but then, men claimed a lot of silly things.

The darkness went from black to gray, and in another few steps they were out of the gap and in an alley.

"Now what?" Ned said.

Jesse Lee motioned toward the rear of the saloon. There was a door but no windows. Just past the door was an enormous pile of empty liquor bottles and other trash. Beyond the pile was a clear space.

"We'll rest there a bit," Jesse Lee said.

Ned muttered something, but he was the first to sink down with his back to the wall.

"We'll make it out, pard," Thal assured him. "You'll see."

Ursula was too worried to sit. She moved next to Jesse, who was staring toward the gap they'd come through. "Do you think they know we're back here?" she whispered.

"Not yet."

"You took awful chances out in the street," Ursula said. "Putting yourself in front of us."

"The others took chances too."

For my sake, Ursula almost said, but didn't. She pressed her shoulder against his and put her hand on his sleeve. "I want you to know I'll make you the best wife any man ever had."

"You pick a strange time to say a thing like that," Jesse Lee said.

Since the others were listening, Ursula changed the subject. "Have you always been like this?"

"This how?"

"So sure of yourself. So confident."

"A man has somethin' to do, he does it," Jesse Lee said. "I learned that from my pa."

More shouts reached them, this time from the street they'd just vacated:

"Where did they get to?"

"I lost sight of 'em."

"Keep lookin'. They can't have gotten far."

"Good," Jesse Lee said. "They don't know where we are."

A troubling thought occurred to Ursula. "What if they rope others into helping them search? They're deputies, aren't they? They could have the whole town looking."

"I doubt it will come to that."

Ursula prayed it didn't. Eight gun hands was one thing. An entire town, another.

To her surprise, Jesse Lee suddenly faced her and put his left hand on her shoulder. "I should have said this at the hotel, but I didn't. It was the best day of my life when you told me that you'd marry me. I wanted to whoop and holler and laugh, you mean so much to me. The days since, I keep wantin' to pinch myself to see if I'm dreamin'. No matter what happens, remember that I care for you more than I've ever cared for anyone."

"What did you say to me a minute ago? You pick a strange time to say a thing like that."

"You deserved to know."

"Why here and now?"

"The livery stable is four blocks away. That's a far piece, with what we're up against."

Fright clawed at Ursula's insides, prompting her to say, "Are you suggesting you might not get there?"

"I'll try my best," Jesse Lee said.

It was rare for Ursula to curse. Her mother had impressed on her from an early age that ladies didn't indulge in improper language. But she cursed now, with a vehemence that seemed to surprise Jesse Lee. "You damn well better."

CHAPTER 35

Thal couldn't help overhearing what his sister and the Southerner were saying. They were talking in low tones, but he was only a few feet away. When they embraced and Ursula whispered into Jesse Lee's ear, he moved to the rear door of the saloon and put his ear to it. All he heard was the drone of voices, and the piano.

About to go back behind the pile of bottles and whatnot, Thal stiffened in alarm. He'd heard another sound — from the gap between the buildings. Footsteps, he was sure. Someone moving quickly, noisily.

Drawing his six-shooter, Thal glided over near the gap, cocked his revolver, and waited. None too soon.

A figure emerged out of the ink. Dyson, one of the special deputies. His revolver was out but pointed at the ground.

The moment Dyson stepped from the gap, Thal jammed the muzzle of his Colt against the man's ribs. "Don't move."

Dyson started to raise his six-shooter, and froze. "Damn!" he blurted.

"Drop it," Thal said, "or I put a hole in you."

Dyson's face was hard to read in the dark. "Easy on that trigger, cowboy," he said, and his six-gun thumped to the ground.

Thal listened for more footsteps. "Are you alone?"

"The others are out lookin' for you," Dyson said. "I came back here on a hunch." He smirked. "Looks like I was right."

The man was much too calm for Thal's liking. "Any tricks, and I'll shoot you. So help me."

"You do, and you'll be in more hot water," Dyson replied. "It's bad enough Bull got shot. Mr. Galt isn't happy. Mr. Galt isn't happy at all."

Thal stepped back and motioned toward the rear of the saloon. "Move. And keep your hands where I can see them."

"Sure thing, cowboy," Dyson said mockingly, and raised his arms halfway. "Enjoy this while you can." He laughed as if it were a joke.

Thal warily moved around behind him and pressed the Colt to his spine. "You're awful cocky with a gun held on you."

"Cowboy, you have no idea what you're in for."

"Quit callin' me that," Thal said, irritated that Dyson made it sound like an insult.

"Whatever you say, cowboy," Dyson said, and laughed.

Jesse Lee appeared as they came up, his Colt leveled. "You caught one of the varmints."

"Ah," Dyson said. "The gun hand."

The others surrounded him, Ned exclaiming, "We've got one, by gosh."

"You've got nothin', cowpoke," Dyson said.

Ursula stood back a little, studying him. "This is wrong, don't you see that? You shouldn't be hunting us down. You should let us leave in peace."

"Are you serious, girl?" Dyson said. "Or just stupid?"

"Be polite to her," Jesse Lee warned.

Dyson looked from Ursula to the Southerner and back again. "So Bull is right. You're sweet on each other, and have been the whole time. Mr. Galt doesn't like that you played him for a jackass."

"We did no such thing," Ursula said.

"Like hell," Dyson said. "He put you up at his hotel and took you out to eat, and you never once told him that you and this

Reb were sweethearts."

"I wasn't trying to deceive him," Ursula said.

"That's not how he sees it," Dyson said. "He thinks you tricked him, and he's mad as hell."

"If he'll give me a chance to explain, I can smooth things over," Ursula said.

"It's too late for talkin', girl," Dyson said.

"What do you mean?"

"You're lawbreakers, and you deserve what's comin'."

"Who are you kidding?" Ursula retorted. "American City doesn't have any laws. Anything goes, remember?"

Dyson gave her a sharklike grin. "We've got a few, girl. No killin' unless it's necessary. No robbin' the banks." He paused. "And no harm is to come to a special deputy. Not ever. That drunk who shot your brother, Myles? We hanged him. After we dragged him into the middle of the street and beat him until half the bones in his body were broken and bits and pieces of his teeth were leakin' out of his mouth."

"That's horrible," Ursula said.

"Mr. Galt can be downright mean when his dander is up, and his dander is up now."

"At us?"

"No, the Sioux," Dyson said, and laughed

scornfully.

"It's all a misunderstanding, I tell you."

"Is that what you call it? You attacked Bull for no reason —" Dyson began.

"He wouldn't let us leave when we wanted to," Ursula interrupted.

"You knocked him out and tied him up and hid him, then lied to Mr. Galt when Mr. Galt asked if you knew where Bull had gotten to. Then you snuck off. And when some of us came after you, the gun hand here shot Bull in the shoulder." Dyson shook his head. "No, girl. This is no misunderstandin'. You assaulted a special deputy, and shot him, and now you'll pay the price."

Thal had a question of his own. "How did Bull get loose and come after us?"

"That was my doing," Dyson said. "I was out front of the hotel, watchin' your window, and saw movement. It got me curious. I came up and found all of you gone, and Bull tryin' to get free behind that bed. I cut him loose and we came after you." He smiled. "And here we are."

"You make it sound like this is all our fault," Ursula said. "But your precious Mr. Galt treated us as if we were his prisoners. Bull wouldn't let us leave when we wanted to, and by your own admission you were spying on us."

Dyson laughed. "That's the funny part."

"What is?"

"Mr. Galt did all that for your own protection. Bull and us were to make sure no one bothered you. Bull wouldn't let you leave because Mr. Galt didn't want you roamin' the streets at night. They're not safe." And Dyson laughed again.

"I don't care what you say," Ursula said. "We're not in the wrong here."

"Wrong or right doesn't matter," Dyson said. "You have to pay for what you did to Bull. That's what this is about now. Nothin' else."

"What if we agreed to pay a fine? Or serve time in jail?" Ursula proposed.

Thal almost spoke up. Under no circumstances would he allow Galt to throw them behind bars. They'd be completely at Galt's mercy, which was the same as being at the mercy of a rabid wolf.

"What jail?" Dyson said. "We deal with lawbreakers with lead or hemp. As Mr. Galt put it, he can't be bothered with feedin' and housin' criminals."

"We're no such thing."

"You are now, girl. All of you." Dyson glanced at each of them in that smug way he had. "Don't you get it yet? Mr. Galt has given orders that none of you are to make it out of American City alive."

"Even her?" Jesse Lee said, nodding at Ursula.

"Especially her," Dyson said.

"But she's female," Ned said.

"She's a lawbreaker. Her being a woman is beside the point."

"It's the whole point," Ned said angrily. "In Texas we never harm a female. It's just not done."

"In case you haven't noticed, cowboy," Dyson replied, "you're not in Texas anymore."

"No," Ned said. "We're in hell."

Thal moved around in front of the deputy. "What will Galt do to her? Have her beaten like he did that drunk? Hang her? Have her shot? What?"

"We're to take her alive if we can," Dyson said. "After that, I don't rightly know. But it won't be pretty."

"And where will my brother Myles be in all this?" Ursula asked. "Surely he won't stand for my being harmed."

"Mr. Galt asked him if he wanted to bow out, with you two being his kin, and all. Myles said he'd like to see it through. That you shouldn't be treated any different than any other lawbreakers."

"No," Ursula gasped.

"Girl, your brother Myles is as cold as they come. He's blown more than a dozen men apart with that scattergun of his. All Mr. Galt has to do is point at someone and say shoot them, and Myles will drop them dead. And now Mr. Galt is pointin' his finger at all of you."

"I refuse to believe my own brother will shoot me."

Thal didn't share her conviction. Myles had turned to the dark side in life, to the worst in human nature. Whatever goodness had once been in Myles had been smothered by the ugliness and vice Myles had willingly embraced.

"You keep on believin' that, girl," Dyson was saying. "You keep on believin' it even as he points both barrels at you and squeezes both of those triggers."

A strained silence gripped them.

Thal had hoped there might be a chance, however slim, of reasoning with Trevor Galt and making it out of American City without having to fight for their lives. That hope had been dashed.

"What do we do?" Ned said, more to himself than to them. "How do we get out of this fix?"

"You don't," Dyson said.

"That'll be enough out of you," Jesse Lee said.

"Or what? You'll shoot me?" Dyson sneered.

"Don't think I won't," Jesse Lee replied.

Dyson wasn't the least bit intimidated. "Oh, I know you can, boy. You're a natural-born shooter. I saw that out in the street. But if you do, the shot will bring the others. So go ahead. Shoot me."

Crawford had been quiet this whole time, but now he said, "I have an idea. We use this one as a hostage. March him in front of us to the livery, and warn them that if they cut loose on us, he'll be the first one to die."

"That might just work," Ned said.

"You're graspin' at straws," Dyson said. "Mr. Galt won't let you get away. He'll shoot me himself to stop you."

"And you work for a man like that?" Ursula said.

"For a thousand dollars a month," Dyson said, "I'd work for the Devil himself."

"Then we fight our way out," Jesse Lee said.

"You can try," Dyson said. "The others will like the sport of it. Bull can't wait to do a few of you in. He owes you for the conks on his noggin and the hole you put in him."

"God help us," Ned said. "We've stepped

401

in it up to our necks, and it's root hog or die."

"It's sinkin' in at last," Dyson said.

"I've heard enough out of you," Jesse Lee said, and taking a quick step, he slammed his Colt against Dyson's jaw. There was a crack and a crunch, and the special deputy sprawled at their feet.

"More cause for Galt to want us dead," Ned said gloomily.

"It had to be done," Jesse Lee said. "This one would have given us away if he could."

"Forget about him," Thal said. "We have somethin' more important to work out." Namely, how to get out of there.

"Blunderin' around in the dark didn't get us anywhere," Crawford said. "I vote we stay here and make a run for it at first light."

"Good idea," Ned said. "We'll be able to see what we're shootin' at."

"And they'll be able to see us," Jesse Lee said, and shook his head. "It's smarter to try now, while we have the dark for cover."

"Thal?" Ned said. "Which do you like?"

Thal had already made up his mind. In the daylight the special deputies could easily pick them off from the rooftops, or from a distance, with rifles. "I like the dark. It works in our favor."

"Then do we do it now or do we wait a

bit?" Ned said.

Jesse Lee answered him. "What use is waitin'? We go while we can, and don't stop this side of the grave. If those special deputies try to stop us, we kill every one."

"Big words," Ned said.

"I'm through with words," Jesse Lee said, and held up his ivory-handled Colt. "This will do my talkin' from here on out." He looked at each of them. "There can't be any holdin' back. Make up your minds, here and now, or you'll be useless in the fight."

"Then it's settled," Thal said. "It's us or them."

"It was never anything else," Jesse Lee said.

Ned swallowed and stared at the figure on the ground. "God help us."

"Amen to that," Ursula said.

Chapter 36

Thal and the others started toward the gap between the buildings, only to be brought up short by Jesse Lee.

"Where are you goin'?"

"Out to the street," Thal said.

"Not that way." Jesse Lee stepped to the rear door, tried the latch, and opened it far enough to peer in. "Through the saloon."

"Were you nicked in the head?" Ned said. "There are people in there. Lots and lots of people."

"So?" Jesse Lee said. "They don't know who we are. Or that the special deputies are huntin' for us."

"You hope," Ned said.

Thal was skeptical too. He wouldn't put it past Trevor Galt to have his deputies go from saloon to saloon and warn everyone to be on the lookout for them. "I don't know about this."

"In a crowd we're less easy to spot," Jesse

Lee argued, "and the deputies are less likely to open fire."

"You hope," Ned repeated.

Shoving his Colt into his holster, Jesse Lee opened the door, hooked his thumb in his gun belt, and strode in.

"Where he goes, I go," Ursula said, hastening after him.

"He's my pard," Crawford said, and was on their heels.

Ned looked at Thal. "Well, hell."

"Get goin'," Thal said, and gave Ned a push. He went last. Since he wasn't Jesse Lee and couldn't draw and shoot in the blink of an eye, he slid his own revolver into his holster but kept his hand on it so he'd be ready, should the need arise.

A narrow hallway led to the front. A hubbub of voices and music, and the clink of glass and of chips, grew louder with every step.

Thal blinked in the sudden glare of the saloon proper. As late as the hour was, dozens of drinkers and gamblers and doves were having a grand time. Over in a corner, a tipsy piano player tickled the ivories.

Jesse Lee made straight for the batwings, ambling along as if he didn't have a care in the world.

The rest of them followed. Ursula and

Crawford were calm enough, but Ned's face twitched from the strain on his nerves.

When a poker player at a table gave a whoop of delight at winning a hand, Thal nearly jumped. It eased his jitters a little to see that no one seemed interested in them. Still, the walk to the batwings seemed to take forever. He was the last to push outside. The others were to his right, hugging the wall.

The people in the street didn't give them a second glance.

"No sign of the deputies," Ned whispered.

Several riders were coming down the street, close to the boardwalk. Prospectors, by the looks of them, out on the town.

"Stick close," Jesse Lee said, and before they could divine what he was up to, he was off the boardwalk and fell into step near the riders.

"Quick. Do as he's doin'," Thal said, and took Ursula's arm. It was a clever ruse, using the prospectors and their animals to screen them from anyone on the other side of the street. "Your man doesn't miss a trick, sis."

"He doesn't, does he?" Ursula said in admiration.

Thal scanned the buildings on their side. The coast appeared momentarily clear. The special deputies, save for Dyson, must have moved on to the next street.

"Thalis?" Ursula said softly.

Thal was still looking for trouble and didn't want to be distracted. "What is it?"

"Don't let anything happen to him."

Thal looked at her.

"I couldn't bear it if something did. I love him, Thal. It might seem strange, your little sister saying that, but I do, with all my heart. Promise me you won't let him come to harm."

Thal was taken aback. She was asking a lot. He was no gun hand. But for her sake he said, "I'll do what I can."

"Thank you," Ursula said, and squeezed his hand.

They came to an intersection. Jesse Lee broke away from the riders and headed up the other street, which was almost empty of people. He didn't skulk or make an attempt to hide.

A saloon was open, but it wasn't as popular as the last. A townsman staggered past them, slurring the words to a song. Two doves, older gals with a lot of powder and rouge on their faces, came out of the saloon arm in arm and merrily made their way homeward.

"I could never do what they do," Ursula

remarked. "Mingle and mix with men to get them to buy me drinks."

Thal marveled that she'd think of such a thing at a time like this. "People do what they have to."

"I'd rather do what I want than what life makes me do."

Thal glanced back and caught sight of a middling-sized man in a bulky coat who appeared to be following them. Another late-nighter? he wondered. Or someone more sinister? He got his answer when the man ducked behind the post to an overhang. "We're bein' tailed," he quietly warned the others.

"Don't look back or he'll know we're onto him," Jesse Lee said without breaking stride.

It was hard for Thal to do. He half expected to take a slug in the back, and his skin prickled.

At the next corner Jesse Lee turned right. The instant their shadow couldn't see him, he darted into a doorway and motioned for them to keep going. "Take your time. Let him see you."

Thal assumed the lead. He pretended to be interested in the windows they were passing, only so he could catch a glimpse of their stalker out of the corner of his eye.

The man came into view. He was hanging

back, moving carefully. Intent on them, he went past the doorway that concealed Jesse Lee. Evidently the man didn't hear the Southerner come up behind him, and he certainly never saw the flash of nickel plating as Jesse Lee brought his Colt crashing down on the back of the man's head. Once, twice, the revolver gleamed, and the man folded without an outcry.

Jesse Lee swiftly caught up.

"Which one was it?" Ned asked.

"Carnes," Jesse Lee said. "He'll be out awhile."

"Good. That's two," Ned said.

"Only six left, and Galt besides," Crawford said, and mustered a chuckle. "We've pretty near got them licked."

"You're pokin' fun at me, aren't you?" Ned said.

"Whatever gave you that notion?"

"Hush," Jesse Lee said, and wagged a hand at the air. "Don't you hear that?"

Thal had. A block or so to the north, someone was shouting angrily. He couldn't make out what they were saying, though.

"That sounds like Trevor Galt," Ursula said.

"What's he so mad about?" Ned wondered.

"Want to bet it's us?" Crawford said.

Thal had realized something else. "Why are we just standin' here? The stable is to the south, and Galt and his assassins are goin' the other way."

Ned snapped his fingers in elation. "That's right! We can get there before they can think to stop us."

"Move your boots," Jesse Lee said, and broke into a run.

Thal exerted extra effort to keep up. In Texas, he went nearly everywhere on horseback. Running was beneath most cowboys. He was out of practice, and the high heels on his boots didn't help.

A few of the folks out and about gave them quizzical looks, no doubt puzzled by why so many men — and one woman — were running down the street in the middle of the night.

At the next junction Jesse Lee turned right. He was out ahead by a good dozen feet.

"Look at him go," Ursula said. "Isn't he marvelous!"

"If you say so." Thal was focused on his breathing. He couldn't afford to become winded and slow the others down.

"The shouting has stopped," Crawford said.

Thal tilted his ear into the wind. As much

noise as they were making, all he heard was the beat of their feet.

"Who's that?" Ursula asked abruptly. She was looking behind them.

Someone was hard in pursuit. A familiar middling-sized figure in a bulky coat. Metal glinted in one hand.

"Carnes!" Thal realized. The man must have a head like iron.

The special deputy thrust an arm at them. Clearly Carnes intended to shoot them in the back.

Thal stopped and drew his Colt. He took deliberate aim just as Carnes's revolver boomed. One of the others cried out.

Thal squeezed the trigger.

Carnes stumbled as if he'd tripped over his own feet, but he didn't go down. Recovering, he snapped another shot and came on faster.

Thal fired a second time. The special deputy was only twenty yards away, but it might as well be fifty. Thal wasn't sure if he hit him. Then Crawford and Ned both fired, and Carnes pitched forward, his arms out-flung. A shriek tore from his throat, and he struck the ground and convulsed.

"We got him, by heaven," Ned exclaimed.

"We should make certain he's dead," Ursula said.

Jesse Lee came running back. "No," he said, grabbing her arm. "Galt and his assassins will have heard. They'll come quick."

Ned swallowed. "Do we stay and fight or skedaddle?"

"What do you think?" Jesse Lee said, and fairly flew.

Thal would give anything for his horse. He consoled himself with the thought that in a few minutes he would be in the saddle and could say so long forever to the Sodom and Gomorrah of the Black Hills. He was never coming back, no matter what happened to Myles. If his brother got shot again, so be it.

Myles had made his bed, as folks liked to say, and now he could lie — or die — in it.

"There it is!" Ned cried.

The livery was at the end of the block. The large double doors were closed, and there was no sign of life.

"Last one in the saddle is a rotten egg," Ned said.

Thal marveled that his pard could joke at a time like this. The last to get there, he lent a hand as they pulled on the doors.

"They won't open!" Ned cried.

Jesse Lee had already figured out why. "They're barred on the inside. The livery must close for the night."

"There has to be another way in," Crawford said. "A side door or a back door. Somethin'."

Thal was puffing by the time they reached a corral at the rear. He nearly lost his balance clambering over the rails.

Ten to twelve horses had been dozing, but now they whinnied and pranced about, rattled by the intrusion.

"I don't see ours," Jesse Lee said. "They must be inside."

To their immense relief, the back door wasn't bolted.

"Find a lantern," Jesse Lee said. "There has to be one somewhere."

Thal groped about in the dark. His fingers brushed a stall and a support beam. He roved his hand higher, to where a peg might be, and hollered, "I found one."

"How do we light it?" Ned said. "I don't have any matches."

"I do," Ursula said. "In my bag."

Exercising care, Thal took the lantern down and set it on the ground. He had lit one often enough that he could do so blindfolded. He succeeded on his first try. As the glow spread, he raised the lantern over his head. "Find our animals."

The others didn't need urging. Jesse Lee and Ursula took the stalls on the right, Ned and Crawlord the stalls on the left.

Midway Ned yelled, "Here's your animal, pard!"

Their other mounts were in adjacent stalls, their saddles and bridles in the tack room.

Toting them out took longer than Thal liked, but presently he led the chestnut down the aisle to the front. Crawford and Ned were already there, and together they removed the heavy bar and carried it to one side so it was out of the way.

Jesse Lee and Ursula brought their horses up.

"Sorry it took me so long," she said. "I can't saddle my horse as fast as you do."

"Let's get out of here while the gettin' is good," Ned said eagerly. He pushed on one door, and Crawford pushed on the other.

Thal smiled, extinguished the lantern and set it aside, and gripped his saddle horn. The worst was over, and good riddance to American City.

The next instant, from out of the dark street, came a shout from Trevor Galt. "Throw down your guns and throw up your hands or we'll wipe you out!"

CHAPTER 37

Ursula felt as if her stomach dropped out of her body. Clutching her belly, she gasped in dismay.

"We're trapped!" Ned exclaimed.

"We can go out the back," Thal said.

As if he had heard, Trevor Galt shouted, "We have the stable surrounded. I won't wait all night. Come out now, while you still can."

"Damn," Crawford said. "This will get ugly."

Jesse Lee was pulling his palomino out of the doorway. "Quick," he said. "Before they cut loose on us."

Ursula led her animal over beside his, then glued herself to him as he returned to the door and peered out without exposing himself.

"We should close these," he said.

The doors weren't open all the way, but close to it. They'd be exposed to gunfire every time they showed themselves. But Ursula worried that if they tried to close them, they'd be fired on. "Maybe we should leave them as they are."

"Too dangerous," Jesse Lee said.

"Let me," Crawford said. Crouching, he sidled along the door, his arm out for the handle.

Ursula held her breath. She prayed that in the dark, Galt and his special deputies wouldn't notice.

A rifle *spang*ed, and Crawford bleated in pain. Grabbing at his leg, he fired, then backpedaled, limping as he came.

To cover him, Jesse Lee stepped out and fanned his Colt twice. Crawford reached him and Jesse Lee got an arm around him to support him as other guns opened up.

"Jesse!" Ursula screamed before she could stop herself.

Five or six slugs seared the air, but Jesse Lee made it back without being hit. Crawford leaned against the wall, and Jesse let go. "How bad?" he said.

"Don't know yet," Crawford said.

On the other side of the doorway, Thal and Ned had drawn their six-shooters.

Ned was in a crouch, and leaning too far out, Ursula thought. "They're movin' around out there," he reported.

"Gettin' into position, most likely," Jesse Lee said.

"For what?" Ursula asked.

"To rush us."

Ursula clenched her fists so tight it hurt. She never in a million years would ever have imagined she would be caught in the middle of a gun battle. That they might all be killed was almost too horrible to contemplate. It didn't seem entirely real, and yet it was. "Give me a gun. I can help. I know how to shoot."

"No," Jesse Lee said without looking at her.

"Give me one good reason why not?"

"They see you with a gun, they'll shoot you."

"They might shoot me anyway."

"You heard Dyson. Galt wants you alive. But if you take part, he might change his mind."

"It's not right that I can't help," Ursula said.

"If it keeps you alive, it is."

Ursula was touched, and upset. This was largely her doing. Thal and his friends had come to American City because of her concern for Myles. The thought of him prompted her to cup a hand to her mouth.

"Myles! Are you out there? Can you hear me?"

His reply was slow in coming. He was somewhere along the buildings on the right side of the street, and hollered, "I hear you, sis."

"Let us go, Myles," Ursula begged. "We only came here on your account."

"It's not up to me, little sister," Myles answered. "You know that." He paused. "I didn't ask you to come. I didn't send for you. You came on your own, the two of you."

"You're our *brother*!" Ursula shouted in anger. "I thought you might need us. Wouldn't you have done the same for me?"

Again Myles was slow in replying. "Probably not," he said.

Ursula was crushed. Her own brother. One of the boys she grew up with. All the fun times they'd had, the playing and working together, had all been for naught. "Oh, Myles," she said softly. She didn't think anyone out there could hear her.

"Don't blame your brother, Miss Christie," Trevor Galt bellowed. "This is on your shoulders. Yours, and those cowboys. You've attacked my special deputies, and killed one. Murdered an officer of the law."

"Hired assassin, is more like it," Ursula shouted back.

418

"Quibbling won't help you," Galt said. "The only thing that will is if you toss your weapons out and step out here with your hands in the air. I give you my word we won't shoot."

Over on the other side of the doorway, Thal yelled, "You expect us to trust you?"

"You'll be taken into custody and put on trial," Galt said.

"And then hanged," Thal said.

"If the jury finds you guilty."

"A jury you'll handpick," Thal said. "With you as the judge, I bet. Nothin' doin', mister. We're not lettin' you railroad us to the gallows."

"Suit yourselves," Trevor Galt said. "We have plenty of space in the cemetery."

Thal surprised Ursula by calling out, "Let my sister go, at least. She didn't shoot anybody. And if you harm a woman, word will get out. There might not be any real law in these hills, but the government might hear and poke their nose in. You want to risk that?"

"A feeble threat," Galt said, but something in his tone suggested the idea troubled him.

"I tried, sis," Thal said.

Crawford had sunk down and sat on the ground and was probing at his thigh. "It missed the bone," he said to Jesse Lee. "And the bleedin' has pretty much stopped."

"We should bandage it," Jesse Lee said.

"After this is over, will do," Crawford said.

After what? Ursula thought, and realized what he meant. After they got out of there. If they got out. "There has to be something we can do." She refused to give in.

Crawford grunted. "We can wait until daylight and fight our way out."

"And be picked off from our saddles like so many flies," Jesse Lee said. "No, that won't do. We have to think of what's best for her."

"Me?" Ursula said. "I'm not the only one trapped in here."

"You're the only one that counts," Jesse Lee said.

"Your lives matter as much as mine does."

It was Crawford who shook his head and gave her a lopsided smile. "No, ma'am, they don't."

Thal was worried sick. Not so much for himself or his friends, but for his sister. They had to get her out of there, but how?

The street outside had gone quiet. After that flurry of movement a while ago, the special deputies were lying low. Probably waiting for them to make the next move.

Leaning back against the wall, Thal contemplated their predicament. They could climb onto their horses and burst out with their six-shooters blazing, but some of them were bound to be hit. He gazed down the aisle at the rear door, which they'd left open, and felt the faintest of breezes on his face. A brainstorm took root. He glanced at the hayloft, and at all the straw strewn around. "It just might work."

"What might?" Ned asked.

"Keep watch," Thal said. "I'll be right back."

"Goin' for a stroll?" Ned said.

Doubled over, Thal moved away from the doors. He stayed close to the stalls so as not to be seen from outside, and when he had gone far enough, he darted to the other side and around to the front, and to his sister and the others. "I've got an idea," he announced.

"We could use one," Jesse Lee said.

Before Thal could share it, Ursula startled him by throwing her arms around him and squeezing him tight.

"I'm sorry for getting you into this."

"It's not as if you twisted my arm," Thal joked, and was startled even more when he felt a tear on his neck and she gave a low sob. "Get ahold of yourself, sis. You'll need your wits about you."

"Sorry," Ursula said, and stepped back.

Thal turned to Jesse Lee. "It's best if we try to break out while it's still dark."

"I said as much my own self."

"Then how about if we help the dark along?" Thal said. "There's straw and hay, and there's that lantern."

Jesse Lee licked the tip of the index finger on his left hand, held it up, and turned his hand from side to side. "Not much in the way of wind."

"But what there is is blowin' in the right direction," Thal said. "It'll carry the smoke out into the street. Once it's thick enough, we use our spurs and fight our way out."

"It's a gamble."

"I'm open to a better idea."

"Wish I had one," Jesse Lee said.

"We go for it, then? You're agreed?"

"I am."

"How can I help?" Ursula asked.

The three of them hurriedly gathered armfuls of straw and piled the straw in the middle of the aisle about twenty feet in from the double doors. Then Thal climbed to the loft and pushed several hay bales over the edge. Two broke when they struck the ground. The third, they had to cut the twine. Once the hay was added, they had a sizable mound.

"This should do," Thal said.

He brought the lantern over. Jesse Lee had brought his canteen and a blanket.

"What are those for?"

The Southerner gave a sly grin. "You wanted to help the dark, remember?"

"Won't they guess what we're up to once they see the fire start?" Ursula asked.

"So what if they do?" Jesse Lee said. "They won't rush us when we can drop them before they reach the doors." Squatting, he spread the blanket out, then opened his canteen and began to wet it. He was careful not to get it so soaked that it would defeat their purpose.

Thal, meanwhile, got ready to light the wick.

"I wish there was another way," Ursula remarked worriedly.

"Quit your frettin'," Thal said. "When we make our break, all you should be thinkin' about is ridin' like the blazes and nothin' else."

"He's right," Jesse Lee said.

A shout from outside caused Thal to stiffen. It was Myles, calling for him by name.

"I wonder what he wants," Ursula said.

"Thalis! Do you hear me in there?" Myles yelled.

Setting down the lantern, Thal went to the door but didn't show himself.

"My ears work just fine, little brother."

"Mr. Galt wants to know what you're up to in there. We can see some of you movin' around."

"We're havin' a jubilee," Thal yelled. "Want to join us?"

"Don't do anything stupid," Myles said. "Mark my words. They will cut you down if you do."

"Does that include you?" Thal said. "Would you shoot your own sister and brother?"

"Only if you force me to."

"What happened to you, Myles?" Thal said sadly.

"Don't start with that again. Give yourselves up while you can. If not for your sake, then for sis's. You won't be shot. Mr. Galt gives me his word. And not all of you will be hanged. Only whoever shot Bull and killed Carnes. Mr. Galt gave me his word on that too."

"Tell your Mr. Galt where he can shove his word."

"What good does that do you?" Myles shouted. "You always were pigheaded. For once try not to be. Do what's best for all of you. Don't only think of yourself."

424

"You son of a bitch."

"I'm doin' you a favor. Mr. Galt is givin' you and your friends one last chance to surrender peaceably. All you have to do is lay down your guns and we'll take you to your hotel rooms and put you under guard. How reasonable is that?"

"We're done, Myles," Thal said.

"You're done talkin?"

"*We're* done, Myles. You and me." Wheeling on a bootheel, Thal returned to the pile of straw and hay and picked up the lantern.

"Are you done tryin' to reason with him?" Jesse Lee said.

"Let's do this," Thal said.

CHAPTER 38

For Ursula, the wait was excruciating.

They had lit the pile. Thal and Ursula and Ned and Crawford had climbed onto their horses and were poised to fan the breeze as soon as the smoke was thick enough.

Jesse Lee was the only one not mounted yet. He stood near the pile, holding the damp blanket, waiting for the right moment.

Ursula's heart was in her throat. The flames were spreading and growing, but much too slowly. The crackling and the acrid odor caused her sorrel to fidget, and she didn't like that either. She was afraid the sorrel might bolt.

It didn't help her anxiety any that Jesse Lee needed to wait until the flames were a lot higher before he threw the blanket on the pile, or otherwise the flames might be extinguished.

Ned was chewing on his bottom lip as if

he intended to eat it, and his reins raised to lash.

Crawford had a hand splayed to his wounded thigh. Blood trickled from between his fingers, and he was gritting his teeth from the pain.

Ursula caught Thal's eye and he smiled encouragement. She returned the favor, wishing she felt as confident as she pretended to be.

"This dang breeze," Jesse Lee said impatiently. "We might as well be puffin' on the fire ourselves."

Ursula had never seen a fire grow so slowly. Or was it just her nerves that made her think that? She did some gnawing on her own lip, and caught herself. She must stay alert. She must be ready. She imagined that most of the special deputies were out in front of the stable. Galt would only have sent a few to the back.

As if he knew she was thinking about him, Trevor Galt chose that moment to call out to them, "What's going on in there? Why in the world have you started a fire?"

Ursula willed the flames to grow, grow, grow.

"What are you up to?" Galt shouted. "You come out those doors any way without your hands in the air, and we open fire. Do you hear me?"

Ursula reflected that they must have heard him in Deadwood, and grinned at her little joke.

Smoke was rising from the pile. Not a lot, but enough that a small cloud hovered.

In another minute the cloud began to spread. Not outdoors, where it was supposed to, but across the aisle, and toward them.

"That's not good," Thal said.

Ursula shared his apprehension. The smoke was supposed to be borne out in the street to cover their flight. Not to fill the stable and make it impossible for them to see anything. Worse, the smoke might drive them into the open and put them at the mercy of the deputies' guns.

"Me and my brainstorms," Thal said.

"Give it a minute," Jesse Lee said. "We're not licked yet."

Of all his special qualities, Ursula admired his determination the most. He never gave up hope. He never quit. When he went at something, he went at it heart and soul, and refused to be stopped this side of Hades. She imagined their life together, imagined how wonderful it would be to have a man at her side who didn't let life ride roughshod over him. Any obstacles they encountered, they would overcome. Together.

Ursula suddenly became aware that her brother was hissing at her. "What?"

"I said to get ready. It will be any moment now."

The flames were growing considerably and giving off a lot more smoke. The cloud above the pile had finally moved, and was slowly drifting toward the doorway.

"I'll ask you one last time!" Trevor Galt hollered. "Surrender or suffer the consequences!"

"Over my dead body," Thal said.

Ursula wished he wouldn't talk like that. She firmed her grip on her reins, watching Jesse Lee, not the fire.

In the street a shot cracked, and a slug struck the outside wall. It was the signal for the special deputies to open up. Rifles and revolvers thundered. More lead struck the walls, other slugs struck the doors, and still others struck the burning pile and sent fiery bits of straw and hay flying.

Ursula was half afraid the sparks would ignite something else. She wished Jesse Lee would toss the blanket but he was still holding on to it. "The flames are high enough!"

Jesse Lee shook his head and coughed. He was closest to the smoke, and it was getting to him.

The shooting stopped, but only because the special deputies must be reloading.

Smoke was drifting out the door.

"Come on, come on," Thal said.

To Ursula it seemed as if time slowed down. The smoke, and everyone around it, moved like turtles. Jesse Lee was raising the blanket, but taking forever. A fugue state, she figured, brought on by her worries.

Then the special deputy called Tiny came around the right-hand door, a six-shooter in each hand. "They've set some straw on fire!" he bawled. In the blink of an eye, he skipped back around.

Ned snapped a shot, but all he hit was the door.

"Jesse, please," Ursula said. A terrible sense of urgency had come over her.

Jesse Lee began fanning the pile with the blanket. Not to cause more smoke, but to move the smoke already there. More crawled out the door and into the night.

"Jesse!" Ursula pleaded.

With a nod, the Southerner threw the blanket on the pile. It only covered a small part, but the flames it snuffed immediately spewed thick coils of smoke that rose to join the rest.

In two strides Jesse reached his palomino and swung up. Bending toward her, he said,

"Stay close." Then he glanced at Thal, Crawford, and Ned and nodded.

All three nodded in return.

Ursula's blood froze in her veins as Jesse Lee let out with a fierce yell and spurred his palomino into the smoke. Forgetting to hold her breath, she lashed her sorrel. Smoke got into her nose, her mouth. She tried to exhale, but a coughing fit seized her.

All around, guns crashed.

The smoke had spread barely twenty feet from the stable. They were in it, and out again.

Ursula burst into the clear and saw the one they called Olivant step out of a doorway to her left, pointing his six-shooter.

Jesse Lee fired twice, and Olivant rose onto the tips of his toes, twisted at the knees, and fell.

Fireflies flared on a roof. Someone was up there with a rifle, Ursula realized. She heard someone behind her yelp in pain. It sounded like Ned.

There were more shots, the din tremendous. A horse whinnied stridently.

Ursula glanced back to see Crawford's bay pitch into a roll. Crawford tried to push clear but didn't make it. His horse came down on top of him and kept rolling. The last sight she had of Crawford, as Jesse Lee led her into a side street, was of the older puncher lying deathly still.

They went half a block and the thunder of guns dwindled. Ursula smiled, thinking the worst was over, and was flabbergasted when Jesse Lee hauled on his reins, bringing his palomino to a sliding stop.

Thal and Ned rode up, Ned gripping his saddle horn to stay in the saddle, a dark stain high on his shirt.

"You've been hit," Thal exclaimed.

"I can ride," Ned said through clenched teeth.

"Where's Craw?" Jesse Lee said.

"His horse went down and took him with it," Thal said.

Ursula's astonishment knew no bounds when Jesse Lee vaulted down and thrust his reins up at her.

"Wait for me outside town."

"What? No!" Ursula cried as his intention became clear. She was so taken aback she didn't resist when he gripped her reins and yanked them from her grasp. "What are you — ?" she began, only to see him thrust her reins at Thal.

"Take her and go."

"You can't do it alone," Thal said. Quickly alighting, he handed her reins back up to her, and when she took them, he smiled.

"Off you go, sis."

"Hold on, now —" was all Ursula was able to say before her brother smacked her sorrel on the rump and fired into the dirt at its hooves. The sorrel exploded into motion, and it was all Ursula could do to cling on.

"Go with her!" Thal hollered, and gave Ned's horse a smack too.

Jesse Lee could reload faster than anyone Thal had ever seen. His own fingers were sluggish by comparison. As he replaced the last spent cartridge, Jesse Lee moved toward the street they'd just left, and he scurried to catch up.

"You should have gone with them," Jesse Lee said. "Crawford is my pard. It's mine to do."

"The Devil you say," Thal said. "You came all this way to help me. Now I can return the favor."

Darkling figures on foot flitted into view. They parted for a pair of riders who came galloping around the corner in pursuit.

Thal recognized Rafer and Dyson. He raised his Colt, but Jesse Lee sprang out and fanned his Colt once, twice. Dyson reared in his stirrups, clutched his chest, and toppled. Rafer, firing on the fly, rode headlong into a slug. The impact flipped him backward off his saddle.

Jesse Lee ducked under an overhang.

Joining him, Thal crouched. "You're hit." He had seen Jesse jerk when Rafer shot at him.

"Worry about the deputies who are still alive," Jesse Lee said, reloading.

Thal had lost count in all the excitement. "How many are left, you reckon?"

"Four, I make it," Jesse Lee said. "Plus Galt."

Thal yearned to run after his sister and Ned and get out of there. But he couldn't, he wouldn't, desert Jesse.

"Here they come," the Southerner said.

Thal's mouth was so dry he couldn't swallow.

"Remember what Wild Bill told you," Jesse Lee said. "Go for their guts. The shock will stop them, if nothin' else."

"I notice you always go for the head," Thal said.

"I'm a better shot."

Across the street a rifle *spang*ed. Farther back, a pair of pistols cracked. Lead chipped at the overhang posts, and a window behind Thal and Jesse Lee broke into shards.

"It's do or die," Jesse Lee said.

Thal flattened behind a post, which offered hardly any protection at all, centered his revolver on the largest of the targets, and fired. A roar of shock told him he'd hit Bull.

A small form rose from behind a trough and charged. It had to be Tiny. Weaving, the small gunman ambidextrously triggered shot after shot. Lead chipped the ground on both sides of Thal as he extended his Colt in both hands so that the muzzle was in line with Tiny's belly, and fired.

"Look out!" Jesse Lee cried.

Mateo had materialized directly across from them and was rushing them as Tiny had done.

Jesse Lee fired, was jolted, and fired again.

Sudden silence fell. Bull and Tiny and Mateo were down. Tiny made gurgling sounds; he was choking on his own blood.

"Reload," Jesse Lee said.

Thal had forgotten to. He clawed at his belt, and turned to ice when a gun hammer clicked behind them.

Jesse Lee froze too, except to glance over his shoulder. "You," he said simply.

Thal dared to look.

Trevor Galt held a nickel-plated pocket pistol in one hand, his cane in the other. He was furious, but smiling. "You bastards killed most of my men, but I've got you now." He pointed the pistol at Jesse Lee.

"You first, Reb. Then him, and her, and whoever else is left."

Thal tensed to spring. He would do what he could, for Ursula's sake.

Simultaneous twin blasts from behind Trevor Galt blew the top of his head off. His hat, his hair, his forehead, everything from the top of his nose, on up, were blasted to bits. The body stood there a few moments, swaying, then crashed down.

"Myles?" Thal said in amazement.

His brother stepped out of a wreath of gunsmoke and broke his scattergun open to reload. "When it came down to it, big brother," he said almost sadly, "when I had to choose between him or you, I chose you."

"Glad to hear it," Thal said.

EPILOGUE

Blood had proven thicker than money. Although much later, Thal was to wonder if his brother hadn't had another reason for blowing Trevor Galt to hell. Myles stayed on in American City, appointed special deputies of his own, and ruled the roost, just as Galt had done. When the gold ran out and the town dried up, Myles drifted to Oklahoma, where he lived on the shady side of the law until a marshal put three holes in him.

American City became a ghost town. Over the course of time, the remaining buildings were torn down. Eventually there wasn't a trace of it to be found.

Crawford survived his spill. He'd suffered cracked ribs and a broken wrist, and returned to Texas with Thal and Ned. They lived out the rest of their days doing what they loved most, cowpokes through and through.

Two months after returning from the Black Hills, Jesse Lee and Ursula were wed at the family farm. After the ceremony, Jesse Lee informed his friends that he wouldn't be going back to Texas. For Ursula's sake, he was unbuckling his six-shooter and taking up a new line of work.

Jesse Lee became a store clerk. Within a couple of years, he and Ursula opened a store of their own. They raised three children and lived a long, happy life.

His ivory-handled, nickel-plated Colt spent forty-four years in a trunk in their attic. Eventually it ended up in the Saline County Historical Museum, with a footnote that it was a relic of the Old West era and was rumored to have been used in a shootout.